SERPENT

Also by Philip Caveney:

Sebastian Darke: Prince of Fools
Sebastian Darke: Prince of Pirates

THE EYE OF THE SERPENT

ALEC DEVLIN

PHILIP CAVENEY

RED FOX
In association with The Bodley Head

ALEC DEVLIN: THE EYE OF THE SERPENT
A RED FOX BOOK 978 1 862 30608 0

First published in Great Britain by Red Fox,
an imprint of Random House Children's Books
A Random House Group Company

This edition published 2008

1 3 5 7 9 10 8 6 4 2

Copyright © Philip Caveney, 2008

The Random House Group Limited supports the Forest Stewardship Council
(FSC), the leading international forest certification organization.
All our titles that are printed on Greenpeace-approved FSC-certified
paper carry the FSC logo. Our paper procurement policy
can be found at www.rbooks.co.uk/environment.

Set in Bembo 14/17pt

Red Fox Books are published by Random House Children's Books,
61–63 Uxbridge Road, London W5 5SA

www.**kids**at**random house**.co.uk
www.**rbooks**.co.uk

Addresses for companies within The Random House Group Limited can be found at:
www.randomhouse.co.uk/offices.htm

THE RANDOM HOUSE GROUP Limited Reg. No. 954009

A CIP catalogue record for this book is available from the British Library.

Printed and bound in Great Britain by
CPI Bookmarque, Croydon, CRO 4TD

*Thanks to Biff Devlin for the use of
just two of her many names . . .
and to Mark Whitaker,
web monkey extraordinaire.*

Egypt, the Valley of the Kings, 1923

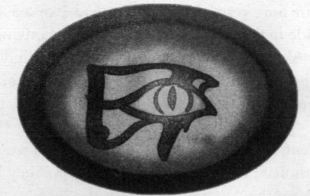

With a growing sense of anticipation Sir William Devlin stood at the top of the long flight of stone steps and gazed down at the massive doors set deep into the sand below him. At his side, his young assistant, Tom Hinton, could hardly conceal his excitement. This was the moment they had devoted so many years of their lives to; the moment they had begun to believe would never come.

The workmen had finished unearthing the steps weeks earlier and, in removing the piles of rubble heaped at the base of the huge gates, had revealed the seals bearing the name of Akhenaten, one of the mightiest pharaohs of the eighteenth dynasty and the father of Tutankhamun. After so much fruitless searching, this was like a miracle.

For four years the two men had worked side by side in the Valley of the Kings, both convinced that Akhenaten's final resting place was hidden not in his desecrated tomb in Amarna, but somewhere in these limestone hills. But in all that time they had discovered nothing more than ancient trinkets: a faience cup, a calcite jar, the occasional piece of discarded jewellery. They had been on the verge of giving up the search when workmen had, quite by accident, uncovered a step, just a few inches beneath the constantly shifting sands.

The resulting dig had unearthed fifteen more steps, perfectly cut from smooth white stone and angling steeply down into the bowels of the earth. But even then there had been a maddening wait while the seals were photographed and artists reproduced every element of them for the archives. Now, as the two archaeologists watched in silence, a couple of their most trusted workmen were finally breaking the seals and pulling open the doors, to reveal the darkness beyond.

Sir William and Tom descended the steps

together until they stood peering into the blackness. Sir William was aware of a thick sweat on his brow: this moment could be the greatest achievement of his life or the greatest disappointment. With a shaking hand he lifted his Eveready torch, flicked the switch and directed a beam of light into the antechamber.

What he saw there made him gasp in amazement.

The large room was piled high with treasures – gilt decorated boxes, gold statues, chairs, couches, even a beautifully ornate chariot. Apart from a fine film of dust, they looked as though they had been placed there only days ago, but Sir William knew that they had been waiting to be discovered for over three thousand years.

'My God!' whispered Tom – and excitement flashed in his blue eyes. He lifted his own torch and added a second beam of light. The two men stood in shocked silence as the twin beams picked out yet more details – intricate necklaces, the threads that bound them long since rotted away, stone jars stacked in orderly ranks, mummified cats, their shrivelled faces staring sightlessly back into the glare of electric light.

At last Sir William took a deep breath. 'It's

going to take us months to make an inventory of all this,' he said. It seemed a terribly lame thing to say after such an incredible discovery, but it was clear to him that their work had only just begun. Ahead of them lay a long stretch of photographing and filing; then the packing of the countless relics for the journey to the museum in Cairo.

'Wait!' said Tom, pointing into the darkness. 'Look – there! Another doorway.'

Sir William redirected the beam of his torch and saw that Tom was right. Beyond the jumble of treasure, half concealed by the sides of the chariot, there was a second sealed door. Before he could stop him, Tom, with all the impulsiveness of his twenty-two years, had run forward into the antechamber and was picking his way nimbly through the litter of treasure.

'Tom, just a minute, we must go easy!' cried Sir William.

'Don't worry,' Tom assured him. 'I'll be careful.'

A few moments later, as Sir William watched, Tom went down on his hands and knees to crawl beneath the chariot. 'The door's intact,' he shouted back over his shoulder. 'No grave robbers have been here. This *has* to be a burial chamber!'

Reluctantly Sir William followed his young

assistant, terrified that he might blunder into some priceless relic and damage it beyond repair; but after a few moments he too was crawling beneath the chariot and staring at what was affixed to the sealed door.

It was a Wadjet eye – an oval of smooth blue faience, onto which had been painted the symbol of an eye. Sir William knew that these eyes were usually representations of the eye of Horus, the hawk lord, son of Osiris – a powerful talisman used to protect precious items from harm. He also knew that in ancient Egyptian mythology, the eye represented the moon and, it was believed, had the power to bring the dead back to life. But there was something different about this one. The painted pupil was a vertical line, making it look more than anything like the eye of a serpent. Sir William noticed how the edges of the stone were rounded and how it stood out from the door in relief, as though it had been used to plug an opening of the same oval shape.

Tom lifted a hand to touch the stone. 'I believe I can pull it free,' he whispered. 'We'll be able to peep through the opening into the room beyond.'

'We shouldn't,' said Sir William nervously. 'Not

until it's been photographed and documented. We could cause damage.'

'It'll be all right,' Tom assured him. 'We could be on the verge of finding the sarcophagus of Akhenaten. You want to look in there, don't you?'

'Well . . .' began Sir William.

'If we do it by the book, it'll be months before we can even get back to this door. We'll have to clear all the artefacts from the antechamber, one by one, catalogue them, photograph them . . . Let's just take a quick peek.' Tom didn't wait for an answer but raised his hand again and took a firm grip of the eye. He pulled once, grunting with the effort, but the thing didn't budge. 'It's jammed in tight,' he said. 'Looks like wax has been set around the edges.'

'Tom, maybe we should wait,' said Sir William.

'No, it's all right, I think I can . . .' Tom gritted his teeth and applied all his strength to the task. There was a brief silence, during which Sir William was aware of his heart beating furiously. Then, quite suddenly, the eye came free with a dull thud that seemed to echo weirdly in the enclosed space, and there was the opening, an oval of the deepest, darkest midnight black.

Sir William experienced a sudden powerful sense of dread. It spilled through him like a wash of Atlantic water, and once again he opened his mouth to tell Tom to wait. But it was already too late. Tom had scrambled closer and was raising his head to peep through the opening.

There was a long, loud hiss, as though a blast of air had escaped from the next room; and beside him, Sir William felt Tom's body flinch.

'Tom?' he gasped. 'What's wrong?'

Tom edged slowly back from the door. His handsome young features were very pale in the torchlight and bore a vacant expression, a look of dull surprise.

'What did you see?' Sir William asked him.

'Nothing,' said Tom, his voice little more than a whisper.

Sir William went to put his own eye to the opening but Tom suddenly placed a hand on his shoulder with a strength that was surprising in one so slight.

'There's nothing,' he said again, and this time his voice was a deep, rumbling growl.

Sir William felt quite unnerved by the incident and decided that enough was enough. 'Come on,' he said. 'Let's get out of here.' He scrambled back from beneath the chariot and helped Tom towards the entrance.

Stepping out into the open sunlight was a shock. The power of the sun hit Sir William like a clenched fist and he almost cried out with the force of it. It seemed as if the two of them had been in the antechamber for days. He turned to look at Tom and felt another shock go through him.

The young man seemed to have aged ten years. His naturally pale skin was now as white and dry as a roll of parchment and his eyes, usually keen and intense, had a flat, blank expression in them. He seemed to react slowly, as though drugged. As Sir William watched, thick beads of sweat on the young man's forehead popped and went rolling down his face.

'Tom, are you quite all right?' he asked.

Tom turned to look at him as though he barely remembered Sir William. When he spoke, his voice was thin and reedy.

'I . . . I feel strange,' he said. He shivered, and more sweat began to trickle down his face.

'I believe you have a fever,' said Sir William, mystified. Only a few moments earlier, Tom had seemed in perfect health. 'Here, let's get you to your tent.' He slipped an arm beneath Tom's shoulder and helped him towards the steps, signalling to the two native diggers as he did so.

'Stand guard here,' he told them. 'Close up those doors and let nobody into the tomb except myself or Mr Hinton.'

They bowed their heads and hurried to obey his orders.

Sir William managed to get Tom to the top of the steps and half dragged him across the ground beyond to the campsite. Once in the safety of the big canvas tent, he laid Tom on his bed and covered him with a blanket. Tom was shivering violently now and the sweat had already soaked through his khaki shirt.

'I'm going to get Doc Hopper,' Sir William told him; then remembered that the expedition's resident doctor had gone into Luxor for provisions that morning. 'Perhaps I can send one of the boys for him,' he added.

'Don't worry,' Tom said. 'It's . . . just a fever. I'll see him when he gets back. I'll be fine once I've had some rest.'

'But . . . to come on so suddenly . . . I'd feel happier if he had a look at you.'

Tom shook his head and sweat rained from his

hair onto his pillow. 'Don't be ridiculous,' he said. 'That will take ages to sort out . . . and . . .' His voice trailed away for a moment and he seemed to grow stronger, his eyes staring up at Sir William with a powerful intent. 'This is your moment, William. It's what you've worked for all these years. Go back to the tomb and . . . get things organized.' The momentary strength seemed to fail him and he flopped back against his pillow. 'I . . . just need to sleep for a while.'

Sir William frowned. 'You're sure you're all right?'

'I'm fine . . . really . . . I only need to . . .'

Tom closed his eyes and seemed to sink immediately into a deep sleep. His chest rose and fell steadily. Sir William stood by his bed for a moment, unsure of what to do. Part of him wanted to get straight back to the tomb and revel in his moment of triumph. Another part felt that something was terribly wrong. Lord knew, they'd all had doses of the fever on this expedition, but this one had struck so suddenly, so completely . . . and Sir William remembered how Tom's body had jolted as he'd peered through that gap in the door, almost as though he'd been shot . . .

A tumult of shouts from outside made his

decision for him. Somehow, news of the discovery had got back to the others in the camp and workers were running around shouting about it. People were spilling out of their tents, eager to get to the excavation. There was no time to waste. The tomb site had to be secured before the news travelled any further.

Sir William stepped quickly out of the tent, letting down the canvas flap behind him and buttoning it closed to keep out the sunlight. Then he hurried back towards the tomb, shouting orders as he went.

It was night before he had a chance to return. By then, he had a whole team of people at work in the antechamber, photographing its contents in position, before separating them for illustration and cataloguing. An area had been set aside where the items could be packed, ready for despatch to the Cairo Museum. It was only as he trudged back through the night towards Tom's tent that it occurred to him that he hadn't seen the odd-looking Wadjet eye since Tom had removed it from its position. Presumably it had been dropped near the door of the adjoining chamber.

He came to the tent and stooped to unbutton the flap. As he straightened up, he was startled to hear a rustling sound coming from within. He threw back the flap and stared in. It was too dark to see very much, so he reached for his torch before remembering that the zinc carbide batteries were exhausted from their earlier use. Instead he located a hurricane lamp and knelt to light it.

The rustling sound went on – a continuous susurration that seemed to grate on Sir William's nerves. It sounded to his heightened senses like a million dry leaves being stirred by the wind – but not the kind of leaves you would ever find in a land like Egypt. He was thinking of the autumn leaves of his native Kent, and for the first time it dawned on him how he missed the place. Perhaps he had spent too many years in this dry, unforgiving heat. It was time he headed home to visit friends and family. He thrust the thought aside and managed to get the lamp alight. Lifting it, he stepped into the tent and looked towards Tom's bed.

He felt a momentary stab of surprise. He remembered throwing a blanket over Tom before he left, but not the dark-brown shiny one that now covered him from head to foot. Sir William stepped closer and then gasped in involuntary horror as he saw that the blanket was moving, swaying back and forth like the tide of some unspeakable ocean. And then he realized that this was a tide made up, not of liquid, but of myriad large, shiny, fat insects that were swarming over what was left of Tom's corpse. Scarab beetles. Millions of them.

Sir William shouted something. He didn't know at the time nor could he ever recall exactly what he'd said; but as he shouted, he thrust his arm forward, directing the pool of light onto the bed, and the great tide of glistening creatures began to scatter before the glow as if it was poison to them. They spilled off the edges of the cot, raining down onto the ground in frantic, wriggling heaps, until Sir William was ankle-deep in them. He stared down in revulsion at the thing they were gradually revealing: a hideous, wasted manikin clad in tattered clothing, the flesh beneath the clothes almost completely consumed, leaving nothing more than bone and a few shrivelled tatters of dried skin.

The eyelids were still there though . . . and as Sir William watched, they slid open to reveal two piercing blue eyes that, most hideous of all, were still very much alive. Tom's ravaged lips curved at the edges to reveal his white, even teeth, set in a hideous grin. He began to laugh, a deep, throaty sound that froze Sir William's blood within him; and then suddenly the scarabs were swarming back, as though Tom had somehow summoned them.

They skittered frantically up the legs of the camp bed and began to stream in beneath his clothing, the fabric rising as if the bones were growing new flesh. Scores of scarabs crawled up from beneath the collar of his shirt and began to flatten themselves against Tom's skull. Instantly their dark covering faded and they turned the colour of pale skin. It was as though Tom had new flesh – flesh that wriggled and squirmed with unspeakable evil.

Sir William began to scream, and as he screamed, loud and shrill like a child, the small part of his brain that remained methodical noticed one last puzzling detail.

The breast pocket of Tom's shirt had been torn open and there, lying against his ruined chest, was the serpent's eye, gazing steadfastly up at Sir William as he lost consciousness.

CHAPTER ONE

Return to Luxor

Alec Devlin stood on the deck of the steamship *Sudan* and gazed thoughtfully across the calm waters of the Nile to the far shore. He and his valet, Coates, had embarked at Cairo three days ago, and though life aboard the *Sudan* was comfortable enough, progress was maddeningly slow. Every inch of Alec's fifteen-year-old frame longed to be at his destination – the archaeological dig in the Valley of the Kings, where he was due to spend his school holidays.

Alec's father, Hugh, was a diplomat, working at the British embassy in Cairo. His busy schedule left little free time to spend with his son; and Alec's mother, Hannah, had been dead more than six months now. During term time Alec attended an English boarding school in Cairo, but holidays had always been a problem; at least until Uncle Will had started inviting him down to help out on his archaeological digs.

It had started when Alec was thirteen. A letter had arrived from Uncle Will (Alec could somehow never bring himself to call him 'Sir William') inviting Alec to go and make himself useful. Alec's father had thought it a capital idea, but his mother had been less impressed.

'He's too young,' she'd argued. 'That's a lawless part of the world. He could get into all kinds of trouble.'

'Nonsense!' his father had answered. 'It'll make a man of him . . . and it's better than having him mooching around the house, bored out of his mind. Look, if you're so worried, we'll send Coates with him – he'll make sure he doesn't get into any scrapes.'

Coates was the family valet. He had been around for as long as Alec could remember, a big, shambling fellow with brilliantined black hair and a face like a slab of granite. Though he

16

seemed tough, Alec knew from experience that he could bend Coates around his little finger if he needed to: taking him along shouldn't be a problem.

So for the past two years Alec had made this trip down to Luxor to work alongside his favourite uncle, and in the process had become totally absorbed in the study of Egyptology. Uncle Will was a brilliant teacher, and consequently Alec knew more about the subject than any other child his age. Everything about it fascinated him: the tombs, the relics, the incredible history of a race of people who had built fabulous temples and monuments when the rest of the human race was still scuttling around in rags. And nothing – absolutely nothing in the world – could ever rival the thrill of finding something that had lain hidden from human eyes for thousands of years.

The previous winter, two things had happened that had changed Alec's life for ever. The first was the death of his mother. He'd been back at school in Cairo, working through some history revision, when he'd been summoned to the headmaster's office. He was initially delighted to find his father waiting for him. But the look on his face had told him very quickly that this was-n't to be good news.

Alec's mother was dead.

She had been bitten by a mosquito, his father said, as Alec listened incredulously. Mosquito bites were nothing – people suffered them on an almost daily basis in this part of the world – but something must have been different about this particular bite, because it had turned septic. She had fallen into a raging fever and within a few hours she was gone. Alec couldn't believe it. A mosquito bite! How could such a silly, innocuous thing be the death of the person he had thought would live for ever?

'It's all right if you want to cry,' Father had told him, but Alec couldn't. He felt like screaming; he felt like smashing the headmaster's office to bits, but try as he might, he could not shed a tear for the mother he had loved all his life.

He had travelled back to the house on Kasr al-Dubara with his father and had gone through the ritual of the burial – the prayers, the hymns, the readings – and he had just felt numb, as though this was happening to somebody else and he was watching it from a distance.

Back at school, he threw himself into his

lessons, thinking that at least he had the summer holidays to look forward to, a chance to immerse himself in the subject he enjoyed so much.

But then a letter had arrived from his father, telling him that something bad had happened over at the dig. Nobody was sure exactly what had transpired, but it appeared that Uncle Will had suffered a complete nervous breakdown and had been taken to a sanatorium. It looked as though archaeology was off the agenda.

And then Alec *did* find some tears. This was the last straw. It seemed to him that everything was lost and he resigned himself to waiting until his schooling was finished before he could devote his life to the subject that so fascinated him.

But then, only a few weeks before the end of term, a revelation! Another letter from his father had arrived, telling him that the dig seemed to be back on the cards. Uncle Will's most trusted American friend, a man called Ethan Wade, had stepped in to take over directorship of the site; and he had extended a personal invitation to Alec to come out and resume his former duties.

So now here he stood at the rail of the *Sudan*,

gazing out at a small herd of camels on the far bank, dipping their heads to drink from the blue waters of the Nile. Alec was asking himself how much longer it would be before he could step off this great floating tub and get his hands into some good Egyptian sand. Coates, a plain-speaking Yorkshireman, who had always seemed able to read Alec's mind, gave him a reassuring pat on the shoulder.

'Fear not, Master Alec. We'll be at Luxor tomorrow afternoon and, all being well, Mr Wade should be at the quayside to meet us.'

Alec glanced at his valet. It always seemed odd to see the big man clad in the unfamiliar garb of a khaki safari suit and pith helmet, rather than his usual black tailcoat.

'I've asked you before, please don't call me that,' he murmured. 'A simple Alec will be fine.'

'Yes, Master Alec,' said Coates, without a trace of irony. 'I shall try to remember that.'

A short distance from the steamer, a large crocodile surfaced briefly, snorted a little water from its nostrils and then sank again, leaving barely a ripple in its wake.

'What do we know about this Ethan Wade?' asked Alec.

'Only that he is a friend of Sir William's and that your father met him some years ago and was, by all accounts, rather impressed with him. I believe Mr Wade was working on an earlier dig alongside your uncle at the time. But he'd moved on by the time you started helping your uncle out.'

'He's an archaeologist, then?'

'No. I understand he is what the Americans like to call "a soldier of fortune".'

Alec frowned. 'What's that exactly?'

'I believe it describes a man who is willing to go anywhere in the world where there is action and adventure. I've heard some reports of exploits in Mexico and Africa . . .' Coates sniffed. 'But of course, if your father thinks he's made of the right stuff, who am I to quibble?'

Alec was impressed. 'Sounds like an interesting fellow,' he said.

Coates allowed himself the faintest look of disdain. 'That's the Americans for you,' he said. 'Probably watched far too many motion pictures. I believe that's what they call them.'

Alec smiled. 'Movies, Coates. That's the American word. And if Father trusts him and Uncle Will trusts him, then he'll do for me.' He paused. 'It's going to seem odd, Uncle Will not being at the dig. I wish we knew more about what happened to him.'

Coates sighed. 'Perhaps we'll learn more in due course,' he said. 'All I do know is that he's not in his right mind and—'

'Excuse me. I trust you will excuse my bold-ness . . .'

Alec and Coates turned in surprise. They had been approached by a complete stranger. He was a hugely obese man, dressed in a white safari suit and a wide-brimmed fedora. Beneath the brim of his hat, his face resembled a great pink blob of blancmange, beneath which a couple of chins wobbled alarmingly. He was sweating profusely and mopping at his neck with a red kerchief.

'I couldn't help but overhear your conver-sation,' said the man, who spoke with a distinct Welsh accent. 'Wilfred Llewellyn, from the *Cairo Herald*.' Llewellyn extended a meaty hand and Alec shook it politely. It felt unpleasantly sticky and he had to make an effort not to wipe his palm on his trousers. 'I'm on my way down to the Valley of the Kings to do a story and I heard you mention a dig and an "Uncle Will" . . . You couldn't possibly have been referring to Sir William Devlin, could you?'

Alec and Coates exchanged glances.

'Umm . . . yes, I'm his nephew,' said Alec cautiously.

'Astonishing! And your name would be . . . ?'

'Alec. Alec Devlin.'

'Of course, Sir William has a brother, Hugh. Your father. That makes sense.' Llewellyn reached into his jacket and pulled out a small notebook and pen. 'I trust, dear boy, you won't object if I make a few notes. For the record.'

Coates frowned. 'What's this all about?' he demanded.

'Oh, just gathering details, my good friend – nothing to be concerned about. We . . . journalists tend to pull in every little thing, so that later we can . . . sift through for the nuggets.' Llewellyn had a soft, syrupy voice that Alec found distinctly irritating. 'So you are on your way to see your uncle?'

'No, we're going to the dig. I've worked up there twice before.'

'Oh, capital, absolutely capital! And if I may say so, how inspiring to meet a young man willing to work in such a dangerous environment.'

'Dangerous?' Coates raised his eyebrows. 'How so?'

'Oh, well, I'm no expert of course, but I would have thought out in the open like that, there must be all sorts of things that could happen. Dust storms . . . wild animals . . . bandits . . .'

Alec grinned. 'Judging from what's happened before, I'd say it's not much worse than camping out with the scouts,' he said. 'And besides, I've got Coates to look after me.'

'Coats?' Llewellyn scribbled a note in his little book. 'Some kind of protective clothing you wear?'

Alec tried not to laugh.

'I'm Coates,' said Coates, with an air of menace.

'Oh, I see! The family retainer, I suppose?'

'I prefer the word "valet".'

'Hmm, yes, of course. And you would have a first name, Mr Coates?'

'Oh, most certainly,' said Coates unhelpfully.

'Look, which paper did you say you work for?'

'Er . . . the *Herald*.'

'It's strange. I've lived in Cairo for many years now and I can't say I've ever heard of it.'

'Oh, well . . . we're quite new. But doing very nicely, thank you.' Llewellyn fixed Alec with a look. 'So you're Sir William's nephew. A terrible thing that happened to him, is it not?'

Alec frowned. 'We don't really know much about it,' he said. 'Only that he had some kind of breakdown.'

'Oh, is that what they told you?' Llewellyn said slyly. 'And did anybody mention anything about a Mr Hinton?'

Alec raised his eyebrows. '*Tom* Hinton?' he asked. He knew Tom well enough; had met him on the two previous occasions when he'd helped out on digs and had found him to be a most agreeable fellow. 'Nobody said anything about Tom. Why?'

Llewellyn leaned closer and Alec wrinkled his nostrils as they caught a curious smell: the odour of cheap lavender water mingled with the sharp tang of sweat.

'I thought it was common knowledge. Mr Hinton disappeared the same night your uncle suffered his . . . *breakdown*. Nobody has seen hide nor hair of him since.'

'Disappeared?' Alec was shocked. 'How could such a thing happen?'

Llewellyn shrugged. 'People are talking about a curse,' he said.

There was a brief silence.

'I think Master Alec has answered enough questions for now,' said Coates.

'Oh, but if I might be permitted to . . .'

Coates put a big slab of a hand against Llewellyn's chest and pushed, gently but firmly, making the man lurch backward several steps.

'If you wouldn't mind,' said Coates, an edge of threat in his voice. 'We were enjoying the solitude.'

'Yes, well, of course, if that's what you wish. Far be it from me to outstay my welcome.' Llewellyn was quite clearly furious, but strove to disguise it with an unconvincing smile. 'I'll leave you to it. I'm sure we'll be seeing each other at the dig, anyway. Perhaps we will have the opportunity to speak again.' He touched the brim of his fedora. 'Master Devlin,' he said. He looked briefly at Coates. 'Mr Coates.' He turned and waddled away across the deck, mopping his sweating face as he went.

Alec looked at Coates. 'What was that about?' he murmured.

'I can't imagine,' his valet replied. 'But if that fellow is a journalist, I'll eat my pith helmet.'

'Then what *is* he, d'you suppose?'

'Somebody too fond of asking questions.' Coates frowned and hunched his massive shoulders. 'And something tells me we haven't seen the last of him.'

CHAPTER TWO

The Tall American

The *Sudan* made dock at Luxor early the following morning. Alec and Coates looked down at the eager press of people on the jetty below them, a mixture of frantically shouting natives, dockworkers in grubby overalls and smartly dressed tourists from just about every part of the globe. Since the discovery of Tutankhamun's tomb a year earlier, Egypt had become an essential addition to every holiday-maker's 'to do' list and it was said that Howard Carter and his team were finding it hard to make any progress whatsoever when they had to deal with a daily influx of British and American visitors demanding that they be allowed to see 'the treasures'.

'I hadn't expected it to be quite so packed,' said an oily voice; and Alec turned his head to see the huge, sweating shape of Llewellyn standing beside him. His heart sank. Since he had introduced himself the previous day, Llewellyn seemed to be following Alec and Coates around like an oversized puppy dog. 'Are you being met by somebody?' he asked.

Alec opened his mouth to speak, but Coates put a hand on his arm to still him.

'We are indeed, Mr Llewellyn,' he said. 'And what about yourself? I'm sure a newspaper reporter of your undoubted calibre will have a fine limousine awaiting his arrival.'

Llewellyn smiled. 'Ah, that's not how I operate, Mr Coates. I believe in slipping in under everybody's guard. That way, I get the *real* story, not something that's been carefully prepared beforehand. The French have a word for it. *Vérité.*'

Coates sniffed. 'I have a word for it too, Mr Llewellyn, but mine's a good old Anglo-Saxon one, which I shouldn't care to repeat in mixed company.'

If Llewellyn understood the remark, he chose

to ignore it. Instead he leaned a little closer as if to confide a secret. 'I was wondering,' he said, 'if you might be able to give me a lift down to the dig.'

Coates stared at the man. 'But, Mr Llewellyn, I wouldn't insult you by offering. I'm sure that what with wanting to get the real story, you'd prefer to travel by *authentic* transport.' He pointed down to where a man in a striped galabiya was leading several donkeys by their bridles.

At that moment the chains across the gangway were unfastened and the passengers began to descend in an eager stream to the quayside. Coates pushed Alec forward and the two of them moved away, leaving Llewellyn staring down open-mouthed at the donkeys. They reached the weathered boards of the jetty and stood for a moment, gazing around. Neither of them had ever met Ethan Wade before and had not the slightest idea what he might look like; but then a man came striding purposefully towards them and Alec knew instantly that this had to be the man they were looking for.

He must have been six foot tall, broad shouldered but narrow hipped, and he was wearing what Alec would have called a cowboy hat, but which he knew was more accurately termed a stetson. He had dark eyes, a sunburned complexion and a red bandana handkerchief tied loosely around his neck. His white teeth were currently displayed in a welcoming grin. Alec couldn't help but notice that the man had a cowboy-style holster around his hips, complete with a six-shooter. To complete the image he wore long, intricately tooled leather boots.

'This must be Mr Wade now,' announced Alec brightly.

'However did you guess?' murmured Coates, rolling his eyes; but he stood up straight and bowed his head respectfully as the big man approached.

'You must be Alec!' said the man, as though Alec wasn't actually aware of the fact. 'I can see the resemblance to your father – and of course your uncle told me all about you.'

'Uncle Will's better?' cried Alec excitedly.

'Uh, no, sorry, this was *before* he was taken ill. But he often sent me letters and he usually mentioned you in them.' He held out a big hand and Alec shook it, trying not to wince at a grip that almost crushed his fingers. Ethan lifted his gaze. 'And I guess you must be Goats,' he added.

'That's Coates, sir, if you'll pardon me correcting you. A goat is a bleating sort of creature that will eat anything, whereas we Coateses rarely speak and are a tad more particular about our food. Very pleased to meet you, Mr Wade, I'm sure.'

Alec had to suppress a grin, because he could tell that Coates hadn't taken too kindly to the mistake, but was doing his best not to show it.

Ethan Wade just looked bemused by the reply he'd received. 'Oh no, call me Ethan, please! We really don't go in for ceremony around here.'

'Very well, Mr Wade. As you wish.'

Ethan looked momentarily puzzled by this.

'Oh, he always does that,' Alec assured the American. 'He's very proper about these things. Don't worry, you'll get used to him.'

'If you say so.' He looked at Coates doubtfully. 'You can stand at ease,' he told him.

'Oh, I am, Mr Wade, I can assure you.'

Ethan looked around for a moment, and lifting his fingers to his lips, let out a whistle of such volume that Alec almost jumped out of his skin. A couple of young Arab boys came running out from the crowd and Ethan pointed up the quayside to where the passengers' trunks were being unloaded. 'Go and sort out the bags, boys. They'll be labelled Master Devlin and Mr Goats . . . er, *Coates*! Hurry on now!'

The two boys raced off and Ethan gestured to his guests.

'Come with me,' he said. 'Let's get you out of this three-ring circus. I swear this place gets busier every time I come here.' He led the way through a packed waiting room and out to the port entrance. On a strip of dust road, two fine-looking convertible automobiles were waiting. Alec recognized the driver of one of them.

'Mickey!' he shouted, and ran forward to shake the man's hand. Mickey Randall was one of Uncle Will's assistants, a wiry little fellow from Bethnal Green who had spent much of his life travelling to the far corners of the earth. Alec had got to know him on previous digs and the two of them were great friends.

'Master Alec.' Mickey grinned, revealing irregular rows of nicotine-stained teeth. 'I'd say you've grown another foot since I last clapped eyes on yer.'

'Maybe a couple of inches,' admitted Alec.

'Whatever, it's good to 'ave yer back.' Mickey glanced cautiously up at Coates. 'You too, Mr Coates,' he said, but his enthusiasm was a little muted: the two of them didn't really get on. It was no secret that the valet thought Mickey a bit of a scoundrel.

'Mr Randall,' said Coates, with chilly politeness. 'May I say you're looking every bit as pugnacious as you did on the last occasion we met?'

Mickey smiled. 'Er . . . thanks, Mr Coates,' he said, but it was quite evident he didn't have the first idea what 'pugnacious' meant and Alec didn't really feel like enlightening him. Mickey turned back to Alec and his sun-grizzled face registered an expression of regret. 'Ain't it terrible about Sir William?' he said. 'I couldn't believe it when they told me what 'appened.'

'What exactly *did* happen?' Alec asked him. 'Whenever I ask, I never seem to get a straight answer.'

Mickey looked uncomfortable. 'Something bad,' he admitted, but seemed reluctant to say anything further on the matter. 'And . . . I believe you've 'ad some terrible news yourself since I last seen yer. I 'eard about your mother, Alec. I'm really sorry. I never met 'er, o' course, but everyone said she was a fine lady.'

Alec nodded. As usual at such times, he couldn't for the life of him think of anything constructive to say. There was an uncomfortable silence.

'Perhaps you might care to change the subject,' suggested Coates; and Mickey obligingly slapped a hand against the shining side of the automobile.

'So . . . whatcha think of the motor, then?' he asked.

'Fantastic! Is it yours?'

'No, these both belong to Mr Wade. Crossleys, they are, made in England – Manchester, to be precise. They say the Prince of Wales drives around in one of these blighters. There's nearly twenty 'orsepower under the bonnet and she's got a top speed of sixty-four miles per hour!'

'Gosh!' Alec tried and failed to imagine a car moving at such an unbelievable speed. Of course, they had a motorcar back in Cairo, but that was a sedate Ford, not a fabulous creation like this. He turned to look at Ethan. 'Must have cost you a pretty penny, Mr Wade,' he said.

'Master Alec, it's considered vulgar to enquire the price of things,' warned Coates disapprovingly.

Ethan waved a hand in dismissal. 'Don't sweat it,' he said.

Coates raised his eyebrows. 'I shall do my very best not to,' he said, 'A quite repulsive habit – though of course, in this climate one cannot promise anything.'

Ethan stared at Coates for a moment as though considering saying something further; but then he shook his head and turned back to Alec. 'A car like that should cost around a thousand bucks, but these are war surplus models. I picked 'em up for a whole lot less. They were made for driving generals around the battlefields, so they could take a good long look at the destruction they'd caused. Thought I might put 'em to better use.'

There was a bitterness in his tone, which prompted Alec to ask another question.

'Were you in the war, Mr Wade?'

Ethan frowned. 'Yeah, I saw some action in France – enough to convince me that I never want to get mixed up in anything like that again.' He glanced up as the two Arab boys came struggling out of the port exit, each of them bent double beneath the weight of a huge trunk. 'You guys don't believe in travelling light,' he observed, grinning.

'One has to be prepared for every eventuality, Mr Wade,' said Coates evenly. 'After all, it's not as if we're just staying overnight.'

'I guess not. Guys, put the two trunks in behind Mr Randall there.'

The two Arab boys did as he asked, standing the trunks upright in the back seat, and Ethan rewarded them with a couple of coins apiece. They grinned delightedly and headed back to the port, in search of more customers.

Ethan turned back to his visitors. 'Mr Coates, if you'd like to get in beside Mickey, he'll take you over to the dig and you can get unpacked. Alec can ride with me in the other automobile. There's a call me and him need to make along the way.'

Coates looked doubtful. 'Oh, I'm not sure about that, Mr Wade. My instructions are to keep an eye on Master Alec at all times.'

'Relax, he'll be fine with me.' Ethan glanced at Alec. 'Is it OK with you?'

'Umm . . . yes, why not?' Alec turned to look

at Coates. 'I'm sure I'll be safe enough,' he said.

'Very well, Master Alec. But be warned, in deviating from the approved procedure you are accepting full responsibility for your own safety.' Coates climbed into the passenger seat beside Mickey, but he didn't look at all happy. He was a man who took his instructions very seriously.

Alec followed Ethan to the other vehicle and got in beside him. 'What's his problem?' muttered Ethan.

'No problem,' said Alec. 'He's just being Coates.'

'Guy needs to relax a little.'

Ethan hit the starter and the car's powerful engine rumbled into life. They were just about to set off when a shout drew their attention back to the port entrance and they saw the hulking shape of Wilfred Llewellyn, dragging a heavy trunk behind him and even more red in the face than usual.

'Mr Wade!' he shouted. 'Just a moment, please!'

'Who's the stiff in the ice-cream suit?' asked Ethan, and Alec had to make an effort not to laugh.

'His name's Wilfred Llewellyn,' he whispered.

'We met on the boat. Claims he's a reporter for a paper in Cairo.'

Ethan scowled. 'A reporter?' he muttered. 'That's all we need.' He didn't appear to have much liking for reporters. 'Those people have been making life a misery for Howard Carter and his team ever since they found Tut's tomb. And since Lord Carnarvon died they've been inventing all this hokum about some ancient curse. I guess it's only a matter of time before we get the same treatment.'

Llewellyn came up and stood beside the Crossley. After his exertion, the sweat was literally pouring from his face. 'This heat!' he observed. 'Quite unreal.' He extended a hand towards Ethan. 'Wilfred Llewellyn,' he said. '*Cairo Examiner.*'

Alec looked at him. 'I thought, on the boat, you said the *Cairo Herald.*'

Llewellyn didn't even bother to look at him. 'No, don't believe so,' he said. 'You must have misheard me, young man. I'm with the *Examiner.*' He fixed his attention on Ethan. 'And you must be Mr Wade,' he said, directing an oily smile at the American while completely blanking out Alec's puzzled expression. 'The gentleman who has taken over the directorship of the site while Sir William Devlin is . . . incapacitated?' Llewellyn still had his hand out, but Ethan either hadn't noticed or had chosen to ignore the gesture.

'You're well informed, Mr Llewellyn. What can I do for ya?'

Llewellyn snatched back the hand, but his smile never faltered. 'I take it you're on your way up to the archaeological dig? I've been sent here to do a story about it and I was wondering if you might have room for one more in your fine automobile.'

Now Ethan turned to look at Llewellyn, his face expressionless. 'Nobody said anything to me about a newspaper,' he said.

'My editor *did* send a telegram. Oh dear, it must have gone astray. You know how communications are in this godforsaken country.'

Ethan shrugged his broad shoulders. 'Well now, see, Mr Llewellyn, we got a problem.' He jerked a thumb back at the Crossley Mickey was driving. 'Ain't no room in there, what with the luggage and all − and me and Alec here, we're heading somewhere else entirely.'

Llewellyn mopped his brow. 'That's all right,' he said. 'I don't mind tagging along. It might make for a more interesting story.'

Ethan shook his head. 'Sorry, but where we're headed, the press ain't invited.' He gestured back towards the dock entrance. 'If you ask around in there, there's a guy called Mohammed Hansa – he has an automobile for hire. Not a very good one, but I expect he'll take you out to the dig if you offer him enough *baksheesh*.'

'Yes, but surely you could . . .'

The rest of Llewellyn's words were lost in the throaty roar of the Crossley's engine as Ethan let out the clutch and they drove off, flinging up a great cloud of sand in their wake. Alec glanced back and saw Llewellyn, half choking in the thick red dust.

'Coates doesn't trust that chap,' said Alec.

'Coates is a good judge of character,' said Ethan. 'I don't like him neither and I only just met him.'

'He definitely told me the *Cairo Herald* back on the boat. Coates says he's never heard of it.'

'Me neither. We're gonna have to keep an eye on that guy if he comes sniffing around the dig.'

The Crossley coasted through the narrow streets of Luxor, passing coffee houses, street markets and whitewashed colonial buildings. Whenever they paused at a crossroads, small groups of Arabs appeared beside them, brandishing pieces of pottery, amulets and figurines.

'*Effendi*, you buy, you buy! Very good price!'

Alec looked at the items they were offering, all of which appeared to be authentically aged pieces.

'Is that stuff genuine?' he asked Ethan as they drove away from one raucous group.

Ethan shook his head. 'Not much of it,' he said. 'Oh, you'll find the odd piece looted from some burial site or other, but most of it they make themselves – they've got real smart at getting it to look authentic. It's got worse since Carter found King Tut. Suddenly every tourist wants to take home a piece of the real Egypt and, for the right price, those boys are more than happy to supply it.'

They soon left the outskirts of the old town and headed out into the desert, the dirt road knifing through sand dunes so white they looked like snow hills. The heat seemed to intensify almost instantly and Alec was glad of the rush of wind that cooled his face. After driving for some twenty minutes, they came to a place where the road forked. Ethan took a left, but when Alec glanced back, he saw that Mickey and Coates had turned off in the other direction, heading towards the Valley of the Kings.

'Where are we going, exactly?' shouted Alec over the rush of wind.

Ethan glanced at him. 'I thought you might like to pay a visit to your uncle,' he yelled back.

'Uncle Will?' Alec brightened. 'I didn't think he was up to having visitors.'

Ethan frowned. He slowed the car a little to make it easier to be heard. 'Tell you the truth, kid, I don't know that he is. But I'm kind of desperate. See, William has spoken barely a word since they found him, the night that Tom Hinton disappeared.' He glanced at Alec. 'You heard about Tom?'

'Not until yesterday, when Mr Llewellyn mentioned it,' he admitted. 'He seemed to think there was something very fishy about his disappearance.'

Ethan nodded. 'We tried to play it down, but the truth is, Tom just up and vanished. You remember him, I guess?'

'Of course, I've worked with him twice before. A nice chap, very level-headed, knows everything there is to know about archaeology.'

'Nobody's seen hide nor hair of him since the

night he took a walk,' Ethan went on. 'His fellow workers looked everywhere they could think of, even talked to the local police, but they weren't any help at all. It's like he just vanished into thin air . . . and as for your uncle . . .' He sighed. 'Well, whatever happened to him, it must've shook him to the core. I thought maybe seeing another familiar face might get some kind of response out of him. Lord knows I've tried everything else I can think of. It's like he just . . . shut himself away from the world. When he does speak, his words seem to make no sense at all.'

Alec frowned. 'But . . . he must have asked for me, otherwise why am I here?'

Ethan shook his head. 'Tell you the truth, that was my idea. I was reading your uncle's journal to see if I could find a clue to what happened. William mentions you a lot. He thinks a great deal of you, Alec – reckons you're going to be a big name in archaeology one day. Heck, I ain't no expert, I can use all the help I can get. Only reason I'm running this circus is because I signed up to come back to work here a month or so back and I agreed to have my name put down on an insurance policy. I was second choice behind Tom. Who would have thought that neither of 'em would be in a position to continue?'

They drove on for a while in silence. Then Alec said, 'From the way you've been talking, it sounds as though Uncle Will *found* something.'

Ethan grinned. 'Oh, he found something all right . . . the very same day he was taken ill.'

Alec could hardly contain his excitement. 'Well, what did he find?' he demanded. 'I know he always hoped to find the last resting place of Akhenaten, but surely you're not saying . . .'

Ethan looked at him. 'He found a tomb, Alec. We're not sure yet, but it could be exactly what he was looking for.'

'You're joking! But that would be . . . an incredible find!'

'Well, sure, the father of Tutankhamun. At the moment we're doing all we can to play it down – at least until we know exactly what it is we've got. I've contacted an expert on hieroglyphics, some Frenchman called Duval. He's due to arrive in the next week or so. Hopefully he'll be able to tell us more. Unfortunately Will and Tom were the only two men in the tomb who had any kind of idea about that stuff. But in his journal Will says you know more than any kid he's ever met.

So I thought it would be good to bring you back on board and . . .'

'And what?' asked Alec.

'And maybe seeing you might just jog something in Will's mind. You might strike a chord. You up for that?'

Alec nodded. 'Sure,' he said. 'I'll give it my best shot.'

'That's the spirit.' Ethan grinned at him. 'You know, I get a good feeling about you, Alec. I figure you and me, we're gonna be pals.'

They seemed to be heading deeper and deeper into the desert and the horizon had that kind of shimmering, melting quality that happens whenever rays of light refract in fierce heat. Alec reminded himself that, beautiful as this landscape was, it could also be deadly. He had heard countless stories of people who had been stranded out here. Very few of the stories had happy endings.

After driving for perhaps half an hour, they saw the outline of a small village on the horizon. Ethan headed into it and brought the Crossley to a halt outside a big, dilapidated whitewashed building.

'This place used to be a governor's residence,' he explained. 'These days it's a hospital.' He opened his door and climbed out. Alec followed his example. They walked towards the entrance of the building – a once grand portico supported by rows of crumbling stone columns. Before they stepped into the shade, Ethan paused and put a hand on Alec's shoulder.

'You'd better prepare yourself, kid,' he said quietly. 'William is . . . well, let's just say he's not the man you'll remember.'

And with that he led Alec up the short flight of steps to the entrance.

CHAPTER THREE

Family Reunion

ANubian nurse, clad in a dazzlingly white starched uniform, led them along corridors and up a flight of wooden stairs. They crossed a landing, their feet echoing on marble tiles, and finally came to a halt at a large mahogany door. The nurse reached into her pocket and withdrew a key, which she used to unlock it.

Alec was surprised by this and a thought ran through his mind: *What kind of a hospital locks its patients in?*

The nurse handed Ethan the key. 'Please secure the door when you leave,' she told him in fluent English, 'and hand the key in at reception.'

Ethan nodded. 'Has there been any improvement since I was last here?' he asked.

She gave him a sad smile and shook her head; then she turned and walked back along the corridor.

Ethan took a grip on the door handle, then paused and looked at Alec. 'Ready?' he asked.

Alec nodded, but he was now feeling horribly apprehensive. He really didn't know what to expect. Ethan swung the door open and stepped into the room, removing his hat as he did so. Alec followed, closing the door behind him.

His first thought was that they had come to the wrong room. Over by the far wall a man was sitting in a bath chair, but this was an old fellow of perhaps seventy or eighty years. He was staring intently at the floor, as though watching something, but when Alec followed the direction of his gaze, there appeared to be nothing there but the bare tiles. Alec noticed that behind the man, the room's single window was closed, the heavy wooden shutters secured with a stout padlock.

The absence of any fresh air made it very oppressive in there and Alec immediately felt beads of sweat breaking out on his forehead, yet the man had a thick woollen blanket over his lap as though he felt a chill. Alec turned to direct a puzzled look at Ethan, but the American's grim expression made him look once again at the old man: a shock went through him as he realized that this was indeed Uncle Will, but changed dramatically since Alec had last seen him.

He had been a tall, rangy, dark-complexioned fellow of fifty, with broad shoulders and striking grey eyes. The man who sat there now seemed somehow shrunken, as though the hot sun had shrivelled his flesh and bones. His formerly dark brown hair was now a mop of snow-white wisps, and his moustache was of the same December hue. Worst of all were the eyes – weak and watery, the colour drained from them; and they seemed to be staring fixedly at something only they could see.

'William!' cried Ethan with forced jocularity. 'I've brought somebody to see you, an old friend.'

Uncle Will lifted his head slightly and those dead eyes surveyed Alec for a moment, but showed no sign of recognition.

Ethan guided Alec forward until he was standing right in front of his uncle. Alec looked down at Will's hands, which were arranged like claws on his blanket. They were shaking as though he was in the grip of a terrible fever.

'Look, Will,' persisted Ethan. 'It's your nephew, Alec. He's travelled down from Cairo to see you. You remember Alec, don't you?'

Uncle Will's eyes continued to stare up at his nephew and he said the name 'Alec' in a flat monotone. Ethan nudged Alec, prompting him to respond.

'Hello, Uncle,' said Alec. 'It's . . . good to see you again. I'm . . . sorry you haven't been well.'

'Alec,' repeated Uncle Will, but once again it was just something spoken parrot-fashion. There was no trace of warmth in that croak of a voice. Like the pale, watery eyes, it seemed completely devoid of life.

'Alec's come to help out with the dig,' said Ethan, crouching down to put himself on the same level as his old friend. 'I know he's been of great assistance to you in the past and I can sure use his skills. I don't know if you recall, but you mentioned him several times in your journal. You said you were completely at a loss to decipher a message and something Alec said gave you the key to it? Do you remember writing that?'

'Key,' whispered Uncle Will and his grey head nodded, but whether this was in answer to what had just been said was anybody's guess, because the head kept nodding slowly long after it was appropriate.

'Father sends his regards,' said Alec. 'I'm sure he'll be over to visit you when he gets the opportunity. Coates is with me too. You . . . you remember Coates, don't you? The valet?'

'Coates.' Again the same dull croak. It was as if the words were meaningless to Uncle Will and he was just acting the role of an echo.

'Yes, that's right. He came with me on the last two trips. You must remember him. He didn't know I was coming to see you, otherwise I'm sure he . . .'

Alec felt ridiculous talking like this and getting no response. He looked at Ethan apologetically.

Ethan nodded, understanding, but was clearly not ready to give up just yet. He put a hand on Uncle Will's shoulder. 'Alec's joining us at an exciting time,' he said. 'We've almost cleared out the last of the artefacts from the antechamber. Any day now we'll be ready to break the seals on the door to the tomb.'

Something happened then. Uncle Will

reacted. His eyes widened and a kind of manic realization seemed to come into them.

'Break them?' he said. 'Break the . . . seals?'

'Yes.' Ethan was delighted to have elicited such a response. 'It won't be long now. Everything you and Tom worked for will be—'

'No!' gasped Uncle Will. 'Don't. *Don't.*'

'Don't what?' asked Ethan, puzzled.

'Go in. Don't. He's not there. Already . . . out. Already out.'

'Who's already out, William?' Ethan was staring into Uncle Will's face, trying to fathom his meaning.

'He's out. Out. I've seen him. The serpent's eye. We . . . we removed it.' Uncle Will's eyes were now staring with a shocking intensity and they suddenly seemed to fasten on Alec, as if recognition had just set in. He reached up and grabbed his nephew's wrist with a strength that made the boy wince. 'Go home!' he bellowed, his voice rising in power. 'You shouldn't have come, Alec. You shouldn't have come!'

'William, you're hurting the boy!' Ethan was trying to prise Uncle Will's fingers free of Alec's wrist, but despite his apparent frailty, he seemed to have discovered an incredible energy and was now talking non-stop, virtually shouting the words into Alec's face.

'He seized the dragon, that serpent of old, the Devil or Apophis, and chained him up for a thousand years! He threw him into an abyss, shutting and sealing it over him, so that he might seduce the nations no more till the thousand years were over! After that he must be let loose for a short while!'

'Uncle, please, stop, you're hurting me!' Alec struggled to pull away from his uncle, but he hung on tenaciously and even the brawny American couldn't seem to break his grip.

'He's out, Alec, don't you see? He's out, and now everything changes – nothing is ever the same again. Tom knows, Tom was there, Tom knows better than anyone what he's capable of. I've seen him, Alec! I've seen what he can do . . .' Then, all at once, Uncle Will's voice trailed away and he seemed to lose all his strength. He let go of Alec and flopped back into the bath chair, his mouth hanging open. The vacant look came back into his eyes and Alec saw that they were filling with tears. 'Out,' he whispered. 'He's out. I've seen him.'

He went back to his silent study of the floor.

Alec and Ethan stood for a moment in silence, staring down at the old, old man in the chair. The sudden transformation had startled them. Alec felt the hairs on the back of his neck stand on end.

'Are you all right?' Ethan asked him at last.

Alec nodded. He rubbed his wrist, where already a ring of dark bruises was appearing. 'I'm fine,' he said. 'I'm not sure what happened there. He seemed to realize it was me at the end.'

'I don't know what got into him – he's never been like this before. What was that stuff he was saying – about a dragon or something?'

'I think it's from the Bible,' Alec told him. 'Except he said . . .'

'What?'

'He said Apophis. The Egyptian serpent god of the underworld. I'm not much of a Bible reader but I'm pretty sure Apophis doesn't figure any-where. And there was something about . . . a serpent's eye?'

Ethan frowned. 'I'm real sorry, kid. I had no idea he'd get all riled up like that. Guess I shouldn't have brought you here.'

'No, that's all right. I'm glad I saw him. Really.' Alec felt badly shaken by what had happened. It was hard to believe that the wretched, wasted creature in the bath chair was the same man he had spent so many happy hours with. 'What can have happened to him, Mr Wade?'

Ethan shook his head. 'I wish I knew,' he said.

He turned and crouched beside Uncle Will again. 'We'll be on our way now,' he said quietly. 'Maybe we'll come and see you again soon, huh?'

Uncle Will said nothing. He was still gazing at the floor and his hands had begun to shake once more. Alec felt so sorry for him – and so totally powerless to do anything to help. He had retreated back to the world he had been lost in when they first entered the room.

Ethan shrugged in defeat. He stood up and led the way back to the door. Just before Alec followed him out of the room, he glanced back at his uncle.

What could make a man change so completely? Whatever had happened to him, it must have been terrifying.

With a sigh, Alec watched Ethan lock the door behind them. 'Is that really necessary?' he asked.

'I'm afraid so. He's . . . unpredictable. They're afraid he might harm himself.'

They began to retrace their steps along the corridor.

'Is there no hope for him?' asked Alec.

Ethan's face was expressionless. 'I'm sorry, kid. The doctors who've seen him say he's a hopeless case.'

'Perhaps if we got him back to Cairo – or even London?' suggested Alec.

'You've seen the condition he's in. I doubt he'd be strong enough to make such a journey.'

Alec rubbed his bruised wrist. 'For a minute there he *seemed* strong enough,' he observed.

They dropped off the key at reception and made their way out onto the street. An inquisitive crowd of natives had gathered around the Crossley and were poking and prodding at it, as though convinced it had just dropped in from outer space. However, they fell back obediently to allow Ethan and Alec to climb into their seats. Some of them reached into their pockets and started brandishing homemade 'relics'.

Ethan got the engine running and then swept off back the way they had come. Soon they were driving sedately out into the desert again.

'Uncle Will kept saying, *He's out*,' said Alec.

'Yeah. Not sure who he's talking about though. Seems to have something to do with the tomb. He didn't want us to open the door. But that doesn't make any sense. It's what he and Tom worked for all those years.'

'*He's already out. I've seen him,*' mused Alec. 'You're sure it's Akhenaten's tomb?'

'Well, the seals on the outer door sure have his name all over 'em. But until we get into the burial chamber, we can't be certain.'

'Akhenaten is interesting,' said Alec. 'He's one of the least known pharaohs. After his death, the people who succeeded him did everything they could to erase his memory. They destroyed his statues, his temples . . . In his official tomb in Amarna, even his sarcophagus was smashed into tiny pieces.'

Ethan frowned. 'Yeah, why was that exactly?'

'Well, most people think that it was because he banished all the popular gods that people had been worshipping for years and made them worship only one, Aten, the sun disc. It was the start of monotheism.'

Ethan looked at Alec doubtfully. 'For a kid, you sure know some fancy words,' he said.

Alec smiled. He was beginning to like the American. He loved the way he didn't try and pretend he knew more than he did. Most adults would have just nodded, as though Alec was telling them something they already knew.

'Uncle Will always believed that Akhenaten's followers must have rescued his mummy and had it reburied in the Valley of the Kings, away from harm,' said Alec. 'Some archaeologists think that his mummy is the one they found in tomb fifty-five in nineteen-o-seven, because all identifying features had been erased; but Uncle Will never accepted that was him. He thinks it's the body of Smenkhkare, another missing pharaoh – and I agree with him.'

Ethan grinned. 'I ain't about to argue with either of you,' he said. 'Sounds like you both know your stuff.'

'Uncle Will kept saying that he was already out . . . Do you suppose he meant that Akhenaten's mummy was gone? Maybe tomb robbers got there before Uncle Will did and stole the remains.'

Ethan shook his head. 'No. As far as we can see, nobody ever broke into this tomb. It was absolutely untouched.'

Alec stared. 'But that's incredible!' he said. 'There's not a tomb been found that hasn't had *somebody* break in and filch some of the treasures. Even King Tut's tomb had been broken into twice over the past three thousand years.'

'Yeah, Carter told me that. I spoke to him the other day.'

'He's a nice chap,' said Alec. 'Uncle Will introduced me to him on the last dig. It was good of him and Lord Carnarvon to allow Uncle Will to excavate in the Valley of the Kings. He had to approach them for permission, years back. Carter could have said no, but he didn't – he said something about there being no harm in a bit of healthy competition.'

'You admire Carter, huh?'

'I was back at school in Cairo when they found Tut's tomb. I would have given anything to have been in on that.' Alec wasn't about to admit it, but Howard Carter was the nearest thing he had to a hero in his life. If he could have changed places with anyone in the world, Carter would have been his first choice.

Ethan smiled. 'Well, Howard's having a tough time of it now. Since Lord Carnarvon died he can't make a move without somebody shoving a camera in his face. All that baloney about a curse.'

'You don't believe it, then?'

'Heck, no! People like to make up that mumbo jumbo – it sells newspapers.'

'But Lord Carnarvon *did* die back in March.'

'Sure, but not from a curse — just an infected mosquito bite.'

Alec nodded. 'Same thing that got my mother,' he said.

Ethan looked uncomfortable. 'Yeah, I remember Will mentioning it in one of his letters. Must've been tough for you, Alec.'

Alec did what he always did in these circumstances. He ignored the sympathy and pressed on with the point he was making. 'Llewellyn said something about a curse, back on the *Sudan*,' he said. 'Not for Tut's tomb; for the one that Uncle Will found. How is it he knows about the find?'

'Not sure. I've only told a few people and I swore them all to secrecy. I guess somebody must have blabbed.'

'Hmm. You have to admit that it's strange that nobody has been near that tomb since it was first sealed. Have they found much in the way of artefacts?'

'Are you kidding? So far, we've only been in the antechamber and that is stacked with goodies. Jars, scrolls, statues, chariots. You name it!'

'Which makes it even more odd. We know that tomb robbers usually turn out to have been in cahoots with the people who organized the burial. Why didn't somebody come and loot this one?'

'Well . . . maybe it was just better hidden than most. From what I read in Will's journal, it was a complete accident that somebody chanced upon it when they did. He said that— Oh, great!'

'What's the matter?' Alec looked up in surprise. Ethan was staring at something in the rear-view mirror. Alec turned to look over his shoulder. The sky behind them was darkening to an ominous gunmetal grey; below, a shifting, stirring brown mass was whipping around in the air.

'Sandstorm coming in,' said Ethan. 'Travelling pretty fast, by the look of it.' He glanced round. 'We can't turn back. We'll just have to keep on for the camp and hope we can outrun it.' He looked at Alec and grinned. 'What were you just saying about a curse?'

He pushed his foot down on the accelerator and brought the Crossley up to its top speed, the metal chassis juddering as the wheels raced across the uneven dirt surface. Already the wind was picking up and Alec could see little flurries of sand gusting across the surface of the road.

'How far is it to camp?' he asked anxiously.

'Maybe twenty miles.' Ethan turned to the boy and winked. 'Not a very nice welcome, Alec. But don't worry, we'll be OK.'

Alec hoped the American was right. He hunched down in his seat and stared out at the seemingly endless ribbon of road unwinding in front of them. Whenever he glanced over his shoulder, he could see that the storm was getting closer by the minute.

CHAPTER FOUR

Hostile Reception

They had just made it back to the fork in the road where they had parted company with Mickey and Coates when the storm began to close in on them, the sound of the wind rising to a howl. Ethan and Alec had already put up the roof and secured it in position and now there was nothing to do but bring the Crossley to a halt and wait for things to improve. Visibility had already dropped to just a few yards and it was hard to even see the road through the rising blizzard of sand. Then the storm struck and Alec could feel the heavy vehicle shifting beneath the force of it. It felt as though it might flip over at any moment.

With the windows closed it grew intolerably hot and Alec and Ethan sat side by side, sweating profusely.

'This is screwy,' muttered Ethan, having to shout over the noise of the wind. 'Damned storm just seemed to come out of nowhere.' He glanced apologetically at Alec. 'Sorry, kid. If we'd headed straight for the dig, we'd be there by now.'

'It's all right,' Alec assured him. 'I'm glad we went to see Uncle Will, even though he wasn't on great form. How did you come to know him?'

Ethan smiled, remembering. 'It was after the war,' he said. 'I'd seen some bad things and I guess it affected me more than I knew. I went off the rails for a while. I had trouble sleeping. Got a little too fond of hard liquor and gambling – couldn't seem to hold down a steady job. My debts got so bad in the end, I had to get out of the country fast. I took work as a deck hand aboard a cargo ship bound for Cairo. I ended up hanging around the docks doing odd jobs to get enough money to eat.'

He shook his head. 'I was at rock bottom,' he went on. 'Then I met Will. He was in town to take care of some business. He weighed me up pretty quick – must have realized I was in a bad way. He said he could always use more help over at the dig. So I figured, what the heck, I'd give it a try.' He shrugged. 'I knew nothing about ancient Egypt, and Will realized that, but he was prepared to give me a chance when everybody else had given up on me, so I'll always be in his debt for that.'

'That's Uncle Will,' agreed Alec. 'Always likes to help others.'

Ethan nodded. 'Well, things finally started to work out for me. Will and Tom gave me more responsibility; I finally felt like I was doing something worthwhile. Oh, we weren't having much success back then, just a few small finds. I worked with them for the first year and a half, but then something came up back in the States. My dad was pretty ill and I needed to go back and settle his affairs. Will made me promise to come back just as soon as I could and even lent me the money to get back to the States. It took a while to straighten things out.'

Alec gave him a questioning look. 'Your father died?' he asked.

'Yeah.' Ethan looked sad for a moment. 'He was a good age, and I guess it wasn't unexpected but . . . well, it's a sad time in anyone's life.'

'And your mother?' asked Alec.

'She was long gone.' He glanced warily at Alec, remembering that the boy had recently lost his own mother. 'Anyhow, I didn't get back to Egypt for a long time. I went up to Wyoming for a year and worked as a cowboy.'

'Wow! Honestly?'

'Sure. There's still big herds of cattle out there, need taking from place to place. It's a hard life, but it can be satisfying. After that I headed down to Mexico and took a post as a mercenary, helping the government put down a revolution.'

'A mercenary . . . that's like a hired gun, isn't it?'

Ethan grimaced. 'I'm not particularly proud of it, but I still had debts to pay off and I knew I couldn't think about heading back to Egypt until they were taken care of. Through it all Will kept in touch. He kept writing me to say there was always a place for me on the team and when was I coming back? Finally, just a couple of months ago, I could see my way clear to do it. I agreed to join up with them for the next season, even let them put my name down on the insurance form, just in case anything should happen to Will or Tom. Then I arrived here three weeks ago to discover that Will had suffered a complete breakdown and Tom had disappeared.' He shook his head. 'Quite a welcome!'

'So that's how you came to be in charge?' said Alec.

'Pretty much. Heck, I'm sure there are plenty of people more qualified to do it, but nobody else on the team seemed willing to shoulder the responsibility. Believe me, I asked them!' He shrugged. 'I feel I owe it to Will to take care of this amazing find that he's made and make sure everything goes as smooth as I can make it.'

He seemed to make an effort to change the subject. 'Devlin's an Irish name, isn't it? I always meant to ask Will, but I never got around to it. Neither of you seem like any of the Irishmen I've ever met.'

Alec smiled. It was a familiar question. 'My great-grandfather came from Mayo,' he said. 'A little place called Westport.'

Ethan grinned. 'I know it,' he said. 'Wonderful people.' He raised his eyebrows. 'Wonderful pubs too.'

'I'll have to take your word for that. My great-grandfather emigrated to London in the early nineteenth century. He made the family fortune in the building trade. We don't have much of a connection with Ireland now, though I believe Dad has some money invested in horse-breeding in County Kildare.'

Ethan shook his head. 'Poor little rich kid, huh?' he said.

Alec nodded. 'I suppose we *are* pretty well off,' he admitted. 'But I'd trade it all to have my mother back.'

He glanced awkwardly at Ethan, surprised by his own words. He didn't usually give so much of himself away to somebody he hardly knew.

Ethan was about to give an answer when something inexplicable happened. There was a last cataclysmic rush of wind and then the sky began to clear as the storm raced on past them across the sand. In just a few moments, everything seemed to be back to normal.

'Well now, if that don't beat everything,' exclaimed Ethan. 'I never saw a storm come and go so fast!' He threw open the door and stepped out into the blazing sun, beating some of the sand off his legs with his stetson. Alec got out too and stared after the fast-disappearing clouds of dust on the horizon.

'Storms like that usually last for hours,' he said.

'Yeah, ain't we the lucky ones?' Ethan got back into the Crossley and hit the self-starter. All that emerged was a dry rattling cough. He tried a few more times, with the same result, and then got out again, walked round to the front and unlatched the bonnet. He tinkered with the engine for a while, then stepped away from it with a grunt of exasperation. 'That's what I was worried about,' he said. 'Looks like sand has choked up just about every moving part.' He slammed the bonnet down and put on his stetson.

Alec took a long look around, turning slowly through 360 degrees. There was nothing as far as the eye could see – only the white dunes stretching to the horizon in every direction. Ahead of them, the hard surface of the road showed only in patches through the fine white sand that had swept in to cover it.

He looked at Ethan. 'What do we do now?' he asked, trying not to think of the terrible stories he'd heard about people who had been marooned in this desert. He could feel the raw power of the sun clawing through his canvas shirt.

'We start walking,' said Ethan, sounding calm and positive. 'As long as we stick to the road, we should be all right. And hopefully somebody from the dig might come out to look for us. They must have seen that sandstorm and they'll know we were on our way back.' He moved back to the Crossley and, reaching into the back seats, pulled out a couple of canteens. 'Luckily I never go anywhere without plenty of water,' he said. He threw one of them over to Alec, who caught it and slung it across his shoulder.

'What about the Crossley?' asked Alec.

'I'll send Mickey back to have a look at it once we reach the dig,' said Ethan. 'He'll be able to fix it – I never saw a better mechanic. Come on, let's stride it out. The faster we walk, the sooner we'll get there.' He set off as if embarking on nothing more daunting than a stroll in the park.

Alec hurried up and fell into step alongside him. 'Coates says you're a soldier of fortune,' he observed.

Ethan laughed. 'Is that what he said? Well, it's as good a description as any, I guess. I kind of got the impression that Coates didn't exactly approve of me.'

Alec shrugged. 'He's like that with everyone when he first meets them,' he said. 'I think it's mostly because you're an American.'

Ethan raised his eyebrows. 'I can't do much about that!' he protested. 'What's so bad about Americans, anyway?'

'Oh, well, I think the main problem is that they're not *English*. Coates dislikes most other nationalities on principle. He's very old fashioned but he's a decent sort when you get to know him. Absolutely devoted to the Devlins.'

Ethan looked at Alec, amused.

'What?' asked Alec.

'The way you talk,' he said. '*Absolutely devoted to the Devlins*. Don't get me wrong, it's kind of neat. Like something out of Charles Dickens.'

'You've read Dickens?' Alec was impressed.

'Some. *Oliver Twist . . . Great Expectations*. You know, the good ones. What's the matter, you think us Yanks only ever go to the movie theatres?'

Alec tried not to look guilty, remembering something that Coates had said back aboard the *Sudan*. 'Of course not,' he said.

'So, what do you read, Alec?'

'Me? Oh . . . I like H. Rider Haggard.'

'*King Solomon's Mines?* Great book. Read it when I was around your age. Loved it. I've even been to some of the places mentioned in it. Didn't find the mines, though.'

'What did you find?'

'Trouble mostly,' admitted Ethan. 'Though in some cases the trouble came looking for me.' He laughed and shook his head. 'So how come you're out here in Egypt, Alec?'

'It's Father's job, mainly. He's been stationed in Egypt for quite a few years now. I attend a boarding school in Cairo and twice a year I spend my holidays with him. Except, of course, he doesn't have an awful lot of time for me, which is where poor Uncle Will came in.' He thought for a moment. 'Actually, this might be our last year in Egypt. Dad says they're planning on making him a roving ambassador, which means he'll be travelling all over the world. He said something about Mexico, the last time we spoke.'

'Mexico, huh? Now that's a wild place. You'll need to be very careful out there. Bandits around every corner.'

'Oh yes, you said you'd been there.'

'Sure have. Got into some trouble last time. I was lucky to get out with my skin in one piece.'

Alec was about to say something else, but he suddenly experienced a powerful sensation of being followed and turned his head to look behind him. At first he saw nothing unusual – just the baking sand dunes, rippling and undulating in the rising heat; but then he saw shapes coming through the heat haze – five or six brownish creatures prowling along the road behind them.

'Mr Wade . . . ?' he said.

Ethan stopped walking and turned to look. As they watched, the rippling shapes seemed to take solid form, as though they had appeared magically from some other dimension. Now Alec could make out the brown spotted fur, the awkward gait of an animal that had longer front legs than back ones. He could see the ugly, brutish heads and the prominent ears. The creatures were staring at the two humans with a steadfast, malignant gaze as they slunk steadily forward.

Hyenas. Alec felt a chill jolt through him. He knew all about hyenas. On a trip to the Serengeti with his father he had once witnessed a pack of them tearing at the carcass of an antelope with jaws powerful enough to splinter the creature's bones.

'What the heck are they doing way out here?' asked Ethan quietly. He glanced at Alec. 'Don't worry, kid. Those things are cowards – they only go for easy prey.'

'And we don't strike you as easy? Two people in the middle of nowhere?'

'Oh, they ain't gonna bother us.' Ethan turned away and began walking on, affecting an air of unconcern, but as he fell back into step, Alec saw that the American had taken his pistol out of its holster and was checking that it was fully loaded.

'That's a Colt forty-five, isn't it?' he asked.

Ethan nodded. 'Yup. This gun has quite a history. Belonged to my dad and his dad before him. Thing must be over sixty years old, but it's never let me down yet.' He glanced briefly over his shoulder, as if weighing up the enemy. 'I gotta say, I'm surprised to see a pack of those things this far north. You ever see 'em before?'

Alec shook his head. 'Not around here. They were around in ancient times, though. The Egyptians kept them as pets. Occasionally they used to fatten them up and eat them. They were considered quite a delicacy.'

'Is that a fact?' Ethan threw a glance over his shoulder. 'Well, I've got six shots for six hyenas. If it comes to it, I should be able to take them all out.'

'That's assuming you don't miss,' said Alec.

'Kid, I *never* miss. Don't worry about a thing.'

Alec tried not to be afraid, but he was horribly aware that the hyenas were steadily closing in on them and, though he knew that most of their species were scavengers who preferred to feed off the kill of other animals, he also remembered being told that the spotted variety were skilled predators who were more than capable of dragging down live prey. He licked his lips and looked at the American. 'Mr Wade . . . ?'

'I told you, kid, call me Ethan!'

'Umm . . . yes, of course. Ethan, I don't suppose you have another weapon I could use?'

Ethan thought for a moment and then reached into a sheath at his belt and withdrew a big broad-bladed hunting knife. 'Think you could handle that?' he asked.

'I suppose so.' Alec took the knife. It was so big he had to use both hands to clasp the bone handle. He made a few jabbing motions in the air.

'That's the idea,' said Ethan. 'But look, I really don't think you're going to need to—'

A low rumbling growl stopped them in their tracks and they turned to see that one of the hyenas, a huge barrel-chested brute, had moved on ahead of the others and was now only a few yards away. It was creeping forward, its head low to the ground, its scraggy tail tucked between its legs. It bared its teeth, revealing rows of dripping fangs. A thick rope of saliva fell from its jaws.

'Get outa here!' yelled Ethan, waving his arms, but the hyena showed no fear, just kept right on coming. Ethan said something colourful under his breath. 'Tenacious sort, huh?' he murmured. He glanced at Alec. 'Watch this,' he said. He lifted the revolver and discharged a shot a few feet in front of the hyena's paws. The creature stopped for an instant. Then it came on again.

'This doesn't make any sense,' muttered Ethan. 'It should have run. Why didn't it run?'

Alec shook his head. He had no idea, but he was beginning to feel very worried about this.

'All right, buster, you asked for it,' said Ethan. 'Time to make an example.'

He lifted the revolver a second time and took aim at the creature's chest. The gun cracked loudly and made Alec jump; and the hyena jolted as though it had been struck across the chest with a cricket bat; but it only faltered for a moment before coming on again. Ethan stared down at it in utter amazement. The other creatures were hurrying forward now, as though moving in to avenge their stricken comrade. Ethan lifted the gun a third time and fired again, blasting another hole in the hyena's chest, inches away from the first. Once again the hyena lurched from the impact, but didn't die. Ethan raised the gun a fraction and put a shot into the beast's head, and this time it dropped in its tracks, its limbs twitching.

'That's four bullets gone!' gasped Alec.

'Yeah, I noticed that too,' said Ethan, sounding ridiculously calm under the circumstances. Two more hyenas were running in to take the place of the fallen beast and Ethan pumped a shot into the first one's head, killing it instantly; but before he could take aim at the next, it had thrown itself through the air and struck him hard in the chest, flinging him backwards onto the sand. The pistol flew from his grasp and he was obliged to throw up his hands and clamp them around the beast's throat in a desperate effort to keep its slavering jaws at bay.

For a moment Alec was frozen to the spot, but then, realizing that he had to go to Ethan's aid, he ran over to where the American was struggling with his attacker and drove the blade of the knife down hard between the hyena's shoulders. The beast gave a high-pitched shriek of agony, then twisted away from Ethan and staggered off, yelping. Ethan sat up and stared frantically around for the gun. He saw it lying several feet away, half buried in the sand, and began to scramble towards it, but another low-pitched growl stilled him. He turned to see that another hyena was closing in for the kill.

Alec acted instinctively. He put himself between Ethan and the beast and raised the knife. 'Go for the gun,' he told Ethan.

'Kid, no, move back!' Ethan begged him.

Alec shook his head. 'It's our only chance,' he said. 'Get the gun, Ethan.'

Ethan nodded, then got onto his hands and knees. The hyena's growl deepened and it braced itself, ready to leap at the boy. Alec took a firm grip on the handle of the knife and waited. He was dimly aware of a strange sound, a wild honking, as though a flight of geese was passing overhead, but he was looking into the hyena's amber eyes and he had to concentrate, because the beast's shoulder muscles were bunching as it steeled itself to leap.

And then Alec heard Ethan's voice from behind him.

'I've got the gun,' he said, sounding calm again. 'Move aside. Gently now,'

Alec swallowed and did as he was told, keeping his gaze fixed on the hyena.

'Now, you brute,' he heard Ethan say.

And then there was the sharp metallic click of a misfire.

CHAPTER FIVE

Mohammed Hansa

The ancient automobile seemed to come out of nowhere, its rusting black chassis clattering on the uneven road, its horn honking repeatedly. Alec realized that this was the sound he had been registering for the past few moments; what he had taken, in his state of confusion, to be a flock of geese.

The vehicle came hammering straight towards him but swerved at the last moment, flinging up a spray of sand. The front bumper clipped the back end of the crouching hyena as it went by, sending the creature tumbling sideways with a howl of pain. The automobile skidded to a halt and the hyena scrambled back to its feet and ran for its life, yelping. Its two companions, unnerved by the automobile's sudden appearance, took off after it. There was a sudden loud bang that made Alec flinch, and a spray of sand was kicked up just inches behind the last hyena's departing legs.

Alec looked back in amazement. Sitting in the rear seat of the dilapidated Model T Ford was an astonished-looking and rather dishevelled Wilfred Llewellyn. In front of him, standing up on the driver's seat, was a young Arab man in a long white galabiya. He was holding an old-fashioned percussion-cap rifle which he had just fired at the fleeing hyenas. He lowered the weapon and turned to look down at the two people he had just rescued, grinning delightedly at them. He was a handsome fellow, with shoulder-length black hair and dark brown eyes that glittered with intelligence.

'Mr Wade!' he cried. 'I *thought* it was you! Are you all right, my friend?'

Ethan grinned back at him. He untied the bandana from around his neck and mopped at a trickle of blood that was moving down his forehead.

'I'm fine, thanks to you.' He walked over to

Alec, sliding the pistol back into its holster as he did so. 'Glad you happened along when you did. Alec, this gentleman is Mr Mohammed Hansa, a trader from Luxor. He's fairly new to the area, so I guess you won't have met him before.'

Mohammed bowed politely. 'Pleased to make your acquaintance,' he said. 'Any friend of Mr Wade's is a dear friend of mine.'

'Pleased to meet you, Mr Hansa.'

'Mohammed. Please, call me Mohammed.'

'When our team needs any luxury items, Mohammed's the guy we go to,' continued Ethan. 'He can put his hands on just about anything – soap, razor blades, cigarettes, whisky – you name it! He's also the closest thing there is to a local taxi service.' He glanced at Llewellyn. 'Boy, am I glad we didn't give you the lift you wanted.'

For the moment Llewellyn seemed to have lost the power of speech. He just sat there, staring open-mouthed at Ethan, who turned his attention back to the driver of the Ford.

'Mohammed, this young man is Sir William's nephew, Alec, come to help us out at the dig.'

Mohammed bowed his head a second time and placed a hand on his chest. 'An honour it is,

young sir,' he said. 'So sorry to hear about your
uncle's illness. Such a fine English gentleman.'

'Would somebody mind telling me what's
going on here?' piped up Llewellyn, who had
finally recovered himself enough to speak. 'One
moment we're driving along nice and quiet, the
next we're thundering towards those creatures—'

'Hyenas,' said Mohammed. 'Attacking my
good friend Mr Wade here. I could hardly sit
there and ignore his plight.'

'Well, no, of course not,' admitted Llewellyn.
'But a bit of warning wouldn't have gone amiss.
I nearly had a heart attack.'

'Alas, sir, there was no time. I had to act
quickly.' Mohammed turned back to Ethan. 'I
had a feeling we might see you, Mr Wade. We
passed your fine English automobile on the road
back there.' He gave Ethan a sly look and sat back
down in the driver's seat. 'Surely it cannot possibly have broken down?'

Ethan chuckled. 'Yeah, Mohammed, I know
what you're getting at. I promise I won't make
any more bad jokes about your Model T, OK?
Right now it looks like the nicest car a man
could ever wish to see.' He patted its rusting
bonnet respectfully. 'Though to be honest, I can't

believe that sandstorm didn't finish off your engine too.'

Mohammed looked puzzled. 'Sandstorm?' he murmured. 'What sandstorm?'

Ethan stared at him. 'Well, you must have seen it,' he spluttered. 'You weren't that far behind us. Near enough blew us right off the road.'

But Mohammed was shaking his head. 'I saw no sandstorm, Mr Wade. It has been like this all the way from Luxor.'

Alec and Ethan exchanged puzzled looks.

'It's all very odd,' continued Mohammed. 'What on earth are hyenas doing so far north? And what made them attack you?' He indicated the dead creatures lying in the sand. 'They are usually such timid creatures. One shot of a gun should have been enough to see them off.'

'Yeah.' Ethan tilted back his hat and stared down at the corpses. 'How do you account for that?' He indicated the biggest of them. 'Took three shots to put that big feller down. Never known anything like it.' He pointed to another dead hyena. 'That guy I got with a head shot.' He lifted his gaze and saw a third hyena lying dead some distance from the others. 'And that one . . .' He seemed to remember something.

His eyes widened and he turned to look at Alec.

'Kid,' he said. 'You . . . you saved my neck. I remember now. That hyena was on top of me and you stuck him with the blade.'

Alec looked down at the hunting knife in his right hand, which was red and sticky with gore. He squatted down and plunged the blade into the sand to clean it.

'I . . . I didn't have time to think,' he said. 'That thing was on top of you and . . . well, I just did what I thought was best.' He handed the knife back to Ethan, who slid it back into its sheath.

'You did great,' he said. 'Really great.'

Alec shrugged. He uncorked his canteen and began to wash the blood from his hand.

Ethan turned to Llewellyn. 'Now there's a story for your newspaper,' he said. 'A story of courage . . . A young boy fighting off a savage beast and saving a man's life! Your readers will love it. And unlike most stories you people print, this one is actually true.'

Llewellyn stared at him for a moment as though he hadn't the faintest idea what Ethan was on about. Then he seemed to remember something. 'Oh, ah, yes, of course! You must, er . . . let me have all the details . . . I shall talk to you when we reach our destination and I'll, er . . . make some notes.'

'Great. Say, which newspaper did you say you worked for?'

'The . . . *Examiner*.'

'Oh, right, so you must know Billy Farnsworth.'

'Umm . . . Billy . . . ?'

'You know, the sports columnist?'

Llewellyn smiled. 'Oh yes, of course. Billy! He and I are great friends.'

Ethan gave him a knowing look. 'Tell me, he still got something going with that little cocktail waitress from the Sphinx nightclub?'

Llewellyn winked. 'I'm afraid so. It's the talk of the office.'

Ethan nodded. 'Well,' he said, 'I guess that settles it. You're no more a newspaper reporter than I am.'

Llewellyn looked appalled. 'What are you suggesting?' he cried.

'Mr Llewellyn, there *is* no Billy Farnsworth and no cocktail waitress neither. I just made 'em up. Now, either you tell me the truth or you can get out of this automobile and start walking.'

Llewellyn's expression turned to one of alarm.

He reached into his inside pocket and produced a leather wallet, which he flipped open and held out to Ethan. 'You must forgive me, Mr Wade. As you say, I am not a reporter but a private detective. I have been hired by the parents of Mr Thomas Hinton to investigate the circumstances surrounding their son's disappearance.' He withdrew a letter from the wallet and handed it over. 'That's from Mr Hinton,' he said, 'explaining the situation. I had hoped that my little deception might help me to obtain information.'

Ethan studied the letter for a few moments in silence. Then he shrugged and handed it back. 'Why didn't you just tell the truth?' he said. 'I don't appreciate being lied to.'

Llewellyn frowned. 'In my experience, Mr Wade, most people have a tendency to distrust detectives, but will tell newspapermen just about anything.'

'Yeah, well, I ain't most people. I hate reporters but I've got a lot of time for private dicks.'

'I beg your pardon?'

'Detectives. One of my favourite uncles is in the business. Obadiah Wade – operates out of Boston. Maybe you heard of him?'

Llewellyn shook his head and his cluster of

chins wobbled alarmingly. 'I'm afraid not,' he said. 'Sorry.'

'That's OK.' Ethan looked at Alec. 'That explains how he knows about the tomb. When I informed Tom's parents that he'd gone missing, they asked for more details, and I had to tell them about the new discovery.'

Alec looked at Llewellyn. 'So Tom's parents told you about the tomb?'

Llewellyn nodded. 'They're very worried about their son. They want some answers.'

'That's perfectly understandable,' said Ethan. 'Tell you the truth, I wouldn't mind a few myself.'

'You surprise me,' said Llewellyn. 'From what Mr Hinton's parents told me, you haven't exactly been yelling about his disappearance from the rooftops.'

'The rest of the team made a pretty thorough search for him before I even got here. They drew a blank. The local police didn't seem to want to know about it. And when I first got here, I made enquiries about Tom too – discreet enquiries.'

Llewellyn frowned. 'Why so discreet?' he asked. 'It's almost as though you don't *want* to find Mr Hinton.'

'That's not true – of course we want to find him! But the thing is, I couldn't open it up too wide: we'd have had the newspaper reporters at the site and then Sir William's great discovery would be splashed over every paper from here to Chattanooga.' He stared at Llewellyn for a moment, his arms folded. 'So what do we do with you, Llewellyn? I confess, my first instinct is to leave you here, and if the rest of those hyenas come back, that's just tough.'

Llewellyn stared at Ethan in horror. 'Mr Wade, I have apologized for my deception. Please, I beseech you, you cannot abandon me to such a fate.'

Ethan scowled. 'I must be getting soft in my old age, but I'm going to give you one chance. Just one, mind you! You can come with us to the dig and you can even ask questions. But I'm warning you – you ever lie to me again and you'll be heading back to Luxor with my boot up your backside.'

Llewellyn was evidently outraged by this remark and Alec had to smother a laugh at the expression on his face, but after a moment he nodded. 'I'm sorry, Mr Wade. I was just trying to do my job.'

'And I'm trying to do mine.' Ethan thought for a moment. 'How long is it going to take, this questioning? You need me to assign you a spare tent?'

Llewellyn looked absolutely horrified. 'That won't be necessary,' he said. 'The Hintons have agreed to finance a room at the Winter Palace Hotel in Luxor.'

Ethan raised his eyebrows. 'Nice. Uncle Obadiah always used to say the best thing about the job was the perks. Maybe I went into the wrong line of work. It's comfortable there.'

'Very comfortable,' agreed Alec. 'Hot showers, ceiling fans, the best food for miles around . . . But of course, you won't be doing it properly like us.'

'I'll live with myself somehow,' said Llewellyn.

'I'm sure you will,' said Ethan. 'But, Mr Llewellyn, I got to warn you. If you're asking questions *anywhere*, please be discreet. Whatever you do, don't go telling people that we found a tomb. It's a sensitive situation and I'm trying to keep a tight lid on it. The last thing I want is for this to get leaked to the newspapers. And listen, the native workers on the dig . . . I've kind of given them the impression that Tom went back to England—'

'You did what?' cried Llewellyn.

'You need to understand, they're a superstitious crowd. If I let them think for one moment that something strange is going on, they'll be out of that site quicker than you can say Abraham Lincoln.'

'And your colleagues?'

'They know something screwy happened, and of course they're all concerned about what might have become of Tom . . . but they also know how important a find this is, and they hate newspapermen every bit as much as I do. I wouldn't think private investigators figure very highly on their Christmas lists either, but if you think any of 'em are holding out on you, tell 'em to come see me and I'll put 'em straight.'

'Thank you, Mr Wade,' said Llewellyn gravely. 'I appreciate that.'

'That goes for you too, Mohammed,' added Ethan. 'Anything you just overheard is top secret. If it gets back to me that you've been blabbing, my team will be getting its goodies from a different trader.'

'I understand, *effendi*,' said Mohammed. 'My lips are sealed. But for now we must decide what we are going to do with you. With all

Mr Llewellyn's luggage, there is no room in the automobile for more passengers.'

'Hmm?' Ethan gazed along the empty road for a few moments. 'I guess we could just dump his luggage—'

'What?' cried Llewellyn, getting up out of his seat.

'Aw, relax, I'm just joshing you,' laughed Ethan. 'No, Mohammed, maybe you could drive Mr Llewellyn on up to the dig and send Mickey back to collect us in the other Crossley.'

'Perhaps, but after the trouble you have just experienced, I am reluctant to leave you out here alone. Those other hyenas might come back. May I suggest that you and this valiant young man come and stand on the running boards of my fine Ford automobile, and in this manner I will convey you to your destination.'

Ethan looked doubtful but he waved Alec to the Ford and the two of them clambered into position on either side of it.

'Think this thing will take our weight?' muttered Ethan, bouncing up and down on the rickety board.

Mohammed gave him a look. 'Mr Wade, did you not just promise to stop making fun of my automobile?' he said. 'We could, of course, drive back to your magnificent Crossley and stand on the running boards of that, but strangely it doesn't appear to be going anywhere.'

Ethan laughed. 'All right, point taken,' he said. 'I guess we'll just have to put our trust in the engineering skills of Mr Henry Ford.'

Mohammed started up the automobile and eased it slowly back onto the firmer surface of the road. 'There now,' he said. 'Are you both quite comfortable?'

'We're fine,' said Alec. He was so pleased to be getting out of these wide open spaces, he wasn't about to start complaining about a little discomfort.

'I'm glad,' said Mohammed. 'And because you are not properly seated, I am only going to charge each of you half fare.'

CHAPTER SIX

The Valley of the Kings

It wasn't a huge distance by automobile but Alec knew that they would have been totally exhausted if they'd attempted to walk through the blazing heat of the afternoon.

After some thirty minutes' drive they came upon an unusual sight. A large grey biplane was parked on a small area of flat land beside the road. There didn't seem to be anybody with it. Mohammed slowed the Ford to a halt so his passengers could step down and take a closer look. Llewellyn declined to get out of the car, saying that it would be too much effort.

'Any idea who this belongs to?' Ethan

95

PHILIP CAVENEY

asked Mohammed as he approached the plane.

'No, Mr Wade. I've never seen it before.'

'Hmm.' Ethan walked around the plane and reached up a hand to stroke its fuselage. 'Not a model I recognize,' he said. 'Foreign, I'd say. I used to fly these things during the war,' he told Alec. 'Spotter planes, mostly. My job was to go out over the enemy trenches and take photographs of their positions.'

'That sounds dangerous,' said Alec.

'It could be,' admitted Ethan. 'Came close to being shot down a couple of times, but I guess my luck held. Say, maybe you and me should take this bird up for a quick spin!'

'Really? Could we?' Alec was delighted at the notion but Ethan just grinned and shook his head.

'I'm only pulling your leg,' he said. 'You can't just up and take somebody's plane without permission. Where I come from, that's called theft.' He tilted his stetson back a little and gazed up at the sky. 'Maybe that dust storm forced the plane down,' he said. Alec didn't say anything but it was already beginning to feel as though they had imagined the whole thing. 'Come on,' said Ethan after a short silence. 'Let's get going.'

The two of them strolled back to the Ford and resumed their places on the running boards.

'Fancy just leaving a plane standing there,' said Alec. 'What d'you suppose happened to the pilot?'

Ethan shrugged. 'Beats me,' he said. 'Maybe it's something to do with Tutankhamun. There's all kinds visiting the site these days. Maybe some Hollywood movie star dropped by to get photographed with Howard Carter. OK, Mohammed, let's drive on.'

They continued on their way and after another half-mile they crested a rise and Alec saw the familiar limestone hills of the eastern Valley of the Kings below him, dominated by the high peak of Al-Qurn, the distinctive pyramid-shaped hill that many historians believed was the chief reason why this valley had been chosen as the burial place for so many Egyptian kings and nobles. Alec knew that there were over sixty tombs in this valley alone, with Tutankhamun's the most recently discovered, and the only one that had survived with most of its artefacts intact – at least, until Uncle Will and Tom Hinton had opened the new tomb. But that was still a secret.

Mohammed took the car slowly down the

tricky winding road. The steep stone cliffs rose up on either side of them, shielding them from the full glare of the sun. The ramshackle car moved with difficulty across the rough terrain travelling at little more than walking speed. They passed a few people on the way – guides from a nearby village escorting tourists around the tombs, some of them mounted on camels, others on donkeys. Alec knew that since the discovery of Tut's tomb the previous year, this site had become the most popular destination on the tourist routes: visitors from all around the world came to watch (and in many cases hamper) the work that was still going on there.

'Luckily, very few tourists make it up to our end of the valley,' said Ethan. 'They get to Tut's tomb and that's as far as they go.'

Sure enough, they soon saw a crowd of people standing at the roadside ahead of them and knew that they were approaching the site of the tomb. A large throng was watching intently as yet another antiquity was brought up the steps from the entrance, the men perspiring in suits and pith helmets, the women dressed in heavy skirts and jackets, shading themselves with dainty parasols. The onlookers ranged from well-to-do tourists to curious locals, with more than a sprinkling of journalists and photographers, eager to be the first to snap and write about each new discovery as it was brought out into the daylight. Alec caught sight of the slight figure of Howard Carter by the tomb entrance, issuing instructions to the two assistants who were carefully emerging with what looked like a large statue of the young pharaoh himself.

As the Ford moved past, Carter glanced up and squinted into the sun; then he smiled and lifted a hand to wave to Alec. He looked tired, Alec thought, and seemed to have aged alarmingly in the single year since Alec had last seen him. Currently the most famous archaeologist in the world, he would probably have given anything to have all those onlookers removed, so he could get on with his work in peace.

'Poor Howard,' said Ethan. 'He looks pooped. But in a way, I'm grateful.'

Alec looked at him, puzzled by the remark. 'What do you mean?' he said.

'He's taking all the heat off us. So far, we haven't had a single tourist coming after us and that's just the way I aim to keep it.' He gave Alec a sly wink. 'Last thing we want is this situation.'

He gestured at the crowd. 'Look at them, standing around like they're watching a matinée at the theatre. I'm surprised they're not selling popcorn.'

'They're selling curios though,' said Alec, pointing to small groups of natives who were moving through the crowd, offering their bogus artefacts. Some of them even seemed to be making the odd sale.

'There's a sucker born every minute,' muttered Ethan.

As the vehicle edged slowly past the crowd, a figure stepped out to greet it, raising a hand to Mohammed to stop.

'Oh, perfect,' muttered Ethan. He leaned forward to whisper, 'Watch what you say to this guy, he's a reporter.' He glanced at Llewellyn. 'A *real* one,' he added.

'Hey, Wade,' said the newcomer. 'Whatever happened to your fancy English automobile?' Another American, Alec decided, a thin, weasel-faced man with a pencil moustache and a cigarette drooping from the corner of his mouth, making him crinkle his eyes down to slits. Despite the heat, he was dressed in a formal white shirt and tie and a grey fedora. Though he had rolled up his sleeves in an attempt to cool off, there were large yellow sweat stains under his armpits.

'Had a little engine trouble back aways,' explained Ethan. 'Mohammed happened by and gave us a lift.'

Mohammed bowed politely. 'Good day, Mr Corcoran,' he said. 'I trust the whiskey was to your taste.'

The man looked annoyed by the remark. 'Er . . . yeah, great thanks.'

'Fine Irish whiskey. Just let me know if you need any more.'

'Oh, that's all right, Mohammed. It was just medicinal. I had a bit of a head cold, that was all.'

'As you wish, Mr Corcoran. And I understand that, with prohibition, you are not able to get hold of such . . . *medicine* in your own country.' Mohammed bowed again as another figure emerged from the crowd. 'Ah, good day, Miss Connors.'

Alec saw that a petite young woman was approaching them. Her blonde hair was cut in a shockingly short bob and her lips were painted a violent shade of red. She wore a khaki shirt, slacks and a pair of heavy walking boots. She was chewing gum like her life depended on it and looked extremely bored, as though visiting the Valley of the Kings was the dullest thing ever. In case there was any doubt about her reason for being here, she was carrying a large, expensive-looking camera.

'Hi, Mohammed,' she said. 'How's business?'

'Business is good,' he assured her. 'I must say that is a splendid-looking camera. I would very much like to get my hands on one.'

'Yeah, well, you can keep your hands off *this* one, buster. It's a Linhof Satzplasmat and it cost me a packet!'

Alec was just wondering how the woman had managed to pronounce Linhof Satzplasmat through a mouthful of gum when he noticed that Corcoran was appraising him as though he didn't much care for what he saw.

'Who's the kid?' Corcoran enquired.

'This is Alec,' said Ethan. 'He's just come to help out on the dig.'

'Yeah?' The man didn't seem interested in the answer, but then apparently had second thoughts. 'Just a minute! Alec . . . Doesn't Sir William have a nephew called Alec?'

Ethan nodded. 'That's right,' he said. 'He

comes here to help every summer.'

The man was suddenly much more animated. He reached across the automobile to shake hands with Alec. 'Biff Corcoran, *Saturday Evening Post*,' he announced. 'Charlie, get a shot of the kid, will ya?'

The woman stepped obediently forward but still managed to make it look as though it was the last thing in the world she wanted to do.

'Say Gorgonzola,' she said tonelessly, and then snapped a shot before Alec could say anything at all.

'Cut that out,' said Ethan irritably. 'Alec only just got here — you trying to scare him away?'

Biff leaned in, a distinctly unconvincing expression of sympathy on his face. 'Say, real sorry to hear about your uncle, kid — tough break. Our readers are all so interested to hear how he's doing. You, er . . . seen him lately, have ya?'

'Er . . .' Alec hesitated, glanced at Ethan, then looked away again. 'No, I'm afraid I haven't had a chance to visit him yet,' he said. 'Only just arrived.'

'But . . . you know what happened to him, don't you?'

Alec frowned and Charlie snapped another picture.

'He, er . . . I believe he was just working too hard. Needed a bit of a rest.'

PHILIP CAVENEY

Biff looked decidedly unconvinced by this. 'That's not what I heard. Somebody told me he's fit for nothing but the booby hatch.' He glanced at Alec apologetically. 'No offence, kid.'

'None taken,' said Alec coldly; but he thought to himself that Biff was one of the rudest men he'd ever met.

'So . . . where is your uncle exactly?'

'Oh now, come on,' interrupted Ethan. 'I told you before, that's not for public consumption. Will needs peace and quiet and he sure isn't going to get it with you two poking around.' He pointed across the heads of the crowd to the entrance of Tut's tomb. 'There's your story, Biff. The greatest archaeological find in history and you're missing it. I only wish we'd made a discovery like that.'

But Biff was shaking his head. 'No, Ethan, I'm looking for the human angle in all this ancient Egyptian malarkey. Oh sure, this stuff is popular – they even built an Egyptian-style movie theatre in Hollywood last year. But my readers wouldn't know a sarcophagus from a duck-billed platypus. Ancient curses now, that's the stuff that sells papers.'

Ethan snorted derisively. 'Oh, please! You

should know better. That's a bunch of hooey! Some dame back in America writes a pot-boiler about an ancient tomb and everybody gets themselves into a flap about it. It's just a new bandwagon to jump on.'

'Maybe you're right.' Biff took the cigarette from his mouth and blew out a cloud of acrid smoke. 'But who cares, if it's what the public wants? And you got to admit, it sounds kind of fishy. First Lord Carnarvon heads for the great museum in the sky. Then Sir William – no offence, kid – loses his marbles and winds up nutty as a fruitcake. What gives?'

Ethan sighed. 'Nothing *gives*, Biff. Lord Carnarvon was fifty-five years old and in poor health. William's no spring chicken either and he hasn't had a holiday in years. The man just needs rest and I'm starting to know how he feels.'

'Relax, will ya? I'm not here to give anybody a hard time.' Now Biff had turned his attention to the fourth occupant of the car. 'Hey, Fats, what's happening?' he asked.

Llewellyn glared at him. 'Are you by any chance addressing me, sir?' he cried.

'Take it easy, mister. I was just saying hello in my own inimitable style.'

'Damned impertinent style, if you ask me!'

'Well, excuse me all over the place.' Corcoran looked at Ethan as though seeking an explanation.

'Biff, this is Professor Llewellyn from . . . the British Museum in London,' said Ethan quickly. 'He's an expert on . . . on dating pottery shards.'

It was a brilliant stroke. The interest went out of Biff's face almost as though somebody had thrown a switch.

'Pottery, huh?' he grunted. 'Well, yippee-doo-dle-day.'

'You want me to take a photograph of him too?' asked Charlie.

Biff shook his head. 'Nah. Go see if you can do the impossible and get a picture of Howard Carter smiling,' he suggested. 'Just for the novelty value.' He glanced up at Ethan. 'How's it going at that dig of yours?' he asked half-heartedly. 'Anything I should know about?'

'Oh, we're doing pretty good. You know, we found a ushabti the other day.'

'A what?'

'A ushabti,' said Alec. 'A small clay figurine.'

'You don't say,' muttered Biff.

'We *do* say!' insisted Ethan. 'Eighteenth

dynasty, for sure. Tell you the truth, we only found a few pieces of it but there's enough to get an idea of what it might have looked like. Say, maybe you'd like to come on over and do a piece on it?'

Biff was already walking back to the crowd. 'Let me know when you find something more interesting,' he called over his shoulder. 'Like a mummy or a . . .'

'A duck-billed platypus,' said Charlie, going after him.

Ethan grinned and gave Alec a sly wink. Mohammed started up the automobile and they were on their way again.

'What a perfectly disagreeable fellow,' observed Llewellyn. 'He had the temerity to call me Fats!'

'Er . . . yeah, Biff isn't the most tactful person on the planet, that's for sure.'

'And why on earth did you tell him I was a professor?'

'Are you kidding? If I'd said you were a private detective investigating a disappearance, he'd have been up the road to our dig before you had time to put your pants on. It's got that human angle he's looking for.' Ethan considered for a moment.

'That's your cover story from now on, Wilfred. Anybody asks what you're doing here, you specialize in dating pottery.'

'But I don't know anything about it.'

'You won't need to. Just start any sentence on the subject and the person you're speaking to will be asleep by the time you get to the end of it.' He glanced at Alec. 'You hanging in there, kid?'

Alec nodded. It had been quite a day and he still hadn't even reached the site. 'I'm fine,' he said. 'You certainly scared off Mr Corcoran. You might as well have invited him to jump into a pot of boiling oil.'

'Works every time. It's only when you start playing hard to get that everybody wants to know what you're trying to hide.'

'So . . . how many people know about Tom's disappearance?'

'There's us, there's the people up at the dig and there's Tom's parents. That's as far as it goes for now. But if people like Biff Corcoran ever get a sniff of it, that site will be like an ant heap covered in honey. Crawling.' He glanced at Llewellyn. 'Remember our deal, *Professor*.'

Llewellyn smiled and nodded. 'I could get used

to that title,' he said. 'Do you know anything about dating pottery, Mr Wade?'

Ethan shook his head. 'I never got much further than dating dames,' he said, 'but I figure that's a whole lot more interesting than a bunch of broken vases.'

They drove on along the valley, the road curving left and right between the outcrops of stone, until finally, at the bottom of a hill, on a flat spread of ground to their left, they saw the tents and vehicles belonging to Sir William Devlin's archaeological expedition.

At the Dig

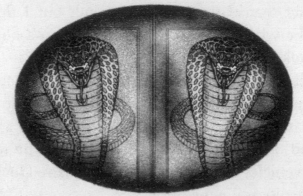

As Mohammed brought the Ford to a halt in front of the encampment, Alec saw Coates emerge from a tent and come hurrying towards them, an expression of concern on his face.

'Master Alec!' he cried. 'You were a long time. I was beginning to get worried.' Then he noticed the ancient car upon which Alec was perched. 'What on earth has happened? Where's the other car?'

'Relax, Coates,' Alec advised him. 'We broke down in the desert, but Mohammed here came along and gave us a lift.'

'*And* saved you from a pack of savage hyenas,' Mohammed reminded him.

'Oh yes, the hyenas,' said Alec sheepishly. 'Forgot about them.' He had hoped to avoid mentioning the attack, knowing exactly what Coates's reaction would be.

The valet's face drained of all colour. 'Hyenas?' he echoed. 'Oh my good golly gosh!'

Alec stepped down from the running board. 'It's nothing to get excited about,' he said. 'Mr Wade shot two of them and I stabbed a third one.'

'Don't forget I hit one of them with my Ford,' added Mohammed.

'You—' Coates looked at Ethan, who was in the process of counting some coins into Mohammed's outstretched hand. 'Mr Wade,' he said sternly. 'A word in your ear, if you don't mind. You assured me that Master Alec would be perfectly safe in your company.'

Ethan looked up and adopted a puzzled expression. 'Well, he's right here, safe and sound. What more do you want?'

'Yes, he *is* here, but it sounds as though he's damned lucky to be alive.'

Ethan dropped the last piastre into Mohammed's hand and turned to face the valet. 'Believe me,' he said, 'luck had nothing to do with it. That's a plucky kid you got there. Sure saved my neck.' He glanced over his shoulder. 'OK, Mohammed, don't forget our deal now.' He lifted a finger to his lips in an exaggerated gesture of silence.

Mohammed nodded, then turned to Llewellyn, who had just got out of his seat. 'What about your trunk, *effendi*?' he asked.

'Oh, you can take that over to the Winter Palace,' said Llewellyn loftily. 'Have them send it up to my room.' He took a watch from his pocket and consulted it for a moment. 'And if you would be so kind as to come back for me at . . . shall we say, five p.m.?'

'Very good, Mr Llewellyn. Of course, after five it costs a little extra.'

Llewellyn rolled his eyes. 'Now why am I not surprised to hear that?' he muttered.

Mohammed gave him an innocent smile, then started up the car and turned it round. He drove off along the valley, honking his horn as he did so, and the Ford's ancient engine protested noisily as it struggled to cope with the steep hill.

'Beats me how that old jalopy keeps going,' muttered Ethan. 'And how come he never saw that storm? It came from right behind us.' He looked at Llewellyn. 'You sure you didn't see anything?'

'Nothing,' said Llewellyn. 'It was clear all the way until we found you and those confounded hyenas.' He suddenly became all businesslike. 'I'll start making my enquiries, if I may.'

'That's fine,' Ethan told him. 'But please confine yourself to this encampment. The excavation site is off limits to anyone who ain't employed by me.'

'Oh, I wouldn't be interested,' said Llewellyn. 'All those old bones and bandages – quite morbid really. Will you be available to answer some questions yourself, Mr Wade?'

'Er . . . later, maybe. Right now I have things to organize. But don't forget what I said earlier. I'm giving you one chance. If I hear a single bad report about you, you'll be out of here so fast your boots won't touch the ground.'

'I'll be discreet,' said Llewellyn; and waddled off towards the rows of tents, looking for victims.

'I'd rather hoped we'd seen the last of him,' muttered Coates, gazing after him disapprovingly. 'How did he persuade you to let him come here?'

'That's a long story.' Ethan looked around

impatiently and then shouted, 'Mickey, where are you?'

The small, skinny figure of Mickey Randall emerged from one of the tents and ran over, nodding to Llewellyn as he passed by.

'Right here, Mr Wade. What's the problem?'

'My automobile broke down some twenty miles back along the road. Full of sand, by the looks of it. I need you to take a tool box and another driver down there and get it working again.'

'Sure thing, boss. I'll get straight onto it.' Mickey started to hurry off, then seemed to remember something and turned back. 'Oh, yeah, that Dr Duval arrived while you were gone.'

'Duval? Here already? How could that be? I wasn't expecting him till next week.' Ethan looked around again. 'Where is he?'

'The doctor wanted to go straight down to the tomb. I thought it would be all right. But, boss, there's something you—'

'That's OK, Mickey, you hurry along and get that car fixed. I'll go down and do the welcome routine.' He grinned at Alec. 'Whaddya say, kid? Wanna come with me and sneak a peek at the tomb?'

'You bet, Mr Wade!' Alec was so excited he could hardly stand still.

'Just a moment,' said Coates loftily. 'Master Alec has had nothing to eat or drink since this morning. Surely there's time for a cup of tea and a buttered crumpet before he goes haring off again.'

Ethan laughed. 'You English and your tea,' he said. 'And I'm not even going to ask what a buttered crumpet is.' He studied Alec slyly for a moment. 'Well, Alec, what do you think?' he said. 'A nice cup of tea . . . or a first look at Akhenaten's tomb?' He started walking confidently away and Alec immediately bounded after him.

Coates stood there for a moment, staring after them, his hands on his hips. Then he sighed, shrugged his shoulders and trudged back to his tent.

The entrance was well hidden, Alec had to admit.

First they had to climb a steep, narrow path that rose between the rocks for some twenty feet. Then the ground dropped away suddenly and levelled out. It was in the midst of this flat space that an opening suddenly descended steeply into the bowels of the earth. Covered with sand, as it had been for thousands of years, it was all but invisible; nobody could have suspected that there was anything down here. It was pure luck, Ethan told Alec, that a workman sent to dig a hole for a new latrine had driven the blade of his shovel in at that precise spot and heard the distinctive clang of metal hitting stone.

'The great thing is that this isn't even visible from the road,' he added. 'That's why we've got everything pitched on the other side, so if any tourists do make it this far along the valley, all they're gonna see is tents and chairs and a few bored-looking people. So far, it seems to be working.' He began to walk down the steps. 'Now watch yourself,' he warned Alec. 'These steps are steep.' He unhooked an Eveready from his belt and switched it on.

The first thing that struck Alec as he gazed down the steps was the scale of the doors that awaited them below. They were huge, ornate, made from what looked like bronze, and dominated by two huge images of serpents – king cobras by the looks of them – their heads raised, their mouths open, revealing forked tongues. Red stones had been set into the eye-sockets and they glittered in the beam of Ethan's torch, giving the momentary illusion that the creatures had somehow come alive.

'Apophis,' murmured Alec, remembering what Uncle Will had said earlier. The serpent god of the ancient Egyptians, often associated with Seth, the god of the underworld, the closest thing the ancient Egyptians had to a devil.

It felt very claustrophobic on those steps: they'd only gone a few feet below the level of the sand and the sun had been extinguished like a snuffed-out candle. It was cool down here – one almost might say chilly – and there was a curious smell in the air, an indefinable odour of dust and decay with a certain sulphurous tone mixed in. Through the open doors a glow of light washed out; and as they reached the bottom of the steps, a shadow fell across the opening.

As Alec watched, the head of a creature emerged from the doorway – the snarling, spotted head of a huge leopard. Alec's blood turned cold within him and he was on the point of turning and fleeing back up the steps when a man's arm came into view, and he realized with a sense of relief that it was simply a painted wooden statue. After a moment the Arab workman moved into view, carefully holding the front part of the statue; his assistant followed, supporting the back legs. Ethan and Alec pressed back against the wall to allow them access to the steps. They bowed their heads respectfully to Ethan as they went by and he gave them a few words of encouragement. Then they began to inch themselves carefully up the steps, well aware that one slip could mean irreparable damage to a priceless treasure.

'No wonder this business takes so long,' observed Ethan to no one in particular.

'What happens to the antiquities once you bring them out?' asked Alec.

'We've got a workshop set up in an empty cave across from here,' said Ethan. 'We get the stuff boxed up there and we take it out by truck at night.' He laughed at his own cunning. 'My idea is, we get everything squared away and *then* we make our big announcement. Come on.'

He led Alec through the open doorway and they stepped into the antechamber. Alec got his first real look at the interior of the new tomb. His initial impression was of a complete mess. There were so many different artefacts in here, piled carelessly one on top of the other. The workmen had hung oil lanterns around the walls to illuminate the treasures; the resulting fumes made it hard to focus on them at first. Alec looked around in wide-eyed wonder. He saw statues and jars and murals and jewellery and scrolls and more jars . . . Behind the almost perfect remains of a battle chariot there was another doorway and he noticed something strange about it: a small oval of midnight-black that must have been an opening into another room beyond the first.

'We've still got a lot to do,' explained Ethan. 'Everything was shut down when Will became ill so we lost the best part of a month. I've only just got things running again.'

There were various people working in the antechamber. A man whom Alec recognized as the team's medic, Doc Hopper, held a sketchpad and was painting a watercolour of a bas relief carving on a wall. Like all members of the team, he had a secondary talent to supplement his main function, and it was his artistic abilities that came to the fore; but at any moment he might be obliged to drop his sketchpad and run to help deal with a broken leg or an infected scorpion sting. He noticed Alec and nodded to him with a welcoming smile.

On the other side of the chamber an Arab workman with a box camera was photographing a statue of Apophis (once again, the snake god, Alec thought), and every so often the space was lit by the brief glare of flash powder, the resulting smoke making it even harder to breathe. Over to Alec's right, a couple more Arabs were carefully brushing away the fine dust that had accumulated around a necklace, the cord of which had long since rotted away, so that it could be photographed intact before being removed bead by bead and reassembled somewhere else.

This was the world Alec wanted to belong to. He realized it wasn't something that would appeal to everyone. It was a world of painstaking research, where the wheels turned slowly and a week's hard work was deemed as nothing when compared to the long passage of centuries. And yet he felt that it was what he had been born to do.

Ethan was looking around impatiently. He spotted a young woman standing alone in a corner, studying an elaborate mural, and he made a beeline for her.

'Say, honey, you must be with Dr Duval. Any idea where he is?'

The woman turned to look at Ethan. She was probably in her mid twenties, Alec thought, strikingly pretty with bobbed black hair and dark brown eyes. She was dressed in a khaki shirt, jodhpurs and brown leather boots and she was looking at Ethan as though she was having trouble understanding him.

Ethan tried speaking louder and slower. 'You go fetch Dr Duval,' he said. 'Tell him Ethan Wade is here.'

'Dr Duval *knows* you are 'ere,' said the woman, in a pronounced French accent.

Ethan did a slow 180-degree turn to look around the tomb, but clearly saw nobody he didn't recognize. The obvious answer began to dawn on Alec and he stepped forward to try and intervene, but he was too late.

'Sorry, sister, you're not making much sense,' said Ethan flatly.

The woman stared at him. '*I* am Dr Duval,' she said.

There was a long moment of silence while the awful truth registered, and Ethan's face went through a silent pantomime of open-mouthed shock.

'You . . . oh . . . my . . . God,' he said. 'I am so

sorry, *madame*, I had no idea. You see, I was expecting . . .'

'A man,' said Dr Duval tonelessly. 'Obviously.'

'Well, yeah, tell you the truth. See, I had no idea that . . .'

'. . . a woman could be a doctor? Perhaps this is against the law in America?'

'Yeah . . . NO! No, not against the law. Just . . . you know, *unusual*. I was expecting some crusty old guy in tweeds, not a woman. Especially such a pretty one.'

Alec winced. Now the look on Dr Duval's face was a picture of pure outrage. 'Oh, so the way I look precludes me from 'aving any brains!' she observed. ''Ow charming.'

'I didn't say that!' protested Ethan. He glanced at Alec as though seeking support. 'Did I say that? I don't think I did.'

'No, *madame*,' said Alec, trying to smooth troubled waters. 'I think what Mr Wade was saying, is—'

'It is *mademoiselle*, not *madame*,' added Dr Duval.

'Er . . . oh, right,' said Ethan. 'That means you're . . . not married, yeah? Well, I can't say I'm surprised.'

Dr Duval stared at him and Alec winced a second time.

'I beg your pardon?' she said.

Alec tried once again to calm things down. 'I think what Mr Wade means is . . . he's sure you'd make somebody a perfectly *good* wife,' he said; and then realized that didn't sound quite right either. 'Er . . . it's . . . it's just that what with you being an archaeologist, it probably doesn't leave an awful lot of time to . . . er . . . you know . . . do wifely things.'

There was a terrible silence while she mulled that one over and Ethan made a desperate attempt to change the subject.

'Dr Duval, please let me introduce Alec Devlin, just arrived from Cairo. Alec is the nephew of Sir William Devlin, who I think I mentioned in my telegram?'

'*Enchanté.*' She stepped forward and shook Alec's hand. 'Your uncle is a genius, Alec. I 'ave read, I think, everything 'e 'as ever published. I was so sorry to 'ear of 'is illness.'

'Thank you, *Mademoiselle* Duval,' said Alec.

'Oh, *non*, you must call me Madeleine, please.'

'Madeleine,' said Ethan. 'Pretty name. Maddie for short?'

Madeleine directed a withering look at him. 'Madeleine,' she said, 'as that is my name.'

'Oh, right.' Ethan laughed. Then, realizing that the remark hadn't been intended as a joke, stopped himself. 'You, er . . . sure didn't waste any time getting here. May I ask how you——?'

'I flew,' explained Madeleine, her voice as cold as a fall of December snow.

'Yeah? You were pretty lucky to find an airline that could bring you so soon. It usually takes——'

'I flew *myself*,' she said. 'In my own plane. I managed to put down on the road a few kilometres from 'ere.'

Now Ethan really was taken aback. He stared at Madeleine in astonishment.

'Whatever is the matter, Mr Wade?' she asked him. 'Are women not permitted to fly aeroplanes in America?'

'Of course not! I mean, of course they are!'

Alec snapped his fingers. 'Oh, so that must have been your biplane back along the road,' he said. 'We stopped to take a look at it, didn't we, Ethan? You even said you'd take me up for a spin in it!'

Madeleine glared at Ethan. 'You told 'im what?'

'I was just kidding, obviously. I used to do a

little flying myself, in the war. Spotter planes mostly – my job was to—'

''Ow long before you open the door to the burial chamber?' interrupted Madeleine, who seemed unimpressed by Ethan's past exploits.

'Hmm? Oh, hard to say. We're making good progress, but it all takes time. A couple of days, maybe three?'

'*Voilà*. For now, we must leave these people to their work. Per'aps you can show me where I am going to be staying?'

'Sure.' Ethan turned to go but then swung back with a worried expression. 'No, wait . . . I . . . I can't show you just yet.'

'Why not?' asked Madeleine impatiently. 'I am tired. I would like to take a little rest.'

'Er . . . sure, I understand. It's just that . . . with me expecting you to be a man and all, I kind of arranged for you to share a tent with someone called Mickey Randall. He's a swell guy, but I expect you'd prefer to have a tent of your own.'

'But of course!' Madeleine looked exasperated. 'A woman sharing with a male stranger? This would not be a suitable arrangement at all.'

'It's not a problem. I'll go and make some changes. Just a case of shuffling people around.

Alec, maybe you'd like to keep Maddie . . . er, Madeleine entertained for a while until everything is fixed up.'

Alec shrugged. 'Whatever you say, Ethan.'

'Thanks, kid. This shouldn't take long.' Ethan shot Alec a harassed look as he hurried out of the antechamber.

Madeleine stared after him. 'What kind of a man is this Ethan Wade?' she asked Alec. "E doesn't seem to know what 'e's doing.'

Alec smiled. 'Oh, I think he's a nice enough chap when you get to know him. He was a little thrown by you, that's all.'

She gave him a puzzled look. 'Thrown?' she said. 'Like a stone?'

'Er . . . no! I mean . . . I think the two of you got off on the wrong foot.'

Now Madeleine was studying her boots with a puzzled look.

'He . . . he's more of a man's man, I think.'

'Ah, yes, I understand this expression. Why does 'e wear a big cowboy 'at?'

Alec thought about it for a moment, remembering how he had been surprised by it but had quickly got used to it. 'I suppose it's just an American thing,' he said.

''E looks like somebody out of a Western film. Beely the Kid or . . . Tom Mix.' Now Madeline was looking around the packed interior of the antechamber. 'You know, this is truly amazing,' she said. 'A find like this is going to make 'istory. This is your first dig, *oui*?'

'Oh no, my third. I've worked with my uncle twice before, but they weren't having very much luck then – we only found a few trinkets. All this' – Alec gestured around him – 'it is rather exciting. When news gets out, it's going to put Tutankhamun in the shade.'

Madeleine smiled. 'I wanted very much to work on Tut's tomb. I 'ad just graduated – it would 'ave been a good opportunity for me . . . but they did not need another expert, so I 'ad to be patient. When this opportunity came up, I said to myself, *Madeleine, you must not waste any time!* I set off just as soon as possible.'

'In your own plane.' Alec couldn't disguise the tone of envy that seeped from his voice. 'That must be marvellous. Did you come all the way without stopping?'

Madeleine laughed. 'Oh no, that is not possible, Alec! I 'ave to make many stops. I go Paris to Lyon, then to Miramas, Pisa, Rome, Otranto,

Potasi, Crete and then to Cairo. This takes me three days to complete.'

'Ethan didn't know what kind of plane it was.'

'It is a Caudron C fifty-nine biplane. Built for the *Aviation Militaire*. Top speed one 'undred and seventy kilometres. Very fast, very smooth. If you like, I take you up for a flight some time.'

'Really? Gosh, I'd love that! I've never actually been in an aeroplane before.'

'*Non?*' Madeleine closed her eyes for a moment. 'But you must try it, Alec. There is nothing else in this world so good! It is like . . . it is like being a bird, you know? You look down on this tiny planet and you feel you can do whatever you want.' She laughed. 'My parents are not so keen on my flying. My mother is quite sure I will come to a . . . 'ow you say? A bad end. I tell her, *Maman, one day, everyone will 'ave a plane of their own – people will fly around the world and think nothing of it*. She is not so convinced.' Madeleine glanced up suddenly as though something had interrupted her thoughts. She took a long look around the smoky interior of the antechamber. 'There is a strange feeling 'ere,' she said.

'How do you mean?' Alec asked her.

'I don't know exactly. It feels like . . . the

people that built this place, they 'ave only been gone a little time and now we 'ave returned to disturb their sleep.'

Something seemed to catch her attention and she pointed. 'And there,' she said. 'Something is missing, I think.'

Alec followed the direction of her finger and saw again the smooth oval opening in the door that led to the next chamber. 'Oh yes, I noticed that when I came in,' he said. 'It looks as though somebody has prised an object off the door. A jewel, perhaps?'

'A priceless jewel if it was that big,' observed Madeleine. She gestured around. 'But nothing else 'as gone. In 'is telegram, Mr Wade says that the seals on the doors were unbroken. I 'ave never 'eard of such a thing.' She shrugged her shoulders. 'Ah well, it is a mystery to solve. I like mysteries.' She licked her lips and indicated the canteen that was still hanging from Alec's shoulder. 'I wonder if I could ask you for a drink of water.'

Alec frowned. 'I'm sure we can do better than that,' he said. 'Do you like tea?'

'Tea is OK,' she told him, 'but I prefer *café*.'

'Coffee? In that case I'm sure my valet, Coates,

will be more than happy to prepare some. He does very good Turkish coffee. He's famous for it.'

Madeleine looked at Alec in surprise. 'You 'ave brought your valet?' she said incredulously.

'Oh, Coates is like my shadow,' said Alec. 'He follows me everywhere. But he does make a cracking cup of coffee. If we ask nicely, he might even offer us a buttered crumpet.' He laughed at the look of confusion on her face. 'Don't ask,' he advised her, and laughing he led her towards the exit.

CHAPTER EIGHT

The Road to Luxor

Wilfred Llewellyn sat in the back of Mohammed Hansa's ancient Ford as it rattled along the dusty road to Luxor. He was sweating profusely and thinking how much he hated this godforsaken country: he wished he had never been offered this thankless assignment.

He had spent the day up at the dig, asking questions to anyone who would give him the time, and he had come up with precisely nothing. Nobody knew anything. Nobody had *seen* anything. It was as if Tom Hinton had simply vanished into thin air. But in Llewellyn's experience, people didn't just vanish: there was always a reason for their disappearance and when you dug deeper, when you peeled back the layers of lies and misdirection, it always turned out that there was somebody else involved.

Tom Hinton had been kidnapped or murdered, of that he was sure; and getting to the truth was simply a matter of persistence.

But Llewellyn had asked enough questions for one day. Now he was heading for the comforts of the Winter Palace, where he could take a cold shower, change his sodden clothing and relax over a good meal and a bottle of fine wine. Tomorrow, of course, he'd have to return to the dig and talk to those people he hadn't interrogated today, but somehow he knew already that the exercise would be every bit as pointless as today's.

He looked up and saw that Mohammed was studying him in the rear-view mirror, as though gearing himself up to ask a few questions of his own.

'You are a private detective,' he said, glancing back over his shoulder.

It wasn't so much a question as a statement of fact; and of course Mohammed had been present when he had been obliged to confess his true occupation to Wade and the boy. Llewellyn nodded, not feeling particularly inclined to waste time on idle chit-chat. But Mohammed was not so easily discouraged.

'How do you become a detective?' he asked. 'Is there a lot of training involved?'

'Oh yes,' said Llewellyn. 'Heaps. I had to study at college for years.'

This was not strictly true. Llewellyn had set himself up as a detective with a minimum of fuss. The simple truth was that the diploma hanging on his office wall was a fake and he had learned most of his tricks from reading classic detective fiction, like Sherlock Holmes; but nevertheless he seemed to be doing all right for himself. He generally found steady work handling divorce cases, the odd bit of fraud, even the occasional missing person around London. This was the first case that had taken him abroad, and he had already decided it would be the last. He had been lured by the easy money and the thought of visiting the country that was currently the talk of London; but he hadn't anticipated just how hot it would be here. It had been a nightmare from the word go. Even getting here had been a trial, a full four days of travel by plane, train and steamer, only to find himself, travel stained and weary, in the most intense heat he had ever experienced. A man of his considerable dimensions had no business travelling in such a climate. He could quite easily make himself ill.

'Supposing I wanted to be a detective,' persisted Mohammed, 'here in Egypt. What would I have to do?'

A tricky question. Llewellyn cast around for a means of changing the subject and was handed one on a plate when he noticed a series of dark shapes flapping and circling in the sky a short distance ahead of them.

'Good Lord,' he said. 'Are those . . . vultures?'

Mohammed nodded. 'Yes, *effendi*. They have been there all day, circling the remains of those damned hyenas.'

As the Ford drew closer, Llewellyn could see that the Arab was right. Three dark bloated shapes lay stretched out on the white sand. The huge birds were coasting low over the dead creatures but none of them seemed willing to land. Llewellyn suppressed a shudder. Everything about Egypt seemed to disagree with him.

'It all looks the same,' he complained. 'The landscape. It's impossible to know if you're making any progress or not. How much further to Luxor?'

'Not so very far, *effendi*. And my fine Ford automobile is not going to break down and leave us stranded like Mr Wade's Crossley.'

'Oh, well, that's a relief,' said Llewellyn flatly.

'You know, *effendi*, I have always thought I could be an excellent detective,' said Mohammed, who was clearly not ready to abandon his previous line of thought just yet. 'I notice things.'

'Is that right?' murmured Llewellyn.

'Yes. For instance, I noticed when I picked you up at the site that you had lost a button on your jacket. That could be important.'

Llewellyn looked down at his midriff to see that Mohammed was quite correct. Another button had given up the thankless struggle to hold Llewellyn's monumental girth at bay and had popped off. He made a mental note to ask the hotel to have somebody sew a new one on. After all, he had his reputation to think of.

'Most observant of you,' he muttered.

'Oh, that is nothing, *effendi*,' said Mohammed, warming to his theme. 'I predict that very soon we shall meet two cars on this road. The first one will have a small English driver, the second a tall

Arab. I also predict that the English driver will have his head under the bonnet of the car.'

Llewellyn stared at the back of Mohammed's head. 'How could you possibly know all that?' he cried. He looked over at the surface of the road for clues, but other than a few blurred tracks in the sand, there was nothing that might yield that kind of information.

'Just call it native intuition,' said Mohammed slyly. Then he pointed ahead. 'Behold,' he said.

Something came into view through the thick heat-haze rising off the surface of the road. At first it was nothing more than a series of black swirls, but as they moved closer, Llewellyn saw to his amazement that two cars were parked at the side of the road. Sure enough, the bonnet of one of them was up and a small wiry figure was bent over, examining the engine. A tall Arab lounged against the second vehicle's side, smoking a cigarette.

'How on earth did you . . . ?' began Llewellyn; then caught himself as it suddenly dawned on him that he'd been suckered. Mohammed had been there earlier today when Wade had despatched Mickey Randall to fix his car; and of course, Mohammed must have passed the two men a short while earlier when he had driven over from Luxor to collect the detective.

'Oh, very clever!' said Llewellyn, and he laughed self-consciously, realizing that he had very nearly made a fool of himself. 'You had me going for a moment!'

'As I said,' chuckled Mohammed. 'Native intuition!'

Mohammed pulled the Ford to a halt alongside the first Crossley and Mickey ducked out from under the bonnet, raising a hand in greeting. He had a spanner in his other hand, his face was streaked with oil and he looked hot and bothered, heavy beads of sweat running down his grizzled forehead.

'Still not working?' asked Mohammed; and Llewellyn thought he detected a note of smugness in the man's voice. He remembered that there had been some kind of rivalry between Wade and Mohammed – something about their respective automobiles.

Mickey shook his head. 'Nah. Looks like the engine's been eating sand,' he said. 'I'm nearly done though. There ain't an engine in the world that I can't bring back to life.' He glanced at Llewellyn. 'I believe I saw you up at the dig earlier,' he said.

'Yes, Wilfred Llewellyn, private detective. I'm investigating the disappearance of Tom Hinton.' Llewellyn extended a hand to shake and Mickey wiped his own on the back of his overalls before dutifully obliging.

'Terrible thing,' he said. 'Young lad like that.'

Llewellyn nodded. 'His parents, as you might imagine, are very distressed.' He turned and pointed back towards the circling vultures. 'What's the story with those brutes?' he asked.

Mickey gazed at them a while as though he'd only just noticed them. Then he shrugged. 'Never seen nothin' like it,' he said. 'They've been circlin' that spot for hours now, but none of 'em ever seems to land and start tucking in – it's almost as though they think something's wrong with the meat.' He shook his head. 'I never 'eard of vultures being that fussy before.'

'Me neither,' agreed Llewellyn, though in truth he hadn't the slightest knowledge of the eating habits of Egyptian vultures, nor did he care to have.

'You 'eading into Luxor?' asked Mickey.

'Yes, I'm staying at the Winter Palace tonight.'

'Lucky you,' said Mickey. 'I wish I was joining yer. They serve the best dinner in Luxor, they do. They do a roast beef and Yorkshire pudding that would put the Ritz to shame. Not that I can afford to eat there very often. But Sir William always used to treat us to Christmas dinner there, every December.'

'They serve some delicious native delicacies also,' added Mohammed. 'For those who are adventurous enough to try them.'

'Well, yeah,' admitted Mickey. 'They'll even serve you sheep's eyeballs if you ask for 'em. But I always say, you can't beat a good old English roast, eh? Even if you ain't in Blighty.' He frowned. 'Anyway, it's only wishful thinking. I've got to get this Crossley back to camp yet.'

Llewellyn nodded. 'A shame,' he said. 'It would have been nice to have a little conversation over dinner.' He thought for a moment. 'I don't suppose there's any point in asking you if you saw anything strange the night Tom Hinton disappeared?' he said.

'None whatsoever. I was busy trying to repair a wireless, tell you the truth. I didn't even know about it until after the event.' He thought for a moment. 'But you might want to talk to Hassan there. 'E reckons he's seen Tom.'

'*Seen* him?' Llewellyn's pulse quickened. 'When was this?'

'Just the other night, I think. I told 'im 'e must have been mistaken, but—'

'Hang on a minute!' interrupted Llewellyn. 'You're telling me that this man claims to have seen Tom Hinton since the night of his disappearance?'

'That's what 'e reckons,' admitted Mickey.

'Well, let's get him over here!' said Llewellyn impatiently. 'This could be important.'

Mickey nodded wearily. He would probably much rather have got on with the job at hand, but he dutifully waved to the Arab and the man stubbed out the butt of his cigarette and wandered over. He was a tall bearded fellow dressed in a black galabiya. He regarded Llewellyn with a sullen expression, as though the last thing in the world he wanted to do was talk to anyone.

'What's this about you seeing Mr Hinton?' asked Llewellyn.

Hassan stared at him. 'Hah?' he grunted.

''Is English ain't so good,' said Mickey. He spoke a few words to Hassan in halting Arabic and after a moment or two received some kind of reply.

'Yeah, 'e says 'e saw Tom two days ago at the bazaar in Sharia el-Karnak.'

'The bazaar – that's like a market, isn't it?'

Mickey nodded. 'Yeah, pretty much. You can buy anything there. Soap, razor blades, antiques, rugs—'

'Yes, never mind what you can *buy*! I'm not planning a ruddy shopping trip. What does he think Mr Hinton was doing there?'

Mickey tried a few more questions, but didn't seem to be getting through, so Mohammed pitched in, talking more confidently and in a lot more detail. He listened to the reply, then turned back to Llewellyn.

'*Effendi*, he says that Mr Hinton was wandering around the antiquity stalls as though he was looking for something.'

'I see. And was anybody else with Hassan who could verify the sighting?'

'No, he says he was alone. He had gone there to try and buy some herbs for his mother, who has terrible backache.'

Llewellyn closed his eyes for a moment and counted to ten. Did Mohammed think he was remotely interested in Hassan's mother's ailments?

'He's sure it was Mr Hinton?'

Mohammed spoke to Hassan again. 'Yes, quite sure. He says he knows Mr Hinton well, has worked with him for many years. He thought of going over to speak to him, to ask what he was doing there, but a camel laden with grain passed between them, and when it had moved on, he looked again and Mr Hinton had gone.'

Llewellyn frowned and stroked his chins. 'Ask him why he didn't mention this to anyone.'

Another exchange of words. Then:

'He says he told Mr Randall when he got back to camp, but because he didn't seem very interested, he didn't bother to mention it to anyone else.'

Llewellyn stared accusingly at Mickey. 'Is this true?' he asked.

Mickey looked rather sheepish. 'I do remember 'im saying that 'e'd seen Tom, but . . . well, I was in the middle of a job, an' besides, I assumed 'e must've been mistaken.' He moved a step closer and lowered his voice. 'I'm not being funny but Hassan ain't the most reliable person in the world – know what I mean? 'E's got things wrong before. I remember once 'e told me 'e'd seen this old fakir turn water into wine. Naturally, I was interested. So we went up to the place where this chap lived and asked 'im to show us 'ow 'e did it—'

'Mr Randall! I am trying to establish the facts here.' Llewellyn tapped Mohammed on the shoulder. 'Ask him again, Mohammed. Is he sure it was Mr Hinton?'

He waited, sweating, as Mohammed spoke to Hassan again. Hassan was nodding, his expression one of absolute certainty.

'He is positive,' said Mohammed. 'He would be prepared to bet money on it.'

'Blimey,' said Mickey, clearly impressed. 'That certain, eh? Well, maybe I misunderstood the situation.'

'Hmm.' Llewellyn considered for a moment. His comfortable hotel was calling to him, but even so, this was a potential breakthrough after a day of no progress whatsoever. 'Mohammed, is this bazaar place anywhere near my hotel?'

'Yes, sir, not far away at all.'

'Good. Take me there first, will you? We'll have a quick look around before we go on to the Winter Palace.' He glanced up at Mickey and Hassan. 'Thanks very much for the tip,' he said. 'I hope it doesn't take you too long to get the automobile fixed.'

'All right, Mr Llewellyn. Enjoy your stay at the Winter Palace!'

Mohammed put the car into gear and they drove away, leaving Mickey and Hassan behind them on the road. Llewellyn glanced back over his shoulder at the parked Crossleys but everything had twisted back into the swirl of the heat-haze, indeterminate black shapes melting into the sunlight. Up above them, in the brilliant blue sky, the vultures continued to circle.

He thought about what he had just been told. Could Tom Hinton really be hanging around a bazaar a stone's throw from his hotel? If only it could be so. He could have this whole case wrapped up and grab the first available berth back to England; back to reliable food, unreliable weather and cases that took him no further than a first-class train ticket. Right now it sounded like heaven.

CHAPTER NINE

Uninvited Guests

It was just before nightfall and Alec was taking his seat at the communal dining table between Madeleine and Coates when Mickey and Hassan got back to camp with the two Crossleys. Everyone was waiting for the Scottish cook, Archie McCloud, to dispense the evening meal. As it was an unusually mild evening, everyone had opted to eat in the open air. Archie had recently replaced the team's veteran cook, Henry Walters, who had retired back to his homeland after a nasty bout of malaria. Alec remembered from his previous visits that Henry had been an excellent chef, capable of creating good food out of the most unpromising ingredients, but Archie was an unknown quantity. A few mumbled remarks around the table soon warned him not to expect the same high standards.

Mickey took his place across the table from Alec, looking harassed, a mood which wasn't helped when Ethan told him that all his belongings had been transferred to Archie's tent so that Madeleine could enjoy a little privacy; but in the best stiff-upper-lip tradition, Mickey assured her that it would be no problem.

'Don't you worry yourself, miss,' he said. 'I'll be fine once I find myself some ear plugs.'

'Ee-yare plugs?' said Madeleine, mystified.

'Archie is famous for his snoring,' explained Ethan. 'On a good night they can hear him in Luxor.'

'Oh, well, Coates might give you some competition there,' said Alec. 'He's an absolutely *phenomenal* snorer when he gets going.'

'Master Alec, may I just mention that it's not the done thing to point out a person's shortcomings?' said Coates coolly.

'Sorry,' muttered Alec. 'I was only making conversation.'

Ethan smothered a grin and helped Mickey to

a large tin mug of the local red wine. 'You were a long time,' he said.

'Yeah. Had to clean out every last bit of that engine. Never seen so much sand. I thought we'd never get the blessed thing going. And as for those dead hyenas . . .' Mickey frowned. 'Funny thing though. Vultures circling them the whole time, but not one of 'em seemed to want to come down and feed. Fair gave me the creeps, it did.'

'I never heard of a vulture that wouldn't eat,' said Alec.

'It's true though,' said Mickey. 'I was telling Llewellyn – they were there the whole time I was working on the car, just wheeling around . . .'

'Llewellyn?' muttered Ethan.

'Yeah, he passed us on the road, heading for the Winter Palace. Lucky blighter.' Mickey lowered his voice. 'At least he'll be eating better than we will tonight.'

Ethan frowned and made a shushing motion. 'Did he ask you any questions?'

'A few. He was more interested in talking to Hassan though.'

'Why Hassan?'

'Because he only went and told Llewellyn that

he thought he'd seen Tom Hinton at the bazaar in Sharia el-Karnak a couple of nights ago.' Mickey raised his eyebrows.

Alec frowned. 'You're kidding!' he said.

'Nah . . . he mentioned it to me the other day, but . . . well, you know Hassan. He can be a bit of a romancer at the best of times.'

Ethan nodded. 'True enough. I remember way back when I worked on that first dig. We found a mummified cat and he told everybody that he'd seen it moving. He had the workmen terrified – they were all for running out on us. In the end Will had to offer them more money to get them to stay. You warned Llewellyn about him?'

'I tried to, but he got very excited about it all. Had Mohammed take him straight over to the bazaar. He must have thought it was worth checking out.'

'Well, I guess it can't do any harm. He can always pick up a few souvenirs to take back to England.' He thought for a moment. 'It's strange about the vultures though . . . And you know, there was something screwy about those hyenas from the word go. You just don't get hyenas this far north. And then I put two bullets into the heart of one of them but it kept right on coming at me. I had to finish it off with a head shot.'

Madeleine nudged Alec in the ribs and surreptitiously made her hand into the shape of a gun. She fired an imaginary shot, then blew on the tips of her fingers, cowboy-style, as though dispersing gun smoke. Alec stifled a laugh with the flat of a hand. He had already decided that he and Madeleine were going to be good friends. Although she had a serious side, there was also a playful, mischievous quality to her that Alec really responded to. Coates regarded her antics with rather less amusement. He had been polite enough when Alec had brought her to the tent for coffee earlier, but it was evident that the valet did not approve of her liberated ways and had been quite scandalized when she lit up a cigarette in his presence. He was of the school that preferred females to sit quietly, look pretty and leave the talking to the gentlemen. But Alec knew that the times were changing – that world was all but gone.

Now Madeleine was looking across the campsite to where the large team of Arab workmen were gathered around a fire, preparing their own meal in a big black cooking pot. Hassan had just joined them and was sitting staring into the flames.

'Such a pity the native workmen can't eat with the rest of us,' observed Madeleine.

'Table is nae big enough,' growled a rough Glaswegian voice behind her. She turned to see Archie McCloud carrying a steaming metal pot towards the table. 'Besides, I don't think they'd much care for the kind of grub we serve.' He was a big, red-faced fellow with a shock of unruly ginger hair and an equally unruly beard. A corncob pipe jutted from the corner of his mouth, emitting clouds of noxious smoke, and when he hefted the pot onto the table, Alec could see a crude tattoo etched into the sunburned skin of his forearm. It read: SCOTLAND FOREVER.

'So, what delights have you got for us this evening, Archie?' asked Ethan, and Alec noted the tone of desperate hopefulness in his voice.

'It's ma very own Highland stew,' announced Archie, ladling out bowls of glutinous brown sludge. He passed the first bowl to Madeleine and gave her a little bow. 'Ladies fust,' he said.

'*Merci beaucoup.*' Madeleine gazed at the contents of the bowl in trepidation. 'What kind of meat is this?' she asked suspiciously.

'The finest that the local suppliers can provide,'

said Archie, leaving the diners to speculate on the awful possibilities.

Probably donkey, thought Alec glumly, but he was too hungry to be fussy and he set to, chewing hard to consume chunks of the gristly meat. Madeleine was clearly not enjoying the experience either, but was gamely chomping away. Coates, on the other hand, was having none of it. As a former chef himself, he had strong views about the preparation of food and was never slow to voice his opinion.

'Mr McCloud, may I enquire where you worked before you joined this expedition?'

'You may, Mr Coates.' Archie stood up ramrod straight, as though standing to attention. 'I'm proud to tell ye that I was a cook in the army for many years. I served with the Royal Highland Fusiliers.'

'Is that right? And is that where you learned to prepare food?'

'That is correct, sir.'

'And this . . . stew. It's been made to your own recipe, has it?'

'Aye, it has. One that's been handed down through the McCloud family for generations.'

'Well, if I may be so bold as to make a suggestion . . .'

'Suggest away, Mr Coates,' said Archie, his expression grim.

'There are, I believe, several hotels in Luxor that for a small extra fee will plate up food and ferry it to the destination of your choice. Perhaps once in a while you should allow yourself a well-earned rest and we could see what the hotel kitchens could provide us with.'

He glanced around the table and was met with enthusiastic nods and hopeful looks. But Archie shook his head.

'Now, Mr Coates, would I let you lot suffer through something like that when it is ma pleasure . . . nay, ma joy to prepare fresh food for ye every morning and evening? The looks of delight on yer faces is all the reward I need.'

'I see. And if perhaps I were to offer my services as your . . . assistant?'

'I wouldn't hear of it, Mr Coates. I have ma own way of working.' Archie looked challengingly around the table. 'Of course, if anybody has any complaints . . .'

Ethan was chewing on a particularly tough piece of meat. He shook his head. 'Oh no, Archie, I don't think anybody is saying that they don't *like* your food. You take this stew now . . .'

'*Please* take it,' Alec heard Coates mutter. 'Take it and give it a decent burial.'

Ethan pretended not to hear. 'It has a . . . really unusual flavour. There's a spice in there . . . I'm not quite sure what it is, but it's got a really distinctive taste.'

'That'll be the cinnamon,' said Archie.

'Yeah, cinnamon, that's it! Very unusual in a meat stew.'

'Well, that was a mistake, Mr Wade. I thought I was adding pepper but ma eyes aren't what they used to be.'

'A happy accident, then.' Ethan gave up trying to chew on a lump of gristle and spat it out, an action that caused Madeleine to push her bowl away with an expression of disgust. 'Why, when I think of poor Mr Llewellyn, forced to suffer through one of those dinners at the Winter Palace . . . He doesn't know what he's missing.' He looked around the table but was greeted by a circle of wistful looks. He made an effort to change the subject. 'So . . . how did it go today? With Mr Llewellyn, I mean? I sure hope his questions weren't too disruptive.'

'He was a pain in the backside,' said Doc Hopper, the team's physician, a plain-speaking

Lancastrian with silver hair and an enormous drooping moustache. 'He spent the best part of an hour grilling me, though I made it plain I didn't know anything about what had happened to Tom. I wouldn't mind, but we already went through all this with the local police.'

'Aye, he had a go at me too,' muttered Archie. 'I told him I was busy making a goat curry the night Tom disappeared. I didn't notice a thing. But I helped him talk to the Arab workers. One of the men who opened the gates of the tomb said that Tom was acting right strange when he and Sir William came out of the antechamber. Looked like he'd taken a fever or somethin'. Sir William helped him back to his tent for a rest and nobody remembers seeing him after that.'

'Will was found in the same tent,' Ethan told Alec. 'Just lying there unconscious. No sign of Tom whatsoever. And when Will came round . . .' He spread his hands. 'Well, you've seen how he is.'

Alec nodded. 'I keep thinking about what he said when we were at the hospital. Apophis. He said something about the great Devil, *the serpent that is Apophis.*'

Madeleine looked at him. 'That *is* strange,' she

said. 'Images of the serpent god are on the doors of the tomb. And, if you look closely, they seem to 'ave been added to the doors, as though it was some kind of afterthought.'

Ethan shrugged. He pushed his bowl of stew away. 'What's so strange about that?' he asked.

'Well, it's supposed to be Akhenaten's tomb,' said Alec. 'The thing about him is that he was a monotheist—'

'There's that word again!' said Ethan. 'I told you, when you speak to me, keep it simple.'

Alec smiled. 'It means he outlawed the worship of other gods and allowed only Aten, the sun disc. He even changed his name from Amenhotep to Akhenaten, to show his devotion to Aten. But Apophis is the enemy of Aten – the great serpent that was supposed to try and swallow the sun every night, putting it out for ever.'

'Alec is right,' said Madeleine. 'Apophis was supposed to 'ave existed since the beginning of time. 'E rose up out of the primeval chaos before creation. It doesn't make sense that Akhenaten would decorate 'is tomb with the symbol of 'is greatest enemy. That would be like . . . Monsieur Coates 'ere, decorating 'is clothes with

Monsieur McCloud's cooking. The thing 'e hates most in the world.'

'Don't spare ma feelings,' growled Archie, and everyone around the table, including Coates, laughed.

'So what are you saying?' asked Ethan. 'That it's *not* Akhenaten's tomb? His name's right there on the door seals.'

'Yes, I 'ave looked at the photographic plates you made,' said Madeleine. 'The name *is* there, but it is saying something like "by order of Akhenaten". As though 'e was still alive when this tomb was sealed.'

'Well, whose is it then? One of his wives'? His children's?'

Madeleine shrugged and took out her cigarettes. 'Pointless to speculate,' she said. 'Maybe we'll know more when we 'ave entered the burial chamber.'

'Tomb it may concern . . .' said Doc Hopper and everybody groaned. It had been funny enough the first time he'd said it, but he repeated it just about every day. Only Madeleine laughed.

'Tomb!' she repeated. 'That is like "to whom", yes? That's very clever!' She looked around the table, perhaps seeking an ally, but everyone else maintained a diplomatic silence.

By now everybody had finished eating. Archie surveyed the bowls of barely touched stew in disgust.

'I don't know why ah bother,' he said.

'It's just that it was so filling,' said Ethan, patting his stomach. 'Really, I couldn't eat another thing.'

'Oh aye. At least Alec has made an effort. Here, perhaps I could offer you a wee bit m—' Archie broke off as something whizzed past his head, striking him across the cheek. He spun aside with an oath, dropping the ladle, and lifted a hand to his face. The fingers came away coated with blood. 'What the bl—?' A second shape sped past him with a flapping of leathery wings and he flung up his arms to beat it away.

Alec began to get up from his seat but something hit the back of his head, almost flinging him across the table. He felt a sharp pain. Then Madeleine gave a shriek of alarm and he saw that she too was lifting her arms to ward something away. He looked in surprise at Ethan, who was jumping up and reaching for his pistol.

'Bats!' Ethan yelled; and then, quite suddenly,

the night sky above them seemed to become even darker. They came flapping down in eerie silence. Fruit bats. Thousands of them. They had large, furry bodies and elongated doglike snouts, and though Alec had never heard of a fruit bat ever going anywhere near a person before, these creatures seemed intent on attacking human targets.

He was dimly aware of Archie running frantically towards the cook tent, his upper torso covered in a mantle of flapping, furry shapes, but there was no time to dwell on that, because now a bat was lunging straight at Alec's throat. He could see the open jaws fringed with rows of sharp little fangs, glittering in the moonlight like shards of broken glass; and then the teeth were snapping at his throat. He grabbed the bat's back legs and swung it down hard against the tabletop, snapping its spine with a loud crack.

Another scream from Madeleine alerted him to the fact that she had a couple of the creatures tangled in her hair. He tried to pull one away, then yelped as the bat's teeth sank into the back of his hand. But he hung on and dragged the bat off, Madeleine's yells of protest telling him that he had torn out some hair in the process. Coates moved to help him remove the other bat and, throwing it to the ground, he stamped down on it with a heavy work boot, stilling its mad fluttering for ever.

The three of them stood there for a moment in a fog of indecision, desperately looking around for shelter, but the air was a blizzard of flying shapes, moving at incredible speed. Alec saw that the native workmen had snatched up burning branches from the campfire and were flailing at the moving shapes around them. One had found a curved scimitar and was lashing about him like a madman, cleaving bats bloodily apart as they sped by.

'Under the table!' yelled Ethan, and everybody moved to obey him. Alec pushed Madeleine under the trailing hem of the heavy canvas tablecloth and then scrambled after her, all too aware that bats were slamming into the tabletop inches above his head; the impact on the wood sounded like the drumming of outsize hailstones.

Coates had snatched a heavy frying pan from the table, and as he moved into position, he started to wallop any creatures that attempted to follow him underneath. Mickey had pulled out a hunting knife and was stabbing at anything that moved, while Doc Hopper was kicking and stamping with his size-eleven feet. Ethan let off a couple of shots but had to concede that there were just too many bats to be deterred by bullets, and he too ducked under the table and pressed his back up against the others. He leaned out and gestured to the Arab workmen to come and join them.

They gratefully accepted his offer and ran for cover. One man, a little slower than the rest, found himself covered from head to foot with writhing, flapping shapes. He fell to the ground as countless jaws went to work on him.

Madeleine screamed and pointed towards him and Ethan reacted without hesitation, dashing out from under the table and running to the man's assistance. He went down on his knees and started tearing the creatures away, slamming them down hard onto the ground. Alec tried to go and help him but Coates grabbed his arm.

'No, lad, stay here!' he hissed.

As Alec watched helplessly, Ethan cleared most of the creatures off and helped the man to his feet. Slipping an arm beneath his shoulder, he half dragged, half carried him back to the table, where his friends helped to remove the bats that were still clinging to him. Alec winced, for when they were pulled off, their teeth ripped away chunks of flesh, making the man cry out pitifully. At last everyone was squashed under the table, those on the outside striking out at anything that attempted to get past them. The bats kept coming, crawling across the sand to be crushed by feet or fists or whatever implement came to hand. Above them, the thuds of bats on the tabletop were rapidly softening as the heaps of the dead provided cushioning.

'Where's Archie?' yelled Ethan, remembering the cook, and everybody craned their heads to look towards the cook tent. At that moment the big Scotsman emerged, dressed in a curious collection of homemade armour. He had an upturned metal colander strapped to his head with a leather belt, and he wore a thick cricket-ing sweater, shin pads and gloves. He carried a cricket bat and grinned like a maniac, his teeth shockingly white against his sunburned face. Patches of crimson on his clothing indicated where he had pulled away the bats that had attacked him earlier.

As the others watched in amazement, he took up a defensive stance and started hitting out at the bats as they came speeding towards him, the willow smashing their bones and flinging them aside like broken toys.

'I believe Mr McCloud used to play professionally,' Alec heard Coates say in a voice that was surprisingly calm, given the circumstances.

'Get under here!' Ethan yelled but Archie just grinned and carried on hitting out, clearly relishing the game. He struck one large bat with such force that it went tumbling through the air in a high arc, clearing the rows of tents and bouncing off the rocks across the road.

'Six!' bellowed Archie.

''E 'as gone quite mad!' Madeleine yelled into Alec's ear and he could only agree with her. But then, quite suddenly, everything stopped. There was a last flapping swirl above them and the remaining bats sped up into the sky and were gone. Archie bent over, gasping to recover his breath, and the people beneath the table began to emerge carefully, ready to dive back under cover at the slightest sign of danger.

But the bats were gone as quickly as they had appeared, leaving behind only the piles of their dead, with here and there the occasional twitching, squeaking survivor, waiting to be put out of its misery.

Ethan stared around in disgust and tilted back his stetson. Alec saw that fresh blood was running down his face where a bat's teeth had broken the skin.

'Would somebody like to explain to me what just happened here?' Ethan muttered. 'Fruit bats! Since when did fruit bats start attacking people?'

'Like those hyenas,' said Alec. 'They don't attack people either, right?'

There was a long silence. Everybody just stood there, gazing about them in mute amazement. It was Archie who recovered himself first. He threw down his cricket bat, took off the colander helmet and marched quickly back to the kitchen tent. He emerged a moment later, holding a handful of hessian sacks.

'Right,' he said, 'let's get some of these wee laddies gathered up. Only choose the plumpest ones.'

Ethan looked at him. 'What's the point?' he said. 'We'll just dig a big hole and shovel them all in.'

'This is nay for burial,' Archie assured him. 'It's for tomorrow's dinner.'

Everyone stared at him.

'Have you taken leave of your senses?' Coates asked him.

'Not a bit of it. These thangs are a bloody delicacy around here. We'll keep enough for tomorrow's grub and sell the rest in the market in Sharia el-Karnak.' He looked around at their appalled faces. 'I'm telling ya,' he said. 'These things are delicious. You go to one of those fancy hotels in Luxor and you'll pay top dollar for curried bat. It would be a crime to waste 'em!'

But it seemed that nobody else was in a big hurry to sample the delights of bat curry, so Archie started collecting up the dead creatures himself. The others watched him in horrified silence and wondered once again just what exactly had been in the Highland stew they'd been served earlier.

CHAPTER TEN
The Bazaar

Darkness was falling when Mohammed and Llewellyn arrived at the outskirts of the bazaar. Everywhere oil lamps were being lit, illuminating the rows of stalls that lined the streets. Here were people selling everything, from fresh fruit to pots and pans. Men in white galabiyas stood calling out their wares; women in black robes and burkas sat at looms, weaving rugs and throws. Llewellyn looked around in amazement.

'I didn't expect this many people,' he murmured.

'Here, everyone likes to shop at night, when it is cooler,' Mohammed told him.

'You call this *cool*?' Llewellyn said incredulously. True, the heat wasn't as intense as it had been earlier, but it was still warm enough to be uncomfortable. The ancient Ford coasted slowly along the packed streets – the bazaar seemed to go on for ever, like a half-remembered scene from a childhood fairy story.

Llewellyn gazed hopefully out from the back seat and saw stalls selling fine leather sandals – hundreds of pairs arranged on bamboo displays; he saw wooden crates stacked one upon the other containing chickens and pigeons, and over to his right, larger cages occupied by goats and sheep. A group of men to his left were standing in a pool of light, haggling loudly over the price of a cockerel, the buyers waving their hands in the air, the seller acting as though he had just received the biggest insult of his life.

The Ford moved on between fruit stalls piled high with multicoloured displays: tiny green bananas and plantains, deep red mangoes and bright orange tangerines, the rich aroma filling the air with a sweet perfume.

Exotic music spilled from gloomy coffee houses where furtive-looking men sat in groups around battered tin tables, drinking, playing cards and enjoying their hookah pipes, the air fragrant with thick clouds of tobacco smoke. Here, a toothless woman crouched behind a huge basket of fish, the stench assailing Llewellyn's nostrils; there, a man offered eggs of every size and colour piled in great precarious-looking heaps; and, of course, there were the inevitable stalls offering tourists so-called relics: stone statues, items of jewellery, lumps of rock that the sellers would claim had come from the tomb of some ancient pharaoh.

It quickly became apparent that the Ford could make no more progress through the press of bodies. The bazaar led onwards into narrow side streets where no vehicle could venture, and even here on the wider streets at the bazaar's out-skirts, people crowded round them, banging on the windows and waving whatever it was they were trying to sell.

Llewellyn wondered glumly why he'd even bothered coming here. He had underestimated the size of the bazaar. How was he ever going to spot Tom Hinton? Mickey had hinted at Hassan's unreliability, and even if Tom *had* been here recently, what were the chances of him coming again?

Llewellyn thought wistfully of his hotel room. He hadn't actually visited it yet, but it would surely be clean and spacious with a ceiling fan overhead to cool the sweat on his brow, and of course it would come with a shower. He promised himself that he would have the water as cold as possible, and when he was dry and tingling, he would douse his body in his favourite lavender cologne. Afterwards he would go down to the restaurant and order himself a delicious meal with a fine bottle of wine, all expenses paid by the Hinton family. His resolve began to crumble. The heat and clamour of the crowded bazaar suddenly overwhelmed him. What was he thinking of, coming here, anyway? What had he expected to find? Tomorrow. He would look around the bazaar tomorrow. He was just about to lean forward and tap Mohammed on the shoulder to tell him to turn round and head for the Winter Palace when, quite unexpectedly, the impossible happened.

He saw Tom Hinton.

At least, he was pretty sure it was Tom. After all, he had never seen the man in the flesh, but this chap looked pretty much like the photographs he had been given by Tom's parents. Llewellyn told

Mohammed to stop the Ford and took out his wallet so he could study the small photo he carried to make a comparison.

The young man was standing at a stall across the street, a display of antiquities, and seemed to be going carefully through the objects arranged on the tabletop, as though searching for something in particular. He was wearing a khaki shirt and trousers and a wide-brimmed hat; the oil lamp on the table cast his face into shadow, so it was hard to make a positive identification and yet . . .

Llewellyn got out of the car. 'Wait here,' he told Mohammed, and began to cross the road towards the stall.

'Mr Hinton?' he called out. 'Is that you?'

The man looked up in surprise and Llewellyn finally got a good look at his face. It was Tom Hinton all right – there could be no mistake, even though the fresh-faced young man in the photograph seemed light years away from the pale, haggard creature that was staring indignantly back at him now.

'Mr Hinton, I—' Llewellyn broke off in alarm as he was suddenly surrounded by a clutch of shouting Arabs, all trying to sell him their wares.

Each of them held a small stone statue. As far as Llewellyn could see, the statues were all identical.

'This very old, *effendi*,' one of them insisted. 'From tomb of Tutankhamun! You buy, only twelve piastres!'

'No, you buy mine, eleven piastres!'

'Get away from me!' Llewellyn pushed impatiently past them, only to see that Tom had turned on his heel and was hurrying away as though he had no intention of speaking to anyone.

'Mr Hinton! Wait!' Llewellyn struggled to the far side of the road and went after Tom. He pushed his prodigious bulk through the people milling around the stall, the exertion bringing beads of sweat to his brow. He could see Tom's head and shoulders some twenty yards ahead of him, his slim frame moving with ease through the crowd, but Llewellyn was determined not to let him get away. He hadn't come all this way to be outrun by some jumped-up Englishman who felt like being secretive.

He hurried past more stalls, ignoring the cries of the vendors. A donkey cart laden with fruit came trotting towards him and he had to press back to one side to allow it to go by. When he resumed the chase, he saw that Tom had gained a few yards on him and he quickened his pace in an attempt to make up the lost ground.

'Mr Hinton!' he shouted, abandoning all thought of decorum. 'Please wait. I don't mean you any harm. I just want to ask a few questions!'

But Tom did not glance back, nor did he slow his pace. He seemed intent on escape.

A couple of ragged children, alerted by Llewellyn's shouts, came trotting along in his wake, pulling at the hem of his jacket, each of them holding out a hand to beg for *baksheesh*. They were grinning up at him like tiny demons.

'Get lost, you little pests!' snarled Llewellyn but they took no notice of his entreaties and in the end he had to put a hand into his pocket and throw a couple of piastres onto the ground beside them. Instantly there was a commotion as the children scrambled to pick up the coins and he was able to leave them in his wake. However, the exertion was taking its toll on him. He was gasping for breath and his shirt was sodden with sweat. It occurred to him that he was in danger of suffering a heart attack, right here in the midst of this crowd, and there would be nobody to help him.

'Mr Hinton!' he cried again. 'Please stop!'

Now he saw that Tom was turning left along a narrow alley. Llewellyn followed, straining to see his way in the darkness. It smelled like something had died in there and the sight of several barrels of rotting fish heads confirmed exactly what that something was. The smell was overlaid with the combined stench of stagnant water and urine. A mangy cat was exploring the fish heads, trying to find something that was still edible. *Good luck to him*, thought Llewellyn as he hurried on by; and he thought once again of the Winter Palace. Even the name seemed cool and reassuring. Why wasn't he there enjoying a glass of chilled champagne? Why was he wasting his time chasing after a man who clearly didn't want to be found?

Up at the top of the alley he saw the dull glow of an oil lamp hanging over a weathered wooden doorway. Tom opened the door and ducked inside, closing it after him.

Right, thought Llewellyn, and his resolve stiffened. *If he thinks he's escaped me, he's got another think coming.* He marched quickly up to the door and reached for the handle. He had expected it to be locked but it turned with a sharp click and swung open beneath his hand. He felt a brief sense of surprise, almost of disappointment. He had expected to have to throw his considerable weight against the door in order to force it open.

He stepped inside and found himself in a small, windowless room made of sun-dried clay brick, the interior lit only by the smoky glow of a hurricane lamp on a rickety wooden table. Tom Hinton was standing in one corner of the room, as though waiting for Llewellyn. His face was expressionless.

'Close the door,' he said quietly.

Llewellyn did as Tom asked. Then he turned back. 'Why did you run away?' he asked, taking out a handkerchief and mopping at his sweat-soaked forehead.

'I didn't know who you were,' said Tom. 'I panicked.' He motioned to a couple of chairs. 'Please,' he said, 'sit down. I see I've caused you some discomfort.'

Llewellyn nodded and moved to the nearest chair, which creaked in protest under the detective's considerable weight, but happily did not collapse. Tom took the seat opposite and sat looking at Llewellyn with what seemed like considerable interest. The detective noticed some kind of charm around his neck on a leather thong, a big chunky blue stone with an eye painted on it. It seemed an odd thing to be wearing, the kind of adornment you might expect to see around the neck of an ancient warrior, not a middle-class British archaeologist.

'Who are you?' asked Tom.

'My name is Wilfred Llewellyn. I'm a private detective. Your parents contacted me when you went missing and begged me to come out to Egypt to search for you.'

Tom's mouth curved into a sardonic smile. 'Missing?' he said. 'I'm not missing.'

Llewellyn allowed himself a sympathetic nod. 'No, I can see that. But you did walk away from the excavation without a word to anybody, the same night that Sir William was taken ill, and none of your friends or relatives have heard from you since. Surely you can see, Mr Hinton, that this would be a cause for concern?'

Tom gave Llewellyn an odd look. 'That's not my name,' he said. 'Hinton.'

Llewellyn was baffled. 'But of course it is!' he protested.

Tom shook his head. 'I *was* Tom Hinton, for a time,' he said. 'Now I answer to a different name. Oh, I still have everything I took from him. I have his voice, his mind, his intellect. Even his bones.'

Llewellyn began to get a bad feeling about this. Clearly Tom had suffered some kind of nervous breakdown, just like Sir William. Whatever had happened on that fateful night, had Tom witnessed it too?

'Come along, sir,' said Llewellyn. 'Of course you are Tom Hinton.' He took the photograph from his pocket and set it down on the tabletop. 'And here is the proof.'

Tom picked it up and gazed at it, a curious expression on his face, as though he had forgotten that he looked as he did. 'It's an understandable mistake,' he said calmly. He stared up at Llewellyn with renewed interest. 'So tell me, Mr Llewellyn. You are known to the people at the dig? They . . . have accepted you?'

'Yes, of course. Why shouldn't they?'

Tom shrugged his shoulders. 'I only ask the question because it has occurred to me that the form I now occupy is awkward for me. People are looking for Tom Hinton and it could cause me problems. But of course, nobody is looking for *you*, are they, Mr Llewellyn? Nobody looks for the one who is looking. You can come and go as you please.'

Llewellyn snorted. 'I haven't the faintest idea

what you're on about,' he confessed. 'But whatever name you answer to these days, I have found my man and I am duty bound to report my discovery to the appropriate authorities.'

'You need not worry about that,' said Tom flatly. 'Very soon now, the form you look upon will be gone for ever and you will no longer be concerned with such trivial matters. I have a favour to ask of you, Mr Llewellyn.'

'A favour?' asked Llewellyn irritably. 'What favour?'

Tom leaned across the table as though to confide something; and Llewellyn became aware of a peculiar smell emanating from him – a sharp sulphuric tang that seemed to catch at the back of his throat.

'Would you mind awfully if I borrowed your body?' whispered Tom.

'Borrowed my . . . ?' Llewellyn stared at Tom in disbelief and then gave an incredulous laugh. 'What are you talking about?' he cried. 'Borrow my body? Is this supposed to be some kind of joke?'

Tom shook his head. 'Oh no,' he said. 'I'm deadly serious.'

Llewellyn stared at him. He didn't understand

any of this. Tom was just smiling at him in a horribly smug way, as though he knew something that Llewellyn could never even guess at. Llewellyn was about to say something else, but just at that moment something strange and rather frightening happened.

Tom's left eyebrow suddenly raised itself up from his face. It thickened, rounded and fell onto the table, where it became smooth and shiny. Llewellyn stared down in disgust as it transformed itself into a large, dark-brown beetle. It scuttled quickly across the table and shot straight up the sleeve of Llewellyn's jacket. An instant later he felt a sharp sting in the fleshy part of his forearm. He let out an oath and tried to move away from the table, but the rickety old chair finally gave up the struggle to hold his weight and collapsed beneath him. He crashed to the floor and lay there, winded, for a moment, staring up at Tom Hinton, who was still sitting at the table.

As Llewellyn gazed at him, Tom's face began to fall apart. Smooth round pieces of flesh raised themselves up, turned dark and shiny and fell onto the tabletop with a plop. At first it was just a few pieces, but then, as if at a signal, his whole face was moving and raining down fat brown beetles, which came swarming down the table legs towards Llewellyn. The mocking face that stared down at him was rapidly turning into a hideous skull from which the distinctive blue eyes glittered with feral malignance.

'First my friends consume the old flesh,' announced the thing that had been Tom Hinton. 'And then the new flesh takes over . . .'

For a second Llewellyn was transfixed, too horrified to make a move, as scores of scarabs skittered beneath the layers of his clothing. Then he felt the terrible pain of hundreds of tiny jaws going to work on his flesh and the agony galvanized him into action. He scrambled to his feet, flinging off his jacket and throwing it aside. He began to tear at his sodden white shirt, aware as he did so that pools of crimson were blossoming on it like flowers of evil. Buttons popped off as he pulled the shirt open and stared down at his chest, gasping in fear. Even as he looked, a glistening dark brown tide of insects was swarming over it.

Pain consumed his body like molten fire and he tried tearing at the creatures with his fingers, but they were locked into his flesh and the tide was rising higher, up around his neck, his chins. He looked down at his feet and saw that the advancing swarm was unstoppable: more and more of the creatures were moving in beneath the hem of his trousers. At the table, a talking skeleton dressed in khaki clothes was speaking to him in a flat, tinny-sounding voice.

'Don't fight it, Mr Llewellyn. Embrace the new flesh. The pain is soon over and then you will begin a new life; a life free from pain and remorse.'

'Stop it!' screamed Llewellyn. 'Please, stop!'

The tide was moving up around his mouth now and he clamped it shut, not wanting to allow the scarabs in. He turned and began to stumble towards the door, but his half-eaten leg muscles no longer had the strength to hold him upright and he fell heavily to the floor, writhing in agony. Scarabs were pushing their way into his nostrils now, preventing him from drawing breath, and then dark shapes were moving to cover his eyes. He rolled onto his back and looked at the table, just in time to see the skeleton collapse and crash to the floor, breaking into pieces on impact. Then darkness descended and there was just pain.

* * *

Mohammed sat in his Ford and wondered how much longer the private detective was going to be. It was all very well working as Mr Llewellyn's personal chauffeur – the money was good – but Mohammed had other work to be getting on with and he couldn't even hope to start on that until he'd delivered Llewellyn to the Winter Palace.

It was funny about Mr Hinton though. Mohammed hadn't got a good look at the man's face, but it had appeared to be him – the same tall physique and straight blond hair; but if it *was* him, why did he rush away as though he had something to hide? Of course, Mr Llewellyn had handled it all wrong. Why had he shouted to the man like that, warning him that he was there? If Mohammed had been on the case, he'd have crept quietly up to Mr Hinton and tapped him on the shoulder, not giving him the opportunity to run away. Mohammed was beginning to wonder just how good a detective Mr Llewellyn was.

As if in answer to the thought, Mohammed saw the Welshman walking back along the crowded street but something about him seemed wrong. He was clasping his white jacket tightly around him as though it was cold; and as he stepped out of the crowd, Mohammed saw that the detective's trousers were covered with dark stains as though he had spilled a glass of wine down the front of them and as he moved closer, Mohammed saw that the collar of his white shirt was also stained.

A couple of children came running after him, hands held out to beg for coins. Llewellyn turned and glared at them and said something under his breath, causing the children to run away, terrified.

Llewellyn turned back towards the car, and now Mohammed was baffled because — and this was really odd — the detective's bloated body didn't seem quite as bulky as it had a short while ago. Oh, he was still a big man but his white jacket hung loosely on his frame, as though he had somehow managed to lose some weight in that short run along the street. Impossible, of course, and yet . . . As Llewellyn approached the Ford, Mohammed, his amateur detective instincts fully aroused, noticed one last puzzling detail. Mr Llewellyn was no longer sweating — indeed, he seemed perfectly cool and relaxed.

'Are you quite all right, sir?' asked Mohammed, puzzled by the apparent changes in his client.

'Of course I'm all right,' snapped Llewellyn. 'Why shouldn't I be?' He climbed into the back seat and the car filled with a disconcerting smell – not the odour of sweat and lavender water that Mohammed was used to; more as though somebody had just struck a dozen matches at once. Mohammed studied Llewellyn in the mirror. His eyes seemed to have a cold, vacant look in them, and when he spoke, even his voice was different, harder, more abrasive.

'What the hell are you staring at, man?'

'I'm sorry, sir, I was merely concerned. Did you manage to catch up with Mr Hinton?'

'It wasn't him,' Llewellyn assured him. 'They had a similar build but when I got a good look at his face, I could see it was somebody completely different. Felt rather foolish pursuing him down the street like that.'

'That's odd,' murmured Mohammed. 'I could have sworn—'

'It wasn't him, I told you! Now, for goodness' sake, are you going to sit around yakking all night or are you going to take me to my hotel?'

'Er . . . of course, sir. Right away, sir.'

Mohammed started up the car and drove slowly off through the throngs of people, sounding his horn whenever somebody got in his way.

'You will collect me from the hotel at sundown tomorrow and take me back to the bazaar,' said Llewellyn. It was not a request but an order.

'Oh, I don't know, Mr Llewellyn,' reasoned Mohammed. 'All this driving — it takes up so much of my time. I have other businesses to run. Perhaps I can send one of my cousins instead.'

'You will come yourself,' snarled Llewellyn. 'How much do you earn in one year?'

'I . . . I beg your pardon, sir?'

'I want to know how much money you earn in a year. I will pay you that amount to be my personal driver for one week. How does that sound?'

'Er . . . very generous, I'm sure but . . . I would need to sit down and work out how much this would be.'

Llewellyn made a gesture of dismissal. 'It's immaterial. You name a price and that's what I shall give you when my business is concluded.'

'But . . . with respect, Mr Llewellyn, you do not know how long that will take.'

'It will not be long,' said Llewellyn; and he turned to gaze dreamily out of the window as they drove away from the bazaar.

Mohammed kept glancing at his passenger in the rear-view mirror. He was convinced now that something was terribly wrong. How could a man change in so many ways in such a short space of time? And why was he lying about finding Tom Hinton?

Mohammed wasn't sure what Wilfred Llewellyn was up to, but he resolved to keep a close eye on him until the truth revealed itself.

CHAPTER ELEVEN
Early Risers

The sun was just peeping over the horizon when Alec took his place at the communal table with the rest of the team. He was used to these early starts from the previous digs, knowing that it was a good idea to get as much as possible done before the heat of the day set in. He'd passed a fitful night, his sleep interrupted by howls echoing around the hills; howls that seemed to descend into maniacal laughter, demonstrating only too well why the creatures making the noise were sometimes referred to as 'laughing' hyenas.

Consequently, this morning he was heavy-eyed

and not all that alert. As he took his seat at the table, Archie dutifully placed a bowl in front of him and he stared at the lumpy grey sludge that filled it. He looked hopefully at Coates, who was sitting beside him.

'I'm not sure what it is either,' said the valet. 'Mr McCloud claims it's porridge but it's not like any I've ever seen.'

'As long as there's no bat in it, I'll eat it,' said Alec.

'The very idea!' growled Archie. 'That's just good wholesome porridge oats with a dash of milk and, of course, my own special ingredient.'

'Demerara sugar?' suggested Doc Hopper hopefully.

'Honey?' suggested Mickey.

'Golden syrup,' offered Alec. He raised a spoonful to his mouth and his expression turned to one of total disgust. 'Salt,' he croaked. 'Lots and lots of salt.'

'That is correct,' said Archie brightly. 'An absolute necessity in this climate. It'll replace all that good honest sweat you're losin'.'

'Mr McCloud,' said Coates. 'About that bat curry you threatened to make for tonight's dinner . . .'

Archie shook his head. 'It's off the menu,' he said with genuine regret. 'The ones in the sack smelled rotten from the word go and it got worse during the night. It was so bad, I had to get up and bury them.'

Everybody at the table let out loud sighs of relief.

'A real pity,' said Archie wistfully. 'Ah could have done something spectacular wi' 'em. Well, eat hearty! There's plenty more porridge in the pot if ye want it.' He wandered back to the cook tent, whistling cheerfully.

Coates pushed his bowl away and looked at Ethan, who was doing his level best to swallow down spoonfuls of the stuff.

'It's not so bad if you get it down quick,' he said.

'Mr Wade,' said Coates, and Alec could see that there was a look of grim determination on his valet's face. 'We are going to have to talk about this.'

Ethan glanced warily over his shoulder. 'What's the problem, Mr Goats . . . er . . . Coates?'

'I'll tell you the problem. That man cannot cook to save his life. It's bad enough that we're out here in this heat and sleeping in tents, but to endure it with nothing edible is going too far.'

'I agree,' said Doc Hopper. He pointed to the ring of Arabs seated around their communal campfire, cooking up something spicy in their pan. 'I wonder what they're having?' he said hopefully. 'It smells a lot more appetizing than this muck!'

Ethan frowned and looked around the circle of faces. 'I can't help feeling you're all being a little hard on Archie,' he said.

'*Hard* on him?' said Coates. 'Why not? He's being *merciless* with us.'

'I feel sorry for him,' said Ethan. 'You know, when I interviewed him, he told me that a lot of his closest friends were killed during the war . . .'

'Probably from food poisoning,' said Madeleine, and Alec had to stifle a laugh.

'Yes,' said Doc Hopper. 'He probably took cookery lessons from Dr Crippen.' When nobody laughed, he added, 'You know, the famous poisoner?'

Coates looked around the table. 'Is *anybody* here happy with the standard of cuisine?' he asked.

Mickey started to put up his hand, but then

changed his mind. 'I was gonna say 'is rice puddin' is just like Mother used to make,' he said, 'but to tell you the truth, she was a terrible cook too.'

That *did* get a laugh.

'And who would like to see an improvement?' asked Coates.

After a brief pause everyone except Ethan raised a hand.

'There you are then,' said Coates. 'He'll have to be told.'

'Uh . . . yeah, OK,' said Ethan quietly. Alec studied him in amazement. The man who had so fearlessly faced up to a pack of deadly hyenas was afraid of hurting Archie's feelings.

'If you feel awkward speaking to him, Mr Wade, I'm more than happy to oblige,' offered Coates.

Ethan shook his head. 'Oh no. I'm director of this project, it's down to me. I'll get him on his own later.' He leaned forward and lowered his voice. 'But listen, I sure wouldn't feel too good about sacking him. I mean, where else would he go?'

'You don't have to sack him,' said Coates. 'Simply tell him that from now on I'll be help-ing him on cooking duties. Which basically

means I'll be cooking and he'll be my assistant.'
He glanced at Alec guiltily. 'Of course, that means
I shan't be able to spend as much time with you,
Master Alec.'

'Oh, what a pity,' said Alec dutifully, but deep
down he was delighted at the news. The last
thing he wanted was Coates following him
everywhere he went.

'Don't worry about Alec, Monsieur Coates,'
said Madeleine. 'I shall make sure that 'e comes
to no 'arm.' She reached over and tousled
Alec's hair affectionately and he felt his face reddening.

'Well,' announced Ethan, trying to sound
more positive, 'today we should get the last items
out of the antechamber. Which means tomorrow
we'll be breaking through to the—' He stopped
at the sound of approaching hooves.

Glancing up the valley, Alec saw an Arab guide
leading a couple of donkeys down the hill
towards the camp. Seated on the donkeys were
two people that he had met outside King Tut's
tomb: the reporter, Biff Corcoran, and his
photographer, Charlie Connors. They looked
quite ridiculous perched on their little mounts.
Biff's boots skimmed the rocky ground by mere

inches. Charlie was carrying her huge camera and looked as bored as she had last time Alec had met her.

'Great,' muttered Ethan. 'Who would have figured they'd be up at this time of the morning? OK, folks, don't forget, we've found nothing.' He went to greet the visitors. 'Biff! Charlie! So you made it up here after all!'

'Yeah.' Biff swung himself down off his donkey and rubbed his backside ruefully. 'Damned uncomfortable way to do it, too,' he growled. He watched as Charlie dismounted. 'Couldn't find anybody to drive us up here. It seems Mohammed Hansa is on permanent call chauffeuring that professor friend of yours around.'

'Huh? Oh, you mean Professor Llewellyn? Yeah, well, there wasn't much for him to do just yet, so he's been getting in a little sightseeing.' Ethan beckoned them over to the table. 'Come and take the weight off,' he suggested. 'Have a cup of java with us.'

'Don't mind if I do,' said Biff. He and Charlie slipped into a couple of empty seats. 'I wouldn't normally be seen dead at this time of the morning but something came to me in the middle of the night.'

'Oh yes?' said Doc Hopper. 'Mosquitoes, was it?'

'Something better than that,' said Biff. 'An idea. A great idea.'

'Hmm. I 'ad one of those once,' said Mickey. 'I wonder whatever 'appened to it.' He winked at Alec, then filled a couple of enamel mugs with coffee, something that even Archie couldn't manage to mess up. Biff took a silver hip flask from his pocket and added a generous measure of the contents to his mug.

'Still got that head cold, I see,' said Ethan.

Biff nodded. 'It's a doozy,' he said. 'Just keeps hanging on in there. You gotta take relief where you can find it.' He took a mouthful of coffee, smacked his lips and looked around at the assembled crew. 'Hope I'm not keeping you people from anything important,' he said.

'Oh no,' said Doc Hopper. 'We were just discussing where we might try looking next.'

Biff nodded. 'Ethan,' he said, 'it's come to my attention that you've been hiding something from me.'

'Huh?' Ethan nearly choked on his coffee. 'What are you talking about?'

Biff was now smiling at Madeleine. 'I'm talking

about this lovely lady here. It's about time you got a looker on your team. The rest of 'em could scare crows for a living.'

'Blimey, you say what you think, don't ya?' observed Mickey.

'It's my job,' said Biff. He looked at Ethan expectantly. 'Well?' he said.

'Oh, er . . . sure. Biff, this is Madeleine . . . Dr Madeleine Duval. She's come over from Paris to help us on the dig.'

'A doctor, no less!' Biff studied Madeleine with evident interest. 'Boy, you Frenchies sure know how to make a subject more interesting, don't ya? What's your speciality, *mademoiselle*?' He pronounced the word as it was spelled – mad-e-moiselle.

Madeleine stared back at him with evident distaste. 'I am an expert in 'ieroglyphics,' she said coldly; then flinched as Charlie snapped a picture of her. 'Please don't do that,' she said. 'I don't like 'aving my picture taken.'

'I can't imagine why,' said Biff. 'Honey, you could give Mary Pickford a run for her money.'

'Mary 'oo?'

'You know. The movie star. She's about the most famous woman in Hollywood right now and she ain't a patch on you, honey.' He turned to look at Ethan. 'So, you sure kept her quiet,' he said.

Ethan fixed him with a look. 'Biff, I'd appreciate it if you didn't talk about Miss Duval like that.' He said it quietly but the menace in his voice was evident.

Biff assumed a look of complete innocence. 'Aw, shucks, Wade, I don't think she minds.'

'Well, I do. Madeleine is a member of my team and I'd ask you to watch your mouth around her, otherwise I'm liable to forget that we're friends.'

Biff stared back at him for a moment. 'Touchy,' he said. 'Very touchy.' He took a sip of his coffee and studied Ethan thoughtfully. 'So you needed a hieroglyphics expert, huh?'

Ethan shrugged. 'Well, not yet exactly, but we live in hope,' he said calmly.

'Hmm. So let me get this straight. Madeleine here came all the way from Gay Paree, just on the off-chance there might be a need for her expertise.'

'In her own airplane,' added Charlie, through a mouthful of gum.

'Oh yeah, nearly forgot about that. Somebody over at the hotel mentioned it. See, call me suspicious, but I figure there has to be a little more to it than you're letting on. You know what? I think you've found something, Ethan. Why don't ya level with me?'

Ethan adopted a hangdog look. He sighed. 'I guess there's no use trying to lie to you, Biff,' he said. 'Yeah, we found something.'

Biff looked at Charlie. 'What'd I tell ya?' he said.

'You said they'd found something,' said Charlie.

'Yeah, and I was right, see. That's what they call reporter's intuition.' He turned back to Ethan. 'Come on, spill the beans,' he said.

Ethan nodded. 'Mickey, go and bring the finds tray for Mr Corcoran.'

'OK, boss.' Mickey got up from the table and headed towards his tent.

'See, this all ties in with my big idea,' said Biff excitedly. 'You know I've been looking for the human interest angle? Well, it occurred to me last night that it was right there, staring me in the face.' He pointed at Alec. 'There he is,' he said.

'Alec?' said Ethan.

'Me?' said Alec.

'Yeah, you! Think of it. Intrepid young English

boy vows to carry on his uncle's work after poor
Sir William gets dragged off to the funny farm.
No offence, kid. Boy heads out to the wilds of
Egypt all alone—'

'Hardly alone,' said Coates indignantly. 'I am
Master Alec's valet. I accompany him everywhere.'

'OK, point taken. He sets off for the wilds of
Egypt with just his faithful flunky at his side.'

'*Flunky?*' Now Coates looked positively horrified. 'That's not a term I approve of.'

'We'll haggle over the words later,' Biff told
him. 'Just listen a minute, will ya? Where was I?'

'Boy goes to Egypt with flunky,' said Charlie
tonelessly, and she snapped a picture of Coates.

'Oh yeah . . . Boy gets to Egypt, joins the
expedition. And to top it all, after weeks of hard
work he makes an exciting discovery.'

'Hardly weeks,' Alec corrected him. 'I only got
here yesterday.'

'The timescale ain't important! It's the
achievement that counts. Our readers are gonna
love this story! Charlie, get some more pictures
of our young hero. Get one with the flunky and
one with Dr Cutie there.'

Charlie obediently started taking more pictures,
but the bored expression never left her face and

her jaws kept chomping rhythmically at her gum. Madeleine meanwhile put her tongue out and made rude gestures at the camera.

'Hey, knock it off, sister,' said Charlie. 'You any idea how much film costs?'

'*You* knock eet off,' snapped Madeleine. 'I told you I don't wish to be photographed. Please respect my wishes!'

'Aw, suit yourself.' Charlie directed her attention at Alec. 'Look heroic, buster,' she told him. He just glared back at her, but she took a picture anyway.

Mickey came out of his tent carrying a small wooden tray, which he brought to the table, walking slowly as if it contained something precious. Meanwhile Biff went right on talking. 'I can see it now,' he said. 'Feature article: THE TUTANKHAMUN KID. We'll have a nice big picture of brave Alex—'

'Alec!'

'Whatever! We'll have a big picture of him standing in front of . . . in front of—' Biff broke off as Mickey placed the carefully prepared finds tray on the table in front of him. It contained a few shards of broken pottery, half a small statue and a mummified cat.

Biff stared down at it in silence for a moment.

'Please tell me this isn't all you've found,' he said quietly.

'Not *all*,' said Doc Hopper. 'Just the best of it.'

'The best?'

Charlie raised her camera to snap a picture of the tray but Biff lifted a hand to stop her. 'Don't waste film,' he told her. 'There *has* to be more than this.'

'We hope there *will* be,' said Ethan. 'But look – that piece of jar there. Eighteenth dynasty: there's no mistaking that.'

'Oh, great,' said Biff. 'That's your big discovery. A broken vase.'

'*D'accord*,' said Madeleine. 'And 'ere – you see this fragment of writing on the clay? The name of Akhenaten himself. Well, it *could* be if it was all there. So you see, we could be on the verge of something very exciting indeed.'

Biff raised a hand to his face. 'On the verge is no use to me,' he groaned. 'On the verge is nowhere. It has to be *bigger* than that.'

'We have some bigger bits of pottery,' said Alec. 'Not quite as old as this stuff, but . . .'

Biff shook his head. His great idea had just crashed up against a real problem. He thought for a moment.

'Wait a minute,' he said. 'Maybe I'll go talk to Howard Carter. Yeah . . . I'll see if he'll agree to me saying that Alex is really working on his dig. Then we can photograph the kid standing in front of a big sarcophagus. Something that will wow our readers.'

Alec glared at him. 'But that would be a lie,' he protested.

'Yeah, sure, but it would be a better story. Let's not get hung up on the details, kid. We photograph you standing next to that junk' – he pointed at the contents of the tray – 'and we don't *have* a story.'

'You're surely not suggesting that Master Alec should involve himself in a total fabrication?' said Coates. 'What about his sense of honour? And where's your journalistic integrity?'

'Forget about honour and integrity: he'd be featured in the *Saturday Evening Post*!' said Biff, as if that was reason enough to do just about anything. 'He'd be in millions of households throughout the USA!'

'What a nauseating proposition,' said Coates quietly.

'Hey, listen, buster, there's plenty of people would give their eye teeth for a place in the *Post*.

Heck, we've featured the biggest stars in Hollywood.'

'How thrilling for you,' said Coates, with just the right amount of contempt.

'I'm sorry,' said Alec firmly. 'I couldn't do it. Uncle Will's dream is to find the tomb of Akhenaten and that's what we're trying to do. Finding Tut was Howard Carter's dream and he's made it happen. I wouldn't do anything to take any of the glory away from him.'

Biff sat there, shaking his head in disbelief. 'You guys are killing me,' he said. 'You know that?' He drained the last of his coffee and stood up. 'To think I gave up breakfast at the Winter Palace to come out to this godforsaken dump and look at a few bits of pottery I could've found in my own back garden. Come on, Charlie, let's get back down the valley to Tut's tomb.' He gave Ethan a withering look. 'A place where they've *really* got something to shout about.' He glared at Alec. 'You ever come to your senses, kid, you know where to find me.'

'I won't change my mind,' Alec assured him.

The team watched as Biff and Charlie stalked off to remount their donkeys. The Arab guide managed to turn the beasts round and they started off up the hill. Biff looked back to shout at Ethan, 'I don't know why I came all the way over here. Wade, you're in charge of a bunch of losers. You'll never find that tomb you keep talking about. Y'hear me? If you find anything of interest, I'll eat my dad-blasted boots!'

Alec felt an overpowering urge to jump up and run after the newspaperman; to tell him to take his boots off and start chewing, because they *had* found something: they had made the most incredible find ever. But Ethan must have sensed what was going on, because he flashed him a warning look followed by a sly wink.

Once the two journalists were safely out of sight, the team let out a collective sigh of relief and had a good laugh about what had just happened.

'Mickey, the tray was perfect,' chuckled Ethan. 'It couldn't have looked more dismal if you'd tried. Maddie, that was a nice touch about Akhenaten – it just added the final straw. Thanks for that.'

Alec waited for Madeleine to protest at the shortened form of her name but she just smiled graciously. 'Thank you for defending me,' she said, 'against that horrible man.'

'Oh, that's OK.' There was a brief silence while the two of them regarded each other; then Ethan made an effort to recall what he'd been saying.

'And Alec . . . you clearly know the meaning of the word integrity. Some kids would have jumped at the chance to be famous.'

Alec shrugged. 'I wouldn't mind being famous for something I really had done,' he said. 'Like being one of the first people to enter the tomb of Akhenaten?'

Ethan grinned. 'Yeah, that would be something, wouldn't it?' He glanced around the table. 'OK, folks, let's get to work,' he said. 'I figure if we go right through we'll have the antechamber cleared by nightfall. Which means that first thing tomorrow morning we'll be ready to open the second door. I don't know about you, but I'm with Alec on this one. I can't wait to get a good look inside that tomb!'

CHAPTER TWELVE

Waiting

He lay on the hotel bed in his unfamiliar body, curtains drawn, windows tight shut against the morning sunlight. From the street below came the hubbub of voices, the shouting of tradesman, the honking of motor horns. Every part of his flesh itched to be out there, pursuing his quest, but he knew that this was not possible. For the moment at least, he could only walk by night.

His name was Sonchis; he was a high priest of Akhenaten and he had waited three thousand years for the opportunity to be reborn. Chance had released him from his sarcophagus hundreds of years ago – a great movement in the earth that had split the copper-lined casket wide open, allowing his ka, or life force, to escape its prolonged captivity. But his joy at being freed from the casket was short-lived because he was still compelled by the magical power of the serpent's eye, created by three of the pharaoh's most powerful magicians, rendering him powerless to break through the wall that separated him from the world. Instead he was obliged to wait in darkness as the centuries rolled slowly by.

But over the long eternity of imprisonment, the hunger for revenge had never left him; nor the certain knowledge that one day he would be free to carry on the work he had started all those years ago. With what excitement had he sensed the arrival of people searching beneath the sand for whatever was hidden there! With what trepidation did he hear the sounds of them moving closer, day by day, inch by inch! And then, at last, the sounds of the doors of the antechamber being opened. The sounds of movement on the other side of the wall!

Finally . . . finally, human hands had taken hold of the serpent's eye and pulled it free, breaking the magical seal and ending the powerful curse that had held Sonchis a prisoner for so long. In its mad rush for freedom, Sonchis's ka had plunged through the opening in the door and had passed through the eye of the young man who was peering through it.

Entering the body of a human host had been his best means of escape, but at first it had been confusing. As well as his own thoughts and memories, he had inherited those of the person whose body he occupied. Hinton was young and strong – he had fought against the invasion and it had taken some time for Sonchis to claim him completely; and then, of course, he had to wait till darkness fell before he could summon his scarab followers – they who had always been his most loyal subjects. Part of him had feared that after so long they would no longer heed his instructions, but he need not have worried. In the darkness they had come scurrying to do his bidding, thousands of them. They had consumed Hinton's body down to the bones and then had replaced his flesh with theirs.

What did it feel like to be free after so long? Incredible! Words could not describe the delight of finally being able to leave his place of interment, to view the world through borrowed eyes.

Up here on the surface, everything had changed immeasurably from the existence he had known, but somewhere, he knew, the great serpent still slept, awaiting the call that would reawaken him; and he had not changed, not one tiny bit – of that Sonchis was sure.

The host he dwelled in now was certainly a better choice than his first hiding place: this was a human who could move freely and ask questions, and moreover, one who was already known to those who had discovered the tomb. Llewellyn's body could be used to take Sonchis wherever he needed to go to regain his former glories.

But it was a process that could not be rushed. After such an age of inactivity, Sonchis knew that certain elements had to be in place before he could enjoy his full powers; and first and foremost he needed to be able to walk by daylight. Even now, more confident in the flabby body of the British detective, he knew that a single ray of sunlight upon his back would cause his scarab flesh to break apart and scurry into the darkest corners.

Tonight he'd go looking again for the amulet that would allow him to brave the daylight hours. He thought he had a pretty good idea where he would find it. Right now he felt a powerful tiredness tugging at him and closing his eyes. He immediately fell into a restless sleep . . .

He woke with a start as manacles were clamped around his wrists – and he looked up in dull shock to see members of Akhenaten's royal guard standing over him, swords raised to cut him down if he tried to resist. He glanced around quickly and saw that he was in his own bedchamber in his fine palace in Thebes. From another room he heard the desperate screams of his servants.

There was nothing he could do. The manacles around his wrist were of forged copper. His powers were nullified and there was no magic he could summon to strike these intruders who had broken into his home in the dead of night. He'd thought he was prepared for something like this. He had kept guards on watch both day and night, but they must have been overwhelmed . . . Either that or they had betrayed him. He had been so tired. The long ceremony of prayers and invocations to Apophis had exhausted him, and before beginning the journey to the Gates of

Apophis, where he planned to summon forth the living embodiment of the ancient god, he knew that he had to snatch a few hours' sleep. That human weakness had been his downfall.

The guards dragged him out of bed and stood him upright, a razor-edged sword against his throat. Then Gila came in, swaggering into the chamber because he knew he had his greatest enemy in his power and was enjoying his moment of triumph. Gila, another high priest of Akhenaten, fat, middle-aged and envious, the man who had watched with jealous eyes as Sonchis drew disciples around him as flies followed honey. Gila it was who had learned of the Apophis cult and had gone running to his master to tell what he had heard, like a schoolchild ratting on a fellow pupil. Gila stood there now, his hands on his plump hips, his eyes outlined in green malachite and gleaming with malice.

'Sonchis,' he said. 'Not quite so high and mighty now.'

Sonchis curled his lip into a disdainful sneer. 'At least I am not a lap dog who goes creeping to his master,' he said; then lifted his head as another scream came echoing from somewhere within the building. For a moment he lost his composure. 'My servants . . .' he gasped.

'. . . are already as good as dead,' said Gila, with some relish. 'My men are putting them to the sword now, every last one of them.' He gestured at the magnificent room, with its fine murals and ornate furnishings. 'And once we've taken out a few choice belongings, what's left here will be torched. Akhenaten wishes to show the world what happens to those who disobey him.'

Sonchis hunched his shoulders. 'Kill me then,' he said, 'and get it over with.'

But Gila was smiling; a cold, mirthless smile. 'Oh no,' he said. 'Too quick, my friend, and hardly worthy of a man such as yourself. We have something much more interesting planned for you.' He gestured to the guards. 'Bring him,' he ordered.

He was dragged, punched, kicked through the many rooms of his palace, and already he could smell the acrid smoke as drapes were set aflame. They brought him out to the street, where an ox cart waited, and he saw his four lieutenants kneeling in the back, tied up like common prisoners. Anger welled through him like a rising tide of water.

'I will pay you back for this, Gila!' he snarled.

'I will have my revenge on you and all who—'
He was punched in the stomach by a burly guard
and sank to his knees with a gasp of pain. He
heard mocking laughter and then he was picked
up and thrown into the cart with the others, as
though he was nothing more than a sack of
rubbish. He lay there, trying to get his breath
back, while his lieutenants spoke to him in
desperation.

'Summon help, Sonchis!' gasped Selim. 'Cast a
spell to hurl these dogs aside and let us make our
escape!'

But he stared down at the copper manacles
that held him and knew that he was helpless. Gila
had prepared well for this night. Sonchis had
never understood why the touch of this metal
depleted his power so dramatically. He only
knew that since childhood it had been his greatest enemy. He had hoped to keep the matter
secret from his rivals, telling only his most trusted
allies, but somebody must have informed Gila
of his weakness and now he was paying
the price.

The ox cart headed out of Thebes, the streets
thronged with staring people despite the lateness
of the hour.

'Help us!' cried one of his lieutenants. 'Help us and you will be richly rewarded!'

But nobody made a move. Nobody dared to resist Akhenaten. Instead they jeered, spat, shook their fists. Even those who had once followed Sonchis were now his enemies. The cart left the outskirts of the town and started out along the desert road. Out there, Sonchis knew, countless demons lurked behind every dune, waiting to feast on the unwary.

'Where are you taking us?' he bellowed, and his voice seemed to echo across the vast expanse that lay before them.

A horse drew alongside the cart and he saw Gila, sitting astride it, looking down at him in glee.

'We are going to give you everything you deserve, Sonchis,' he said. 'Tonight you will take your place with the most powerful men in the kingdom. Tonight you will be laid to rest in the Valley of the Kings.' And, laughing, he spurred his horse forward.

Sonchis closed his eyes and began to pray to Apophis, asking him to send him the courage he needed to get through the night without showing fear.

Help me, great serpent. Give me the courage to know that I—

He opened his eyes again and he was back in the hotel room, lying on the bed in the strange wriggling body of the fat detective. For a moment all was confusion. He lay there, staring around at the strange furnishings, unsure of who he was and what had happened. Then he remembered. He got up off the bed, stumbled to a mirror and saw the great white blob of a face staring back at him. Yes. He understood now. He had been dreaming and yet it had seemed so real . . .

He put on the pair of dark glasses he had found in Llewellyn's luggage and went to the window to peep out through the curtains; but the instant the sun touched him, he reeled away, aware that his temporary 'skin' was ready to burst apart.

He waited a moment for the scarabs to settle themselves; then he lay down on the bed again, telling himself he would have to be patient. He looked at the clock on the bedside locker and the part of him that was still Wilfred Llewellyn told him that he had another six hours to wait until nightfall. He was afraid to sleep because of the terrible dreams that awaited him, so he lay there, staring up at the ceiling, watching the fan moving round and round and round . . .

As far as Alec was concerned it had been a near-perfect day. He had helped to photograph the last remaining items in the antechamber. He had prepared a drawing of an interesting detail from a mural. He had helped the Arab workmen to manoeuvre some awkward parts of the battle chariot up the steps to the daylight, where they could be quickly carried out of sight for packing. He had painstakingly removed the dust from a statue with a fine paintbrush.

And through all this he had watched with interest the developing friendship between Ethan Wade and Madeleine Duval. It was subtle, yet obvious. Though their first meeting had been disastrous, something between them had changed; some invisible barrier had now gone. Madeleine no longer bristled when Ethan spoke – instead she listened intently and seemed to give his ideas due consideration. When she made a joke, he laughed. Now Alec noticed the way they spoke about things, their voices soft and conspiratorial; the way they leaned slightly towards each other as they talked. Once, when Ethan asked her to pass him an eye-glass, their hands touched for just an instant longer than they needed to; and Alec saw the way they pulled apart as though an electric shock had run through them.

He was pleased this was happening. He thought of them both as his friends and it would have made life extremely difficult if they had remained enemies. They were so different . . . But didn't people always say that opposites attract? And the attraction *was* there – you could see it in their eyes whenever they looked at each other. He was too young to think about such things himself, but in a few years, he knew, that would change; and it was nice to think that one day he might end up with someone like Madeleine.

As evening approached, the last few items were carried out of the antechamber and Alec, Ethan and Madeleine stood before the doorway to the tomb itself. In the lower part of the door, the dark oval opening was beckoning. Alec knelt to peep through it.

'Can you see anything?' Ethan asked him.

Alec pulled away and looked up at the American, realizing that he was quoting the very words that Lord Carnarvon had spoken to Howard Carter when they had first peered into the tomb of Tutankhamun.

'I'm supposed to say "Wonderful things",' he said with a rueful grin. 'But it's as black as pitch in there. Perhaps if we shone a torch into it?'

Madeleine smiled. 'You know what?' she said. 'It's late and we've all worked very 'ard today. Why don't we wait until morning and come to it fresh?'

Ethan nodded. 'Yeah, that makes sense. I'm pretty pooped myself. And hungry.' He looked down at Alec and ruffled his hair. 'Guess you're gonna have to be patient, pardner.'

Alec scowled, but nodded his acceptance. 'All right,' he said. He got back to his feet and then stared at the opening in the doorway. 'I wonder what happened to it,' he mused.

'To what?' asked Madeleine.

Alec pointed to the opening. 'To whatever was there. You can see that something was sealed around the edges with wax, almost like a cork in a bottle. Must have been something oval, about the size of a golf ball. But where is it? We've taken everything out of here, but there's nothing that could have fitted there.' He pointed to the floor along the base of the door where he had spent some time digging, hoping he might find the object buried in the hard earth. 'I even looked down there, but no luck.'

Ethan frowned. 'That *is* odd, now you mention it,' he admitted. He thought for a moment. 'Well, the only people who were in here before us were Sir William and Tom Hinton. Maybe one of them took it.'

Alec shook his head. 'Uncle Will would never do a thing like that – he does everything by the book. I remember on one dig I found a small piece of jewellery and suggested he just put it in his pocket, take it as a souvenir. He went up the wall at me! Gave me a whole lecture about how everything had to be carefully documented. And . . . and from what I remember of Tom, I don't believe he would do it either.'

'Well, *somebody* 'as taken it,' said Madeleine. 'It 'as not just walked out of 'ere by itself.'

'It might help if we knew what it was we're talking about,' said Alec.

From outside came the clanging of the large pan lid that Archie used as a makeshift dinner gong. The evening meal was ready.

Ethan looked somewhat uncomfortable. 'That

reminds me,' he said. 'I have to tell Archie that this is the last meal he's making without being supervised by Coates. I'll go and grab him now, before we get too much of an audience.' He hurried out of the tomb and they heard him running up the steps.

'Good luck!' Madeleine shouted after him. She looked at Alec. 'He's going to need it,' she said. 'I wouldn't like to tell Monsieur McCloud the truth about 'is cooking.'

Alec laughed. 'You like him, don't you?' he said.

'Monsieur McCloud?' she said playfully.

'You know who I mean! Ethan.'

Madeleine shrugged her shoulders. ''E is . . . interesting. When I first meet him, I think 'e is a big cowboy, like Tom Mix. Now, I still think 'e is like Tom Mix, but maybe I am just starting to like Westerns a little bit more.' She laughed self-consciously. 'I liked the way he stood up for me when that newspaperman was so rude. And did you notice, when those bats came after us, 'e was the first to run to 'elp that poor worker? 'E didn't stop to worry about saving 'is own skin. So yes, I think maybe I misjudged 'im.' She chuckled. 'But don't worry, Alec. You are still the only man for me!'

She reached out and hugged him. He felt his face reddening, but couldn't deny he was enjoying the experience. It was a long time since a woman had hugged him. The last one had been his mother, he thought, and a great wave of melancholy passed through him.

Madeleine seemed to sense that something was wrong. She pulled away from him and regarded him with a sad smile. 'Oh, but now you are sad,' she observed. 'You know, I think your mother would be proud to see 'ow you 'ave turned out, Alec.'

He shrugged. 'Think so?' he said.

'I know she would. It is what any mother wishes for 'er son. To be strong and fearless and doing the thing that 'e loves most in the world. I was watching you work today. You take a great delight in archaeology, yes?'

Alec nodded. 'It's the best,' he said.

'Then, Alec, you must pursue it with all your 'eart and never let anybody tell you that it is not for you.'

'I intend to,' he said.

'Good. Now . . . I suppose we 'ad better go and see what 'orrors Archie 'as concocted for us,' suggested Madeleine.

Alec affected a look of dread. 'Do we have to?' he muttered.

'Try to be brave, *mon ami*,' said Madeleine, and they both laughed. She put her arm around his shoulders, and side-by-side they left the antechamber.

CHAPTER THIRTEEN

The Search

Sonchis did not like the way the driver kept glancing at him in the rear-view mirror. The man had the cold, cunning eyes of a jackal and it was evident that he sensed something was wrong. But, Sonchis told himself, he could not possibly have an inkling of what had *really* happened to his client, Mr Llewellyn; and even if he guessed at the truth, who out there would believe him?

The sun had been down for less than an hour, and under the covering of his clothes Sonchis felt his supernatural skin itch maddeningly. He longed to make his flesh real again, to inhabit his own body; but he understood that it would take a little more time.

He knew exactly what was required to rectify the situation and was pretty sure that he would find it back at the bazaar. He had already spent several weeks there in his former body, searching the various souvenir and curio stalls for the item he needed. Indeed, the previous night he had just received a valuable tip-off from a stallholder.

'There is a man who calls himself "the Algerian",' the stallholder had informed him. 'He has a shop in Kasr al-Birkir and deals in *real* curios, not this fake tourist stuff. If anybody has what you are looking for, it will be him. But he doesn't come cheap. Expect to pay top dollar for anything you want.'

Sonchis had handed the man a few piastres and the stallholder had told him exactly where to look for this shop. He had just been on the point of heading Tom Hinton's form off in that direction when the fat detective had called out his name; and then, of course, everything had changed.

His first thought had been to simply escape, but Llewellyn had followed him back to the rat-infested hovel in which he was staying and, in doing so, had unwittingly offered Sonchis a better, safer way of getting around. If Tom Hinton suddenly turned up after so long away, there would be all kinds of awkward questions to answer; much better to be the one asking the questions – and who would expect anything else of a detective? So the transfer was made. Sonchis had taken possession of the man with no great difficulty, but had found he needed a few hours to walk Llewellyn's bones around, to get used to being somebody else. Soon, if everything went according to plan, Sonchis would be walking around as nobody but himself.

Mohammed brought the battered old Ford to a halt and pointed along a narrow street. 'Kasr al-Birkir is just through there,' he said. 'Would you like me to walk along with you, sir?'

'No. Wait here,' snapped Sonchis; and then, realizing that he had not sounded like Llewellyn at all, he softened his tone, forced himself to smile. 'I shouldn't be long,' he added. 'If you would be kind enough to wait for me?'

'Of course, *effendi.*' Mohammed bowed his head politely, but his eyes told a different story. Once again he had noticed that something was different about his passenger, something that didn't tally with the man he had met only a couple of days earlier. But Sonchis didn't have time to be worried about such details. He told himself that if the Arab driver became too difficult to handle, the scarabs were always ready to eat – and there were surely other drivers for hire in Luxor.

He turned away from the car and headed along the crowded street. In his right-hand pocket, the serpent's eye seemed to hum with a life of its own. For so long the item had held his ka prisoner; now it was his amulet, his touchstone, from which he derived a sense of power. But it could not arm him against the light. He was condemned to walk only by night until he could find something that would enable him to brave the sunlight.

He pushed his way through the crowded bazaar, the stalls lit by a succession of hurricane lamps. There were a lot of tourists here, he noticed, and nearly all the stalls sold souvenirs and curios. As he passed by one stall, he noticed a cheap and inexpertly carved figurine of Apophis: the Arab stallholder was telling a middle-aged couple that this was a genuine curio, thousands of years old. Sonchis felt a sudden urge to grab the man by the throat and throttle the life out of him for daring to cheapen the name of the one, the only true god, but he consoled himself with the thought that when he had regained his power, such people would be amongst the first to be made an example of.

Now, up ahead, he saw a row of shops, their interiors lit by gas lamps, and he peered in through the open doorways. He quickly identified the one he was looking for. A long wooden counter ran the length of the place and, on the wall behind it, rows of shelves were stacked with more expertly crafted pieces. He went into the shop and scanned the rows of objects, noting that some of them were genuinely old, but he didn't see anything like the item he was searching for. Two people stood behind the counter – a middle-aged fellow and a bored-looking teenager. The older man had a grey moustache and wore a striped woollen galabiya and a red fez – to impress the tourists, no doubt. He was chewing handfuls of cherries and kept spitting out the stones onto the floor. The youth, who had curly black hair and deep-set brown eyes, was obliged to keep hopping out of the way for fear of getting the discarded stones on his sandals.

The older man studied Sonchis for a moment; and Sonchis had to remind himself that he was not seeing the great wizard in his true form, but a fat, hapless westerner. Sensing a potential sale, the man spat out a last few stones and approached, rubbing his hands together.

'Good evening, sir. Can I be of assistance?'

'Perhaps. You are the one they call "the Algerian"?' asked Sonchis.

The man bowed his head in agreement.

'I have been given your name by another trader. I am searching for a particular item and he told me that you might be able to supply it.'

The Algerian considered the question for a moment, then gave an oily smile. 'Your friend is most kind to consider me,' he said. 'But it would rather depend upon which item you are seeking.'

'A small statue of Apophis. Small enough to fit into the hand. And of genuine antiquity.' Sonchis waved a dismissive hand at the items on display. 'Not elaborate fakes like these,' he added, so there could be no mistake.

Again the Algerian smiled, but his eyes were cold. 'If I knew of such an item for sale, I would have to be sure that you were a genuine collector,' he said. 'There are of course people employed by the government who make it their business to go around seeking such items; and when they are produced, the seller invariably finds himself in hot water.'

Sonchis nodded. 'I appreciate your concern,' he said. 'I am not such a man. My only interest is to procure a genuine artefact for a museum in London, England.'

The Algerian frowned, then nodded. 'If such an item existed – and for the moment, you understand, I do not say that it does – but if it did, it would of course be a very expensive piece. And the seller would understandably require cash.'

'Understandably.' Sonchis reached a hand into the breast pocket of Llewellyn's jacket and pulled out his wallet. He opened it to display the large wad of British banknotes that he had found in Llewellyn's luggage the previous night. 'Would this be suitable currency?' he asked.

The Algerian's smile deepened. Clearly, money was a language that he understood and spoke fluently. 'I believe we might be able to do business together,' he said. 'Of course, such a valuable item could not be kept on display here. But my rooms are only a short walk away. One moment, please.' The man moved aside to leave instructions for his young assistant. Then he came out from behind the counter and led the way along the street.

'It is a fine evening, is it not?' he said, making small talk.

Sonchis couldn't be bothered to give a reply to such a pointless question. He was impatient to reach the man's rooms, to see if what he had to offer was genuine. Beneath his shirt, his scarab followers twitched and twisted.

'I don't believe I caught your name . . .' said the Algerian.

'I don't believe I threw it,' said Sonchis; but then forced himself to be more agreeable. 'Llewellyn. Professor Llewellyn.'

'Ah yes, you mentioned a museum! I must say it's refreshing to find that somebody of your standing is prepared to obtain their exhibits by less . . . proper channels. Mind you, you're not alone. Even the famous Howard Carter has been known to deal in ancient artefacts.'

'Really?' Sonchis tried to look interested.

'Oh yes. I am honoured to report that he has bought the occasional piece from me over the years. Why, only the other day I read in an English newspaper that the late Lord Carnarvon has left a vast collection of Egyptian relics to his dear wife. It seems he instructed her to sell them to the British Museum for the sum of twenty thousand pounds sterling. But the enterprising lady sold them instead to an American museum for considerably more.' He raised his eyebrows. 'It seems everyone understands the principles of business,' he said.

'I believe in using any means available to give our public what they wish to see,' said Sonchis. 'We're mounting an exhibition of the gods of Egypt, and Apophis is the only one we're short of. So the museum made some funds available to rectify the situation and despatched me to take care of it.'

The Algerian looked impressed. 'What a refreshing attitude,' he said. He stopped in front of an open stone doorway, where a hurricane lamp hung from a hook. 'Through here,' he said, taking up the lamp and holding it out in front of him. He led the way along a stone-flagged hall-way and up a flight of stairs. They came to a landing with several mahogany doors. The Algerian produced a heavy iron key, unlocked one of the doors and entered the room. He set the lamp down on a table. 'I keep reading about the wonderful electric lights they have in

England and America,' he said. 'The world is changing fast, is it not?'

Sonchis regarded the man expressionlessly, tired of his prattle. 'The item?' he prompted.

'Of course. Please wait here.' The Algerian went through into another room, and after a few moments a glow of light appeared from within. Sonchis heard the sound of another key in a lock and a second or two later the man reappeared with a wooden tray bearing several small cloth bundles. He set it down on the table beside the lamp and waved a hand at the bundles.

'These objects are of great antiquity,' he said. 'The man I obtained these from came from a long line of workmen who lived at Deir el-Medina, the village of the tomb workers. You can still see the ruins of it today.'

Sonchis grunted. The man was telling him ancient history now. He waved a hand in dismissal but the Algerian kept prattling on.

'Over the centuries, these workmen had access to the tombs of the pharaohs and were able to help themselves to all manner of items, which were then passed down from generation to generation.' He smiled. 'Occasionally, when times were hard, such items would be sold. Indeed, many of the great museums of the world have been stocked with treasures bought from such people.' He gestured at the tray. 'Not much is left to sell, but here there are still a few rare items . . .' He stroked his chin. 'Now, you mentioned Apophis, did you not? If my memory serves me correctly . . .'

His hand moved to and fro across the wrapped bundles and then stopped to pick one of them up. He unwrapped it slowly, with infinite care, and Sonchis began to think that the object really might be of genuine antiquity. The Algerian removed the last layer to reveal a small stone idol, which he placed in Sonchis's hand.

Sonchis gasped. He stared down at the small figurine in stunned amazement. He could never have dared hope for such an outcome, not even in his wildest dreams; for he was looking down at his own personal charm, an item he had not seen since the day he was arrested by the royal guard three thousand years ago. What powerful fate had ensured that he would be reunited with it after so long? What irresistible magic had ensured that their paths finally converged? He could feel the power of it discharging along his arm and spreading into every part of his insect-clad body, which seemed to stir and strengthen beneath his clothing; and a vivid memory came to him. He was a small child, lying in his bed, the reassuring coolness of the powerful charm clutched in one tiny fist. He had not thought of his childhood for a very long time and an involuntary tear spilled from the corner of his eye. The amulet had been his for as long as he could remember, a gift from his mother, who had also been a follower of Apophis.

The Algerian was puzzled by his silence. 'The object pleases you?' he asked.

'Yes, very much.' Sonchis could hardly control his voice. 'You have no idea,' he added. He couldn't stop staring at the figurine.

The Algerian coughed politely, a reminder that they were here to do business. Sonchis nodded. He took out Llewellyn's wallet, removed the entire wad of money and placed it in the Algerian's outstretched hand. The man counted the notes thoughtfully and then frowned.

'This will do as your deposit,' he said after a pause. 'Bring the same amount tomorrow and you may have the charm.' He held out his hand for it.

Sonchis stared at him. 'What are you talking

about?' he snarled. 'It's mine now. I've just paid you, haven't I?'

'With respect, sir, that's not enough. I did warn you it would be very expensive. But don't worry, I shall keep it safe for you until you return with the rest of the money.'

'There's no more,' Sonchis told him flatly. 'It's all I have. Just be grateful I have paid you for something that is rightfully mine.'

The man laughed. 'Rightfully yours?' he cried. 'How could that be? You are simply buying this for your museum, are you not?'

Sonchis shook his head. 'That's what I told you,' he admitted. 'But the truth is, this charm is mine. It was given to me by my mother when I was a child and now I am reclaiming it. So I warn you, take the money or take the consequences.'

'I've never heard such nonsense,' said the Algerian. 'How could it be your property? It's three thousand years old! Now, I'm telling you that the piece has a price affixed to it and it shall not be yours until I'm paid what I am owed. Give it back and you can return with the rest of the money tomorrow.'

He tried to prise the charm from his client's hands. A mistake.

Sonchis concentrated for an instant and felt new strength flowing through him. He grabbed the man by the throat, picked him up as easily as if he were a bundle of dried sticks and flung him against the wall. He crashed into it so hard that chunks of plaster rained down with him as he fell to the floor and lay there, gasping for breath. He began to fumble in his coat pocket and pulled out a revolver; but before he could aim it, Sonchis had stepped across and kicked it out of his hand. He leaned over to prise the wad of money out of the man's other hand.

'You should have taken my offer when you could,' he said. 'Now you will have nothing. Do you hear me? Nothing.' He lifted a foot and placed it across the man's throat.

The Algerian's eyes widened in shock. 'Who are you?' he gasped. '*What* are you?'

'I am vengeance,' said Sonchis quietly; and he pressed his foot down hard.

Sonchis let himself out of the apartment and went downstairs again. He stepped out into the street and headed back the way he had come, taking a short detour so he would not have to pass by the Algerian's shop. He was well aware that the man's body would be found soon enough and that his assistant would tell the authorities about the fat man in the white suit who had accompanied the Algerian to his apartment to look at some curios he had for sale. But it mattered little. By the time the local police organized themselves to look for Wilfred Llewellyn, he would have vanished from the face of the earth.

As he walked back to the Ford, Sonchis could feel the power of the Apophis statue throbbing in his breast pocket; while in the pocket on his right hip the serpent's eye emitted a strange power all of its own. Now he knew he could come and go at any hour of the day or night, and the first place he intended to visit was the tomb that had for so long been a prison – but was now a temple.

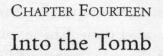

CHAPTER FOURTEEN

Into the Tomb

The time had come at last. Alec, Ethan, Madeleine and Mickey stood in the now empty antechamber and watched as two Arab workmen broke the seals on the inner door. It had been decided that the four of them would enter the tomb now and the others would take their opportunity later. Pointless for everyone to go in together. Nobody knew what they might find in there, and the last thing they needed was over-excited groups of people blundering into priceless relics and destroying them.

Ethan was there as director of the expedition, Madeleine as hieroglyphics expert, Mickey was

235

going to take photographs for the records and Alec . . . well, as Ethan had explained to the others, he was there to represent Uncle William, who for obvious reasons could not be present in person. Alec felt tremendously honoured and rather guilty, because in his heart he believed that there were others who deserved the place more than he did.

As they watched in expectant silence, the men struggled to open the heavy doors; but gradually they began to part, creaking slowly back onto darkness. Ethan and Alec switched on their torches and sent rays of brilliant light into the swirling dust that rose in the rapidly widening space in front of them. Then the dust began to settle and they could finally see what lay within.

'My God,' said Ethan; and they stepped into the burial chamber.

It was a large rectangular room, dominated by a huge sarcophagus that rested in the very centre. But this was unlike any Egyptian sarcophagus that any of them had ever seen before, a big oblong wooden box with no decoration whatsoever. Furthermore, the box had been damaged. Not by human hand, Alec could see, but by a major shift in the earth that had torn a great crack in the ground beneath it, creating a gap of some six inches or more. This had caused the heavy sarcophagus to split across the middle. The thick wooden lid had snapped diagonally across and as Alec approached, he saw that the top half had slid aside to reveal the mummy's bandaged face staring sightlessly up at him. Alec felt the hairs on the back of his neck prickle. The bandages had merged so completely with the face that the expression was quite visible, the features frozen in what looked like a grimace of hatred. Alec felt as if the mummy could see him; as if the look of hatred was directed at him.

Could this really be the body of Akhenaten? he asked himself. Why no decoration on the outer sarcophagus? And why no inner sarcophagi? Tutankhamun's mummy had been enclosed in three separate coffins, each fitting inside the other like Russian dolls. This man had nothing: his bandaged body lay inside one plain wooden box.

Then Alec noticed a puzzling detail. The lower edge of the diagonal split had exposed the mummy's waist and he could clearly see that the man's arms were clamped with what looked like heavy manacles.

'Come and look at this!' he said. Ethan and Madeleine hurried to his side. 'This is so strange,' he gasped. 'This man was chained when he was put in here!'

'Why would anybody do that?' asked Ethan, but neither Alec nor Madeleine could think of an answer.

Mickey had set up the camera and was busying himself snapping pictures, the occasional burst of flash powder lighting up the interior of the chamber. Ethan and Madeleine had meanwhile moved to inspect the other sarcophagi. There were four of them in all, undecorated in any way, just plain black boxes propped upright in each corner of the room and facing inwards, as though the mummies were looking at the central sarcophagus. The earlier tremor had also disturbed one of the upright boxes and the lid had shifted to reveal a glimpse of another wizened bandaged face, this one frozen in an expression of absolute agony.

Madeleine made a sound of revulsion. 'It looks as though 'e was still alive when 'e was entombed,' she said.

Ethan was shaking his head and gazing around

the room. 'This is nuts,' he muttered. 'I'm not sure what I expected to find in here, but it was nothing like this.' He looked at the other two. 'Have either of you ever seen anything like it before?'

Alec looked puzzled. 'It isn't like any other burial chamber,' he said. 'I've studied books on all the tombs, but this . . .' He struggled to find the word. 'It's so . . . *plain*,' he said.

Madeleine too seemed taken aback. 'It is very strange,' she said. 'I cannot believe this is the tomb of a pharaoh. Where are the murals, the nested shrines? It is almost as if these people 'ave been placed 'ere . . . as some kind of punishment.'

Alec had returned to the main sarcophagus and was directing the light of his torch into the opening. 'This thing is lined with metal,' he said. 'Looks like . . . copper.' He studied the manacles once more. 'I'd say those manacles are copper too.'

'Really?' Madeleine moved over to join him. 'Yes, I think you are right, Alec. That is interesting. Many Egyptians believed that copper 'ad protective qualities. Placing it around something would keep whatever was inside from harm.'

'Yes, but' – Alec thought for a moment – 'if that was the case, wouldn't they have put the copper on the *outside* of the sarcophagus?'

'An interesting point,' she admitted. 'Could that be it, Ethan? 'Ooever was buried in there was considered evil. Nobody wanted 'is spirit to escape.'

Ethan frowned. 'Could be, I guess. Alec, you said something before about how Akhenaten was unpopular . . . how people tried to destroy all record of him.'

Alec nodded. 'Well, yes, that's true. And after his death his son Tutankhamun even changed his name to reflect the god Amun. He wanted to distance himself from his father's beliefs because they'd proved so unpopular. But . . . surely this can't be the resting place of one of the greatest pharaohs in history? This . . . black box? It just doesn't seem right.'

'I don't think this is Akhenaten's tomb,' said Madeleine flatly. She looked at Alec apologetically. 'I know that is what your uncle was 'oping to find, Alec, but I really don't think that is what we 'ave uncovered. Remember what I saw on the outer door seals? "*By order* of Akhenaten". I believe 'e 'ad these people buried 'ere. All the artefacts you found in the antechamber must 'ave been their belongings, but in this chamber there are none of the things you would expect to find in the tomb of a pharaoh. It is so bare . . . almost like a prison chamber.'

Alec looked around the tomb and nodded. 'And yet there were so many artefacts in the antechamber . . . more than were ever found in Tut's tomb. But no tomb robber ever came in here. You have to ask yourself why.'

'The Ancient Egyptians were superstitious people,' said Madeleine. 'Maybe they were afraid to take this man's possessions.' She pointed to the grimacing face in the sarcophagus. 'It is almost as if this was a man that Akhenaten feared. One of his rivals for the throne per'aps?'

'Let's see what we've got in here,' said Ethan. His torch beam had just revealed a large storage jar standing against one wall. He kneeled down, lifted the lid as gently as possible and set it on the ground. Inside the jar he could see several papyri, tightly rolled into tubes. He extracted one and carefully unrolled it to reveal closely written text on what looked like a well-preserved sheet of papyrus.

'Maddie, this is your territory, I think,' he said. He handed her the sheet and she took it gently, handling it like the priceless relic it was. 'What does it say?' he asked her.

She gave him a scornful look. 'I cannot read it just like that,' she protested. 'It is not like reading a page in the *New York Times*! It is going to be a while before I can tell you anything.'

'How long?' he asked her.

'I don't know. There are so many scrolls 'ere, it could take weeks to translate them all.'

Ethan frowned. 'Well, I suggest you get straight on to it. We need some answers and I'll bet my bottom dollar that this is where we're going to find 'em.' He gestured around the room. 'There's nothing else here that's going to give us a clue. Mickey, get some pictures of these scrolls in position, will ya? Then Maddie can take them away and study them in detail. Maybe they'll tell us something more about this place.'

Alec had moved back to the central sarcophagus and was directing his torch onto the grimacing face of the mummy within. He still could not shake off the conviction that the creature was looking at him.

Who are you? he thought. *And what made people hate you so much that they buried you like this?*

Sonchis sat in the back of Mohammed's car as it trundled down the road to the Valley of the Kings, marvelling at his newfound ability to venture forth by daylight. Beneath his shirt, his temporary skin still shifted and squirmed, but the combined power of the two talismans he now wore on a thong around his neck ensured that it would not burst asunder. His eyes still felt sensitive to sunlight and he had put on the dark glasses he had found in Llewellyn's room. Now he needed to get closer to the people at the dig and there was an obvious way to do that.

The Ford bumped along the winding road, passing occasional groups of tourists on the way. Some of them were mounted on donkeys; a couple of wealthier travellers, a husband and wife, perched ludicrously on the backs of two camels, clinging on for dear life.

Sonchis allowed Llewellyn's lips to curl in a sneer. When he was back to his full power, no foreign travellers would dare return to this valley, for he would rule it and deal with such fools accordingly.

Up at King Tut's site there was the usual crowd of gawping imbeciles, currently watching as a rather ordinary-looking chair was brought out into the daylight. From the reaction of the crowd, you'd have thought that they had just brought out a heap of precious jewels.

As they cruised by, the newspaperman, Biff Corcoran, stepped forward and raised a hand for Mohammed to stop. He regarded Sonchis with interest.

'Professor Llewellyn, ain't it?' he said. 'You finally decided to head back to your friends at the dig, huh?'

Sonchis decided that Biff had a gift for stating the obvious but refrained from commenting on it.

'I thought I'd see what progress they've made,' he said.

'Me and Charlie was up there yesterday,' said Biff. 'They got some swell little pieces of pottery for you to look at. Bet you can hardly contain your excitement, huh?'

Again, Sonchis said nothing.

'By the way, what museum did you say you were with?'

'I didn't,' Sonchis assured him.

'It's just for the record. You wouldn't want me to get it wrong, would ya?'

'Well, Mr Corcoran, just for the record . . . it's the *British* Museum.'

'Hmm. Beats me why an institution as important as that would send somebody all the way out here to look at a few scraps of pottery. Or is there something else they're not telling me about?'

Oh yes, there's something else, all right, thought Sonchis. *Something that your tiny brain couldn't hope to comprehend*; but he smiled thinly and said, 'They may be little pieces of pottery to you, Mr Corcoran, but to a man such as myself, they are the building blocks of history.'

'Is that right?' muttered Biff. He pulled the stub of his cigarette from his mouth and blew out a cloud of smoke. 'And there was me thinking that they were just broken vases.'

The woman called Charlie appeared from out of the crowd and walked towards the automobile. As she approached, she raised her camera.

'One for the family album,' she said. And she snapped a photograph of Sonchis, who raised his hands to cover his face an instant too late.

'Please don't do that!' he snapped angrily. For a moment he had felt the creatures that made up his flesh poised to scatter in all directions. He concentrated and they settled down.

'Hey, keep ya shirt on,' said Charlie. 'I never met such a bunch of prima donnas. First that French dame and now you! Don't you wanna be famous, Professor?'

'Oh, I *shall* be famous,' he assured her. 'But not for the reasons you think.'

'Yeah, I can see the cover now,' sneered Biff. 'Professor deciphers code on ancient pot.' He lifted a hand to frame an imaginary piece of text. 'A GIFT FROM MACEY'S!' He sniggered and Sonchis had to quell an impulse to throttle the life out of him.

'Hey, Biff, you're missing all the excitement over here,' said Charlie. 'They just brought out a *chair*. Imagine that, a chair! I got half a dozen in my apartment back home.'

'Yeah and I bet they're nearly as old as King Tut's too,' said Biff and then laughed at his own poor joke. He turned back to Sonchis. 'Say, Prof., if you see Ethan Wade, tell him he's to let me know if he finds anything new.'

'I'll tell him,' said Sonchis, and he tapped

Mohammed on the shoulder. 'Drive on,' he ordered. Mohammed put the Ford into gear and started to move off, but Biff walked alongside for a moment.

'Say, Mohammed, that's another thing,' he said. 'I'm running a little low on provisions, if you know what I mean. I could do with another bottle.'

Mohammed nodded. 'Leave it to me, Mr Corcoran,' he said. 'I'm a little busy right now, but I'll get what you need just as soon as I can.'

Biff lifted a hand and the Ford accelerated away. It rounded a bend in the road and began to climb the hill beyond, the ancient engine protesting all the way. Sonchis became aware that Mohammed was studying him in the mirror again.

'How is your search progressing?' asked Mohammed after a decent interval.

'My search?' growled Sonchis.

'For Mr Hinton. Did you find out anything at the bazaar last night?'

Sonchis shook his head. 'I found nothing,' he said.

'And we shall return there tonight?'

'No. I've decided to concentrate my efforts in another area.'

'But . . . I could have sworn that was Mr

Hinton we saw, the night before.'

'You are mistaken. There were some similarities, for sure, but—'

'I *know* Mr Hinton very well and I would be willing to swear—'

'Mohammed, why don't you stick to driving and leave the detective work to me,' said Sonchis, loading enough venom into his voice to make the insolent driver close his mouth.

They drove on in silence, and soon came to Wade's camp. Few people were around. A group of native workers were standing around drinking cups of tea, and the cook, the man called McCloud, was wiping down the large dining table with a filthy-looking wet cloth. He looked up as Mohammed's automobile ground to a halt.

'Ah, Mr Llewellyn,' he said. 'You're back, are you?'

'So it would appear. Where is everybody?' asked Sonchis, climbing out of the vehicle and taking a quick look around.

'Depends who you mean by everybody,' said Archie evasively.

'Mr Wade?'

'He's, er . . . not around at the moment. I

think he went into Luxor with some of the others.' He was lying, that much was obvious. Both Wade's automobiles were parked nearby. Wade must be up at the tomb, Sonchis decided, but of course there was no way Archie was going to mention that.

'I was hoping to get a look inside the tomb,' he said quietly.

'What tomb would that be?' asked Archie.

'I think you know. Oh look, it's quite all right – Mr Wade told me I could have a look at it any time I liked.'

'He didn't say anything to me about that,' Archie told him.

Sonchis considered his options. He hadn't anticipated this. 'So who else is around?' he asked.

'Mr Coates is in the mess tent preparing lunch.' Archie rolled his eyes despairingly. 'And Doc Hopper's in his tent.'

Sonchis evaluated the situation quickly. He had already thought about claiming Wade as his host, putting himself in control of the dig in one fell swoop; but since the American wasn't around, perhaps he would settle for the big shambling Lancastrian doctor, who would probably prove to be just as useful. As a valued member of the team, he would be granted full access to the tomb; and of course, everybody trusted a doctor, didn't they?

'I'll just have a quick word with the doctor,' he said. 'Something I forgot to ask him before.'

He started walking towards the medic's tent.

'Aye. Well, you must stick around for luncheon, Mr Llewellyn. Mr Coates is preparing a soufflé.' Archie shook his head. 'I ask you, a bloody soufflé. He must think he's working at the Ritz or something!'

Llewellyn ignored him. There was no time to waste on this. He had to be quick and quiet. One scream from Doc Hopper could ruin everything. Wilfred Llewellyn had proved useful for a while, but clearly there was no way the rest of the team would allow him near the tomb. As Hopper, he could live right here at the dig and go in and out of the burial chamber at his leisure.

He looked in through the open flap of the tent and found the doctor sitting at his improvised desk, writing in what looked like a journal.

'Excuse me, Doctor. I hope you will forgive the intrusion . . .'

Doc Hopper looked up from his work a little

wearily. 'Mr Llewellyn,' he said. 'You again. What can I do for you?'

'It's a rather delicate matter,' said Sonchis, stepping into the tent. 'I've been bitten by an insect and the bite is looking rather nasty. I wondered if you might be kind enough to cast an eye over it.'

'Of course.' His professional instincts aroused, Doc Hopper turned away from the desk to find that his patient was closing and buttoning the tent flaps. 'There's no need for that, surely?' he said.

Sonchis moved closer. 'I wanted a little privacy,' he said. He took off his jacket and threw it into a corner, then began to unbutton his shirt. 'I was bitten in an awkward place, on my back, somewhere very hard for me to inspect.'

'I see.' Doc Hopper stood up. 'Where exactly?'

'Here,' said Sonchis. And his left hand grabbed the doctor around the neck, exerting prodigious pressure. Meanwhile he clamped his right hand across the man's mouth. Hopper's eyes widened in surprise — a surprise that deepened immeasurably as Sonchis's hand suddenly came apart and swarmed outwards to cover his entire face.

Doc Hopper tried to struggle but Llewellyn's grip was too powerful, and now he felt hard-bodied *things* skittering across his face and into the openings of his ears and nostrils, followed by a blossoming of incredible pain as tiny jaws went to work on the soft flesh within. He opened his mouth in a desperate attempt to drag in some air, but more of the things spilled down his throat, making him retch. His head was spinning; he could no longer breathe and the pain was rising within him like an unspeakable tide from which there was no escape.

He sank slowly to the ground, his body quivering, and when death finally came, it was a merciful release.

CHAPTER FIFTEEN

Luncheon is Served

Alec, Ethan, Madeleine and Mickey walked back from the tomb, carefully carrying the papyrus scrolls between them. Ethan spotted Mohammed's car by the roadside and sent Mickey on ahead to distract him, while the rest of them took the scrolls straight to Madeleine's tent and laid them out on her desk. She found a towel and draped it protectively across them to shield them from sight and from harm.

'It is very irregular doing it like this,' she told Ethan. 'These are very fragile documents – they could easily be damaged.'

'I'm sure you'll be gentle with them,' he

reassured her. 'I need answers, and everything around here seems to move like molasses in winter. But listen, both of you, let's not say a word about this until we know what we've got. I've already warned Mickey to keep his trap shut. I don't want everybody getting all excited and then we find we've got nothing more interesting than Akhenaten's shopping lists.'

'Madeleine doesn't even think it is Akhenaten,' said Alec gloomily. 'And I'm sorry to say I agree with her. What a shame if Uncle Will searched all those years for nothing.'

'Not for nothing,' Madeleine assured him. ''Ooever that tomb belongs to, it is a very exciting find that is going to set the world of archaeology on fire. Nobody 'as ever found something like this.'

From outside there was the sound of a gong being struck.

'What the hell is that?' muttered Ethan. He stuck his head out of the tent to see Coates standing by the dining table, looking faintly ridiculous in a white apron and tall chef's hat.

'Luncheon is about to be served,' he announced dramatically.

Madeleine gave a tut of irritation. 'Per'aps I

skip the food,' she said. 'I would rather get on with my translating.'

'Are you kidding?' Ethan stared at her. 'Coates is in charge of the cooking now. This could be the first decent meal we've had since we started this dig. Come on, Maddie, what difference will another half-hour make?' He took her arm and led her out of the tent. Alec followed, marvelling at the fact that Madeleine, who not so long ago could have been counted on to shout at Ethan for being so forward, just smiled and went obediently after him.

The three of them took their places at the table.

'Archie, you appear to have prepared an extra place setting,' shouted Coates.

'Aye, that's for Mr Llewellyn.' Archie came out of the tent, carefully carrying a huge soufflé. The smell of it caught Alec's nostrils, reminding him that he had skipped breakfast that morning because he was so eager to enter the burial chamber.

'Where's he got to?' asked Ethan.

Mohammed approached the table with Mickey. 'He wanted to ask more questions. I think he went to talk to Doc Hopper.'

'Oh yeah? I bet the doc was delighted about that.'

Mohammed moved closer. 'Actually, Mr Wade, I wanted to talk to you about Mr Llewellyn. There's something very strange going on—'

'Hey, now look at that!' cried Ethan delightedly. Archie had just set down the soufflé. 'Mr Coates, that looks absolutely delicious!' He glanced apologetically at Archie. 'No offence,' he added.

'None taken,' growled Archie but he looked far from happy about the situation. 'Of course, if I'd realized that this was the kinda grub you wanted, I could have provided it. You only had to say.'

An incredulous silence followed this remark. It was evident that nobody believed he had the first idea how to make a soufflé.

'Oh yes,' said Archie, warming to his theme. 'Many's the time, back in the war years, ah'd send my lads over the top wi' a good hot helping of soufflé in their guts. It might be the last meal they ever ate, so it had to be top notch! The sergeant major said to me once, he said, "Archie, an army fights on its stomach, and thanks to you, our lads have stomachs to beat the band".'

Madeleine looked puzzled by this last remark.

'You are saying that Scotish soldiers 'ave the big bellies?' she said; and Alec had to stifle a laugh.

'Forget it,' said Archie, and went to get the cutlery.

Ethan turned back to Mohammed. 'Sorry – what were you saying about Llewellyn?'

'I can't explain it exactly. It's a feeling. There's something odd about him.'

'You're telling me!'

'No, I mean something *different*. It is as though he has changed somehow, ever since that night in the bazaar, when we saw Mr Hinton—'

'You saw Tom?' cried Alec in amazement.

'Yes . . . at least, I was sure it was him. Mr Llewellyn said no, it was somebody else. But you see, he went after Mr Hinton. He was gone for some time and when he came back, it was like he was a different man.'

Ethan frowned. 'Well, maybe we should ask him about that. If he's seen Tom, I want to know about it. Where is he, anyhow?' He lifted his head to shout, 'Doc? Mr Llewellyn? Grub's up out here! You coming?'

Coates was spooning out generous portions of soufflé onto plates. It did look magnificent – thick and creamy and beautifully browned on the top. Alec reflected that Coates was capable of producing delicious food in the most primitive of kitchens and remembered that he had worked as a professional chef before taking up his role as valet to the Devlin family. He couldn't help feeling sorry for Archie though. Coates had taken over his very reason for being here.

Mickey took a seat at the table, rubbing his hands together gleefully. 'This looks very good, Mr Coates,' he said. 'Almost as good as roast beef and Yorkshire pud.'

'It's not all my own work,' said Coates, trying to be modest. 'Mr McCloud was equally responsible for this. And as we cook, I'm making sure that he makes notes about the whole process, so he'll be able to create the same wonderful meals after I'm gone.'

Archie came out of the cook tent rolling his eyes. 'That's a relief then,' he muttered.

'Furthermore,' said Coates, 'I've decided that from now on, we chefs should eat with the rest of you, so we can hear your reactions first hand.' He and Archie settled themselves at the table.

'Good idea,' said Ethan. He looked out towards Doc Hopper's tent and started to get up from his seat; but then the tent flap opened and the doctor came out and closed the flap behind him. He walked slowly towards the table.

It struck Alec instantly that there was something odd about Doc Hopper. He seemed to be moving awkwardly, with a slow, precise gait that was quite unlike his usual shambling stride; and Alec noticed that he had changed his jacket and had buttoned it tightly around him, as though he felt cold. For some reason he was wearing a pair of dark glasses that Alec had never seen before.

Alec glanced at Ethan, about to say something, but the American was scooping up big mouthfuls of soufflé and eating with an expression of sheer bliss on his face. Alec shrugged his shoulders and started eating too. It was, he thought, the best thing he'd tasted since he'd left Cairo.

Doc Hopper reached the table and slipped into a vacant seat. His food was already in front of him, but he just sat there looking down at his plate as though he wasn't quite sure what it was.

'Where's Mr Llewellyn?' asked Alec.

'Hmm?' Doc Hopper looked up in apparent surprise. 'Isn't he with you?'

'No. Mohammed said he went to your tent to ask you some questions.'

'Well, yes, he did. But . . . he only stayed a few moments and then he left.'

'What did he ask you about?' asked Ethan, through a mouthful of soufflé.

'He had an insect bite on his hand and wanted me to have a look. It was nothing serious.'

'Did he say anything about Tom Hinton?'

Doc Hopper shook his head. 'He just asked about the bite.'

'Aren't you hungry, Doctor?' asked Coates. 'You haven't touched your food.'

'Oh . . . yes.' Doc Hopper picked up his fork and began to toy with his food but made no effort to put any in his mouth. This too was odd, Alec thought, for Doc Hopper usually had the heartiest appetite of them all.

Ethan indicated the plate that had been set out for Llewellyn. 'Mohammed, looks like Llewellyn isn't around, so why don't you take his place? It's about time you sampled some good western cooking.'

Mohammed bowed. 'You are most kind,' he said and took a seat at the table. 'It looks very good, Mr Coates. This is made from eggs, yes?'

'Correct,' said Coates. 'Eggs and cream. It has

to be whipped really well and then the oven temperature must be—'

'Just a moment,' interrupted Alec. 'The food is lovely and everything, but where can Mr Llewellyn have got to?' He gestured around. 'I mean, there's nowhere to hide around here, is there? If he'd come out of the tent, surely we'd have seen him.'

Doc Hopper cleared his throat. 'I believe he said something about going back to the King Tut excavation. He wanted to speak to that newspaperman, Mr Corcoran.'

Everyone stared at the road leading back up the hill, its stony surface rippling in a rising heat haze.

'You're saying he *walked*?' said Ethan. 'In this heat, when he had a car waiting for him?'

Doc Hopper made a gesture of irritation. 'I'm only telling you what he said,' he snapped. 'It's of no interest to me where that bloody idiot has got to.' He glared at Alec. 'Or perhaps you're suggesting that he's still in my tent?'

Alec felt his cheeks reddening. 'No, of course not,' he said. He was shocked – the doctor had always seemed such a genial, easygoing character.

'Perhaps you think I murdered him,' said Doc

Hopper. 'That I tore all the flesh from his body, dumped his bones in an old sack and hid it under my bed.'

There was a long, uncomfortable silence. Then Madeleine said, 'I think this is what you English call the wishful thinking, yes?'

That broke the tension and everyone laughed; everyone except Doc Hopper, who for some reason seemed out of sorts today.

'Anyway, never mind about Wilfred Llewellyn,' said Coates once the laughter had died down. 'Wherever he is, I'm sure he'll turn up sooner or later. Tell us about the burial chamber.'

'Aye,' said Archie. 'What did ye find in there?'

'Never mind me *telling* you,' said Ethan. 'Just as soon as we finish up here, you can go and take a look for yourselves. Mr Coates, Archie . . . Doc – I guess you'll want to see what all the fuss was about?'

Doc Hopper nodded. 'I've been waiting a long time for this,' he said.

'And Mohammed,' added Ethan.

'Me?' Mohammed looked astonished. 'You . . . you would grant me that honour, *effendi*?'

'I guess I'm just feeling extra generous today,' said Ethan. 'But I'm holding you to your word of honour that you won't speak of this to a soul outside the team . . . at least, not until I say it's OK.'

'I promise, Mr Wade, my lips are sealed.'

'Then you can go in with the others.'

Mohammed bowed. 'I thank you,' he said. 'From the bottom of my heart.'

'That's settled then.' Ethan lifted a tin mug of red wine to his fellow diners. 'Congratulations, everyone. We're not quite sure who we've found up there, but whoever it is, he's going to make history, you can be sure of that.'

Everyone else raised their mugs, all except for Doc Hopper, who sat there silently, staring at Alec through the dark lenses of his sunglasses.

Sonchis approached the tomb with a strange feeling deep within him. When his life force had finally escaped from here only a few weeks earlier, his only thought was to get as far away from his prison as possible. But he had always known that he must return to claim his rightful body. His temporary 'skin' had served its purpose but he could not tolerate it for very much longer.

He passed through the empty antechamber without hesitation, leaving his companions

PHILIP CAVENEY

behind to speculate about its size and shape and rich decoration. None of it had been prepared for him, of course. Sonchis well knew that this tomb had been intended for one of Akhenaten's most favoured nobles. The next room had not even been finished but had been hastily pressed into service when a tomb was needed to contain the soul of a powerful magician.

He passed through the open door into the burial chamber and paused for a moment, a sense of shock running through him and making his flesh quiver for an instant. There was the sarcophagus in which they had imprisoned him; and there was his own mummified body, his manacled hands clamped together like some common prisoner; and there was his own wizened face, the features set in a grimace, as though imploring him to return to his own flesh, to restore the life that had been so cruelly taken from him.

Sonchis stepped closer and reached out a hand to touch his own face. Once again, his supernatural skin shuddered in anticipation; but he knew he had to be patient a while longer. There were certain rituals to be observed before he could become whole again; and of course, once that

264

was achieved there was the little matter of summoning Apophis – something he had planned to do all those years ago. Before that could be accomplished a suitable sacrifice was required; but he already had somebody in mind for the role.

'Ugly bugger, isn't he?' said a cheerful voice beside him and he turned to see the ruddy features of Archie McCloud grinning at him. He felt a powerful urge to snap the man's neck like a twig, but quelled it, telling himself that he could not afford to do anything that might compromise his plans. So he forced a smile, nodded and called forth Doc Hopper's distinctive tones.

'Yes, he wouldn't win any prizes for looks.'

'I wonder who he is,' said Coates, coming over to join them. 'And who, do you suppose, are these four characters?' He waved a hand at the upright sarcophagi that surrounded them.

Sonchis gazed at them impassively. He knew who they were – his four most powerful and loyal followers, who before much longer would be called back to aid him once more.

'And where are all his possessions?' asked Mohammed. 'Whoever this man was, he must have been despised.'

Sonchis allowed Doc Hopper's mouth to curve into the ghost of a smile.

Yes, he thought. *Despised, feared and hated. The man who had nearly brought down a pharaoh and his empire.*

'Look at his expression,' murmured Coates. 'It's almost as though he's trying to speak to us across the millennia.'

Sonchis remembered his last few moments, as they had brought the lid down upon him, plunging him into total darkness. He remembered how he had cursed them for all eternity and how he had promised that one day he would return to take his revenge. That time was almost at hand.

He turned and headed for the exit.

'Where are you off to?' Archie shouted after him.

'I've seen enough,' said Sonchis; and he walked out of the burial chamber, through the room beyond and up the steps into the light.

CHAPTER SIXTEEN

The Scrolls

Alec couldn't relax that night. He was thinking of Madeleine translating the scrolls and wanted to know what progress she was making. He kept pacing up and down the tent, disturbing Coates, who was studying a recipe book, planning the next day's meal.

'What do you think about beef wellington?' he asked Alec.

'I don't know,' said Alec doubtfully. 'It's nice, of course, but . . . don't you think it's a bit . . . fancy? I mean, we are supposed to be roughing it.'

Coates looked puzzled by the remark. 'The stroganoff was very well received this evening,' he

267

said. 'Everyone seemed to enjoy it apart from Dr Hopper.'

'Hmm.' Alec remembered his misgivings about the doctor. 'Actually, he's been behaving strangely all day. He was really off with me at lunch time. Ever since Mr Llewellyn called on him, he—' He stopped pacing and looked at Coates. 'There's another thing,' he said. 'Whatever happened to Mr Llewellyn? It's as though he just disappeared.'

'And you're complaining?' muttered Coates. 'Let's face it, that man is a nuisance. Everybody groans when they see him coming.'

'Well, true . . . but I wouldn't want anything bad to happen to him.'

'I'm sure nothing has, Master Alec. I've no doubt he's over at King Tut's dig, asking annoying questions of everyone he bumps into. Didn't Mohammed drive up there to look for him?'

'Yes, and we've heard nothing since.'

'Which probably means that Mohammed found him and took him back to the Winter Palace for the evening, so anything I might add would sound distinctly like sour grapes. He's certainly more comfortable than we are.'

Alec frowned. No matter how much he tried to reassure himself that this must be the only explanation, he just couldn't picture the huge Welshman trudging up that baking hot hill when he had a car and a chauffeur waiting for him. And how was it that nobody had seen him leave? *Just like Tom Hinton*, he thought.

He began to pace up and down again, filled with a restless energy that he couldn't seem to shake off.

'For goodness' sake, Master Alec, can't you relax and read a book?' asked Coates. 'You're ruining my concentration.'

Alec sighed. 'I think I'll go out for a while,' he said.

'Then I shall accompany you.'

'There's absolutely no need . . . I'm just going to Madeleine's tent to, er' – Alec remembered in the nick of time that he was not to mention the scrolls to anyone else until they knew what they contained – 'ask her something about hiero-glyphics.'

'Hmm.' Coates's expression was one of profound disapproval. 'I'm not sure that's appro-priate, Master Alec – a young man like yourself hanging around the tent of an unmarried woman.'

Alec glared at his valet. 'What are you talking

about?' he cried. 'I'm only going to ask her a few questions about translating.'

'Yes, but don't forget, Master Alec, she is . . . well, forgive me for saying it, but she is *French*.' He said the last word as though it was some obscure curse.

'I know she's French,' hissed Alec. 'What's wrong with that?'

'I'm only saying, the French are not like us. They have . . . dubious morals. Perhaps smoking cigarettes and flying aeroplanes is considered acceptable practice for young ladies in Paris, but where I come from, it is definitely beyond the pale.'

Alec shook his head. 'Coates, you really must try and step into the twentieth century,' he said. 'You are simply too old-fashioned. Women are different these days. They can vote. Some of them even have *jobs*.'

Coates sniffed disdainfully. 'Who knows where it will all end?' he said bleakly.

'Now, please stay right where you are,' Alec told him. 'I won't be long and I'll try not to come back smoking cigarettes and waving a French flag!'

He pulled aside the mosquito screen and stepped out into the night air. He stood there for a moment, gazing around. The night was very still, and a huge luminous moon was riding serenely in the cloudless sky. Around it, billions of stars glittered like tiny diamonds scattered across dark blue velvet. The stars here never failed to amaze him. In Cairo, where there was so much reflected light from every building, only the biggest stars were visible, but out here on the edge of the desert, they seemed to be literally fighting each other for the space to shine.

He turned his head at an unexpected noise over by the road – something scuffling – but he saw nothing; and a few moments later, the long cackling howl of a hyena seemed to offer an explanation. They were always around these days, bold and inquisitive, and his memory of the attack warned Alec to be on his guard. He found himself wondering what the creatures could possibly find to eat out here in this wilderness.

As he turned towards Madeleine's tent, he saw Ethan emerge from under his own canvas.

The American grinned. 'I guess you're thinking the same as me,' he said.

'I couldn't sleep,' Alec told him. 'Surely Madeleine must have found out something by now.'

'Let's see,' said Ethan.

They approached Madeleine's tent and peered in through the mosquito screen. She was sitting at her makeshift desk, studying one of the rolls of papyrus by the light of a hurricane lamp. Ethan pulled aside the screen and they stepped inside. She lifted her head to look at them for a moment and then went back to her studies.

'I'm busy,' she told them.

'Aw, come on, Maddie, you must have found out *something*,' said Ethan impatiently. 'You've been locked up in here since lunch.'

She sighed, sat up and lifted a hand to rub her neck. Then she turned her chair round to face them.

'Long enough to know whose tomb we are dealing with,' she admitted. She gave Alec an apologetic look. 'I am sorry, Alec, it is as I suspected.'

Ethan pulled over a couple of canvas seats and he and Alec sat down. 'Whose then?' he said.

Madeleine frowned. 'It is the tomb of a man called Sonchis.'

Alec and Ethan exchanged puzzled looks.

'Sonchis?' echoed Alec. 'I never heard of a pharaoh called Sonchis.'

'That is because 'e was not a pharaoh. 'E was a 'igh priest of Akhenaten, a very powerful man, the leader of a religious sect who worshipped the great serpent, Apophis. According to this text, 'e 'ad many followers.'

'That explains all those serpents in the tomb,' said Alec thoughtfully. 'But . . . I thought that Akhenaten stopped the worship of any god other than Aten.'

Madeleine nodded. 'That is correct. Sonchis and his followers met in secret against the pharaoh's wishes. Sonchis told them that 'e knew where the great serpent slept in a chamber deep beneath the ground, and that 'e 'ad the necessary rituals to awaken 'im and bring 'im back to the surface, where 'e would take 'is place as the rightful ruler of the world.'

Ethan let out a low whistle. 'Guy must have been as nutty as a fruitcake,' he said.

Madeleine shrugged. 'There were many people who believed 'im,' she said. 'Some'ow Akhenaten found out about 'is plans. 'E gave orders that Sonchis and his four most devoted lieutenants should be arrested in the dead of night. Akhenaten 'ad already ordered the tomb to be prepared for one of 'is wives, but decided instead to use it as a place of imprisonment.'

Alec raised his eyebrows. 'Imprisonment? Don't you mean burial?'

Madeleine shook her head. 'Sonchis and 'is four lieutenants were brought to the tomb. They were given a powerful potion to make them sleep and then their bodies were wrapped in bandages and oils and they were sealed up alive. A wall was built between them and a protective talisman – something they call the serpent's eye – was specially blessed and prepared by Akhenaten's priests. This was placed upon the door as a means of keeping Sonchis's *ka* – 'is spirit – contained within the tomb. Akhenaten must 'ave believed that this man's spirit was so dangerous, it must never be allowed to escape, even after death.'

Alec frowned. 'That accounts for the copper-lined sarcophagus,' he said. 'And the manacles . . .' He thought for a moment. 'And it also explains the opening on the door of the tomb: that must have been where this serpent's eye thing was placed!'

'And yet we didn't find anything like that in the antechamber,' said Ethan. 'So where did it go to? We know there haven't been tomb robbers . . .'

'We've already talked about this,' said Alec. 'I'm sure Uncle Will would never have taken it. Maybe Tom,' he suggested. 'Maybe taking the eye had something to do with his going missing. Maybe it . . . affected him in some way?'

Ethan shrugged his shoulders. 'Sounds crazy, but at this stage I'm prepared to consider just about any idea.' He frowned. 'Anything else we should know, Maddie?'

She nodded. 'Yes, but you aren't going to like it.'

'Try me,' suggested Ethan.

'As Sonchis was being sealed in the tomb, 'e woke from the drug-induced sleep and cursed those who 'ad arrested 'im. 'E cursed Akhenaten and anybody else who entered the tomb . . .'

'Oh, great,' sighed Ethan. 'Another curse. Perfect.'

''E also said that death could not keep 'im . . . that 'e would return one day to fulfil 'is destiny. 'E said 'e would walk the earth and 'e would go to the Gates of Apophis and awaken the great serpent from 'is sleep.'

Ethan smiled. 'The Gates of Apophis, huh? Well, that ain't too far away.'

Alec stared at him. 'You've heard of it?

'Sure. A big old cave system out in the desert, due west of here. One of the rocks above it does kind of resemble the head of a cobra. Some of the older locals still call it by that name and I remember one guy telling me he'd heard a story about it when he was a kid. Looking at the guy, that must have been like a hundred years ago. He said that under the cliffs, Apophis slept; and one day he would be called and return to the surface.'

Alec looked at him. 'Do you think there's anything in it?' he asked.

Ethan gave a snort of derision. 'Do I think there's a giant snake asleep under the desert?' he asked. 'No, and I'm surprised at you for asking such a stupid question!'

Alec felt his cheeks redden. 'But I read somewhere that all legends start with a fact,' he argued.

'Yeah, maybe somebody did get bitten by a snake there, down the centuries – but just an ordinary-sized one. Then, over the years, it got exaggerated. Heck, Alec, you know how these things work!' He turned back to Madeleine. 'Good job, Maddie. OK, so now we know who we're dealing with. It ain't Akhenaten, but it's a pretty amazing find all the same and we shouldn't lose sight of that.'

'And the curse?' murmured Madeleine.

'Don't even give it a second thought.'

'No, but wait,' persisted Alec. 'Just think for a moment. You heard what Madeleine said. A serpent's eye was placed in the door to keep this high priest's spirit locked up. But the eye is gone . . . and the sarcophagus was smashed open by an earthquake, who knows how many centuries ago? There have been some very rum things happening around here. Tom Hinton's disappearance. Hyenas in a place where you don't normally find hyenas. Fruit bats that attack people. Now nobody knows what happened to Wilfred Llewellyn. I know it sounds crazy, but . . . suppose something *did* get out of the tomb? Suppose Sonchis's spirit is already out here, causing bad things to happen?'

Ethan stared at Alec for a moment in silence. Then he threw back his head and began to laugh.

Sonchis lifted his head at the unexpected sound of laughter coming from one of the tents. *Yes, laugh*, he thought, *while you still have something to laugh about!*

He waited for a moment in the darkness until

the sound had died down, and then he carried on, moving the still unfamiliar shape of Doc Hopper into the dark hills beyond the road. The hessian bag he carried over his shoulder bumped against his back with a dry, rattling sound. He reached a spot on the edge of the darkness and paused, listening intently. After a short while he was rewarded with a low growl and he saw the glint of a pair of feral eyes regarding him from the shadows. A moment later, another pair appeared, and then there were more, as a whole pack of hyenas came creeping out from their hiding places.

They had always been his loyal servants – and these ones had travelled hundreds of miles to carry out his bidding. Such loyalty deserved to be rewarded occasionally. He lifted the sack from his shoulder and upended it at the edge of the road, sending a grisly collection of bones and tattered clothing tumbling down to where the hyenas waited. The mortal remains of a fat detective called Wilfred Llewellyn would soon be nothing more than a memory. Sonchis could not allow his plan to be disrupted by somebody stumbling upon the sack that he had temporarily stored under Doc Hopper's bed.

He listened for a while as the hyenas began to snap ravenously at the bones and then he flung the bloodstained sack into the darkness too, knowing that not a trace of it would remain by morning. Hyenas were not particular about what they ate. He returned to his tent, impatient to begin the next part of his task – to inhabit his own body once more; but he was all too aware that he could not start until everyone in the camp was asleep.

Then it would begin, the process that he had waited thousands of years to complete. He slipped a hand inside his shirt and felt each of his talismans sending fresh power through his spirit, and he told himself that he would not have to tolerate this artificial body for very much longer . . .

With an expression of disgust, Biff Corcoran pulled the sheet of paper from his typewriter, balled it up and threw it at the waste bin on the other side of the hotel room; it glanced off the edge and rolled away to join half a dozen other similarly discarded attempts that littered the floor.

Not for the first time, he asked himself what was he doing here. The room was intolerably hot, despite the clattering ceiling fan, which was vainly trying to stir the humid air around. Meanwhile his attempts to scare up some kind of a gripping travel article seemed equally doomed to failure. He thought again about the Devlin kid: what a great little story that would have been – but no, that interfering flunky had made sure that it just wasn't going to happen. Typical uptight Englishman – the kid could have been in the *Saturday Evening Post*!

Trouble was, what other angle did he have? It was no good sending his editor a bunch of hooey about mummies and tombs and ancient artefacts. That wouldn't wash for the average *Post* reader. No, he needed to find 'the human angle' but it just wasn't coming and time was fast running out.

To make matters worse, Biff's supply of whisky was fast running out too, and Mohammed Hansa, the best contact for the stuff in these parts, had been hard to get hold of since he'd started chauffeuring that Welsh professor around. Biff poured himself a small shot and savoured the feel of it on his tongue, telling himself that if things didn't pick up soon, he'd have to start thinking about another line of work.

A furious hammering on his door made him

jump and he almost spilled the precious contents of his glass.

'Come in!' he growled. The door opened and Charlie swept into the room, carrying a photograph. The last time Biff had seen her she'd been heading for the improvised darkroom she had set up in one of the Winter Palace's linen cupboards, but now her face was ashen and for once in her life she looked anything but bored.

'Biff, there's something screwy going on,' she announced.

'You're telling me,' he said. 'It's called Egypt. The whole place is screwy. You know, I watched *The Sheik* three times and at no point did you ever see Valentino pulling sand out of his duds – but I swear every item of clothing I brought with me is full of the stuff.'

'Never mind about that! I want you to look at a photograph I took.'

'That's above and beyond the call of duty, kid. You know I do the words; I leave the images to you.'

'Yeah, but you know the English guy, Llewellyn?'

'The *Welsh* guy. That's why he talks the way he does.'

'Yeah, whatever you say. I took this photograph of him and it's *hideous*!'

Biff sniggered. 'Oh, you only just noticed? I could've told you he's no oil painting. The British Museum clearly doesn't employ professors on the basis of their looks. He's got the kind of puss you'd put on the mantel to keep the kids away from the fire.'

'No, look, will ya! What do you make of this? I did an enlargement, just to be sure I wasn't hallucinating or something.'

Charlie thrust a sheet of photographic paper into his hands and he gave it a cursory glance; then looked again as he registered what he was looking at.

'Holy moly!' he said.

A face stared up at him from the print. The eyes were covered by a pair of dark glasses, but they were the only normal-looking things in the picture. They hung from a face that was a fright mask made up of what appeared to be hundreds of fat black insects.

'Is this some kind of joke?' gasped Biff.

'If it is, nobody's laughing,' Charlie assured him.

'It's a little early for Halloween, wouldn't you say? Aw, come on, Charlie. He must have put on some kind of a mask.'

She shook her head. 'Uh-uh. You were there when I took it – he was sat in the back of Mohammed Hansa's automobile and he looked completely normal. Well, as normal as a guy like that ever looks. But I remember he wasn't too pleased about having his picture taken. He kicked up about it. Say, maybe he knew it would come out like this.'

Biff felt a sense of excitement stirring within him. Charlie had chanced on something here. He didn't know exactly what it was yet, but he was pretty sure it would make more exciting reading than some dry old stuff about digging up relics. Not so much human interest as *inhuman* interest – but what the heck. It would transfix readers from Hoboken to Colorado.

He slammed down his glass of whisky and stared at Charlie. 'Great day in the morning!' he shouted excitedly. 'This is incredible. This has to be the story of the century!'

'You figure?'

'Yes, I figure. This is gonna be bigger than the *Titanic!*' Biff thought for a moment. 'Say, what room is the professor staying in? We'll get some hired muscle and go and have a little word with him.'

Charlie shook her head. 'He ain't there,' she said. 'I bumped into the desk clerk a little while ago and he asked me if I'd seen anything of Professor Llewellyn. Seems he went out early this morning and never came back. Told the clerk he was headed for Ethan Wade's dig.'

'You're kidding me! Well, don't just stand there, go and find us some transport!' he cried. 'Get Mohammed Hansa if you can. We're going up to the dig.'

Charlie stared at him. 'At this time of night?' she cried.

'Yeah, shake the lead out of your boots! I can see it now . . .' He lifted a hand to frame an imaginary caption. 'ANCIENT TOMBS HAUNTED BY INSECT—MAN HORROR,' he said. 'Exclusive feature by Biff Corcoran.'

'Photographs by Charlie Connors,' added Charlie.

'Yeah, sure. Now skedaddle! I want to get up there before that weirdo professor disappears on us.'

She turned and ran for the door. It was the first time Biff had seen her hurry over anything. He turned back to his glass of whisky and gulped it down in one before looking around for his jacket and boots.

CHAPTER SEVENTEEN

The Return of Sonchis

Sonchis paced anxiously up and down, telling himself that he had waited long enough. He had returned from feeding Llewellyn's bones to the hyenas some time ago and had made himself sit quietly in the doctor's tent. It was late now and he was pretty sure that everyone in the camp must be asleep. He stooped, picked up a hurricane lamp and the heavy bolt cutters he had set aside earlier, but he did not light the lamp yet. He went over to pull aside the mosquito netting and peered outside. Not a soul in sight, but from a couple of tents he heard loud snores. He wondered how the whole camp had not been awakened by it.

He stepped out into the open and, aware of how the slightest sound carried at night, began to creep towards the road, moving the doctor's clumsy feet as quietly as he could. He crossed the road and picked his way carefully between the rocks in the pale moonlight. Once he was a good distance from the tents, he walked more quickly, climbing down into the gully and crossing the intervening space.

Ahead of him, beside the entrance to the tomb, he saw Hassan, the arab worker who had alerted Llewellyn to the presence of Tom Hinton, dozing fitfully beside a small campfire. As he moved closer, the man snapped awake and directed a lazy smile at the approaching figure.

'Dr Hopper,' he said in his poor English. 'You up late.'

Sonchis arranged the doctor's features into a reciprocal smile. 'Something I needed to check on,' he said. 'How long before somebody comes to take your place?'

'Hours,' said Hassan glumly. 'I just come on watch.' He stood up. 'Hassan go inside with you?' he asked.

'No need,' said Sonchis. 'In fact, now I come

to think of it, I have no further need of you at all.' He flung out a hand to seize Hassan by the throat and the Arab's dark eyes bulged in surprise. He opened his mouth to cry out but all that emerged was a brief hiss of expelled air. Sonchis exerted all his supernatural strength and felt the bones in Hassan's neck snap beneath his fingers like dry twigs. Hassan's eyes became vacant and he went limp, his life extinguished. Sonchis regarded him for a moment, not wanting to make any mistakes; he couldn't allow Hassan to recover and go shouting for help while he was inside the tomb. But the man's eyes were already glazing over. Sonchis stepped over the body and, taking a box of matches from the doctor's pocket, stooped to light the hurricane lamp. Then, holding it aloft, he went quickly down the steps into the tomb.

Alec was running for his life. It was night and he could see very little, but he knew that behind him in the dark shadows something ancient and evil was following him on silent feet.

Ahead of him lay a vast expanse of desert, pale and unwelcoming in the moonlight. The sand seemed to cling to his feet as though it was damp; he could feel it sucking at his ankles and feared that if he slowed his pace, he would sink to his knees and be held there, a helpless captive. He tried to cry out for help, but his voice seemed to have gone and he could manage nothing more than a dry rattle of despair. From behind him a pair of skeletal arms were reaching out to grab at his shoulders—

He woke with a start and lay sweating on the camp bed, trying to get his breathing back to normal. At first he was surprised to find that he was dressed, but then he remembered he had been so tired when he finally turned in, he could do no more than pull off his boots. The dream had been so real, he could still feel the unspeakable touch of those dried fingers clawing at his flesh. He shivered, despite the heat, and gazed around the gloom of the tent, reassured by the sound of Coates snoring loudly nearby. But then he realized that something else had woken him: the sound of footsteps passing by.

He got up and went to peer outside. The campsite looked deserted in the eerie wash of moonlight. For a moment he thought he saw a shadowy shape moving amidst the jagged rocks on the far side of the road – it looked like the tall shape of Doc Hopper; but then it was gone and he decided he must have been mistaken.

Whatever the answer, he could feel sleep plucking at him again and he was too tired to resist for long. He stumbled back to his bed and lay down, listening to Coates – an infernal racket that was somehow oddly comforting. Eerily, from Archie's tent across the way he could hear more snores, the deeper tones seeming to provide some kind of answer to Coates's more high-pitched ones. If he had been more awake it would have seemed funny, but he was so tired and sleep was pulling at him with irresistible power. He closed his eyes and was asleep again in moments. This time there were no dreams to trouble him.

Sonchis approached his own mummified corpse, drinking in the wonder of this moment, one he had anticipated for so many years. At last the time of his rebirth was at hand. He set down the lantern and pushed aside the remains of the wooden lid. Then, turning back, he took the powerful bolt cutters and sliced through the clasps that secured the copper manacles. Pointless to return to his own body only to find himself once more a prisoner of that despised metal. He picked up the manacles and flung them aside.

He stood for a moment, looking down at the shrivelled, mummified corpse in the sarcophagus, a body that had once pulsed with strength and vitality and magical power beyond the comprehension of mere mortals. He told himself it was of little matter. He now held the life forces of three men within him, and once they had been transferred to his own body, together with his own *ka*, he would soon begin to regenerate flesh and blood and muscle. He would be as strong as ever, if not more so. From around the doctor's neck he took the thong that held the two amulets. Then, leaning forward over the sarcophagus, he slipped the thong around his own neck and draped the two talismans on his lifeless chest. He was ready to begin.

He placed Hopper's hands on either side of the bandaged head, moved Hopper's face closer and began to recite the words of transference; the words he had held in his mind for so very long.

He spoke softly, muttering them under his breath, and almost instantly he felt the change occurring within him. As he looked down, his hands began to melt away, the scarabs peeling off in agitation, revealing the bare bones beneath. The insects swept over the still body below him, then up and over the edges of the wooden sarcophagus, raining to the floor and skittering across the sand at his feet; and now his wrists were dissolving, his arms, his shoulders; and as he looked on in wonder, the eyes of the body beneath him suddenly flicked open and regarded him in silent triumph.

Now the rest of him was bursting apart in a flurry: he could feel Doc Hopper's body collapsing, no more than a collection of bones in a set of clothing; then his final thoughts transferred themselves to their new home. And he was no longer looking down, but gazing up from the sarcophagus, just in time to see the last of Doc Hopper's wasted body bursting apart in an explosion of shiny, wriggling shapes.

He sat up and looked around. After so many unsuitable hosts, he was at last in the place where he belonged. He was Sonchis again. He lifted a hand to look at it, watching in awe as the flesh of his palm began to regenerate, stretching the slackened bandages taut again. He lifted his other hand and tore the bandages away; they came apart easily beneath his eager fingers and he could see the black flesh beneath swelling, the colour lightening as blood flowed to long-dead veins and arteries. He tore the other hand free and pulled the wrappings from around his face. He explored the flesh beneath with his fingertips, feeling his proud nose reshaping itself, his shrivelled lips filling with moisture. There was no mirror here for him to see the transformation, but he knew he had more than enough life to power him; for he was more than just Sonchis – he also had the knowledge, the experience and the strength of three other men at his disposal.

He peered over the edge of the sarcophagus and saw the swarms of scarabs running this way and that in confusion, away from the fallen bones of Doc Hopper. They had served him well, these simple creatures. They had provided him with a means to walk the earth again while he drew up his plans.

He stood up in the sarcophagus and climbed over the side, crushing several scarabs beneath his feet as he did so. A poor reward for what they had done, but he wasn't about to get sentimental over a few insects. He had more important matters to attend to. He walked to the nearest of the standing sarcophagi and, taking the wooden lid in his hands, wrenched it aside as though it was made of nothing stronger than balsa. He propped the lid against the wall and studied the occupant of the sarcophagus.

A shrivelled, bandaged face greeted him and he was shocked to note that he did not even remember the name of this man. It mattered little. His four lieutenants were here to aid him, though they would never be as complete as he was. He tore the bandages away from the man's closed eyes. Then he raised his arms and placed his hands on either side of his lieutenant's head, and muttered the words of regeneration.

After a few moments, with a dry click, the man's eyes opened and Sonchis saw in them an expression of absolute loyalty, undimmed by the passing centuries. This one he would leave behind, he decided, to take care of any who tried to follow him. The other three would accompany him to the Gates of Apophis, where they would help him to perform the sacred rite that he had planned three thousand years earlier.

He moved to the next sarcophagus and removed the lid. He lifted his arms and spoke the words, and as he did so, he remembered one other little detail that he needed to take care of. Apophis would require a suitable sacrifice, and luckily, Sonchis knew exactly where to find one.

Mohammed Hansa was far from happy. He was not used to being roused from sleep at this time of night and told he must make a tricky journey across the desert. He had tried his very best to dissuade the journalists from making the trip now; had even warned them that he would have to charge them triple fare; but nothing seemed to put them off. Mr Corcoran had agreed to his demands with barely a protest, and that had instantly made Mohammed suspicious, because the American was not known for his willingness to spend money.

The ancient Ford rattled along the road to the Valley of the Kings, its acetylene-gas headlights sending two weak and watery beams into the darkness.

'Can't you get this old jalopy moving any faster?' barked Biff from the back seat. 'And why don't you have electric headlights yet? *Everybody* has electric headlights!'

'Not in Luxor,' Mohammed shouted over the rush of wind. 'And I must go carefully, Mr

Corcoran. This is a bad road.' He studied the reporter in the rear-view mirror, noticing how fired up he was. Beside him, Charlie Connors, usually the most indolent person in Egypt, was sitting bolt upright, staring ahead, her expensive camera cradled in her lap, ready for action. Something important must have happened to get these two out of their hotel beds at such a late hour. 'I can't imagine that anyone at the campsite will be awake at this time of night,' he warned them.

'We'll wake 'em up,' Biff told him. 'When they hear what we have to say, they'll wake up all right.'

Mohammed frowned. This didn't sound good. 'Is something wrong, Mr Corcoran?' he shouted, keeping his eye on the mirror.

Biff's face was expressionless. 'I was about to ask you the same question,' he said.

'Whatever do you mean?'

'You've been driving Professor Llewellyn around for the last couple of days, ain't that so? You notice anything . . . odd about him?'

'Well, he is certainly an unusual gentleman, but—'

'See, while I was waiting for you to turn up, I

checked at the hotel reception. It seems they ain't seen Llewellyn since yesterday, when you picked him up and drove him off to Wade's dig. How come you didn't bring him back?'

'Oh . . . er, well . . . he . . . he disappeared.'

'He's *disappeared*?' Charlie nearly jumped out of her seat and Mohammed noticed that Biff gave her a warning nudge with his elbow to calm her down.

'Yes, Miss Connors. I drove him over to the archaeological dig only yesterday, as Mr Corcoran said. I dropped him off and he went to talk to Doctor Hopper. After that, I didn't see him again. When it was time to return to Luxor, there was no sign of him. I checked every tent. In the end we thought that he must have decided to walk to the Tutankhamun site.'

In the mirror he could see the two journalists exchanging bemused looks.

'You think that's likely?' asked Biff after a while.

'No, sir, most *un*likely. But we couldn't think of any other explanation – unless he simply wandered off into the desert. Funny, though. That's the second person to—'

Mohammad broke off, realizing that he had just made a terrible mistake and hoping that

Biff might have missed it. But of course he hadn't.

Biff leaned closer. 'Go on, finish what you were about to say,' he snapped.

'It's . . . nothing.'

'Sure it is. Come on, spill the beans. Listen, Mohammed, withholding evidence is a crime: you could wind up in a whole lot of trouble. You might even lose your precious car. Tell me, who else has gone missing?'

Now Mohammed was truly horrified. Without his Ford he wouldn't be able to make a living. He licked his lips. 'Well . . . only Mr Hinton.'

'Tom Hinton? Sir William's assistant? He's missing too?'

'Yes. Didn't you know?'

'No, I didn't! Say, wait till I see that Ethan Wade. He sure kept that quiet. When did this happen?'

'He . . . he disappeared the same night that Sir William Devlin suffered his breakdown. But—'

'I don't believe this. It's a conspiracy!'

'No. Mr Wade just thought it would be better if people didn't panic.' Mohammed felt terrible. Now he really had let the cat out of the bag. And after he'd promised Mr Wade he wouldn't give the game away.

'But I don't get it,' persisted Biff. 'What's the

connection between Tom Hinton and some professor from the British Museum?' he asked.

Mohammed shook his head but Biff was still staring at him in that intense way he had.

'You know more, don'tcha?' he said. 'Come on, Mohammed, I'm telling you, you can give it to me the easy way or we'll stop this car and I'll beat it out of you.'

'I promised Mr Wade,' he said.

'Don't think Wade's gonna help ya!' snarled Biff. 'I'm giving you to the count of three and then we'll stop this car and we'll really see how much you know.'

Mohammed didn't doubt that the American would make good on his threat given half a chance. He realized it was pointless to keep up the pretence any longer.

'He's not a professor, Mr Corcoran. He's a private detective, sent from England by Mr Hinton's parents. We spent time looking around the bazaar in Luxor. I think he found Mr Hinton too . . . only when I asked him about it, he said it was somebody else, somebody who only *looked* like Mr Hinton. But you know, after that, Mr Llewellyn, he began to behave very strangely . . . as though something had happened to him.'

'Something like what?' interjected Charlie.

'I cannot say. He came back to the automobile and . . . he was like someone else entirely. As though some spirit had possessed him.'

'Say, did he have a face that looked like it was made up of hundreds of bugs?' asked Charlie.

'I beg your pardon?' said Mohammed.

'Just put your foot down!' snapped Biff. 'Something screwy is going on at that dig and we need to find out what it is.'

Mohammed nodded. He pushed the old Ford up to its top speed, crashing and shuddering along the uneven road to the Valley of the Kings.

Madeleine sat at her desk reading through the hieroglyphs on the scroll. She realized that she should have gone to bed long since, but what she was reading was simply too riveting to abandon. If this account of Sonchis's exploits was to be believed, she could understand why Akhenaten had wanted him put where he could do no harm. Whoever had written this latest text was making some pretty wild claims.

Sonchis had an affinity with wild animals; could make them obey his every whim. She thought about the hyena attack and the fruit bats that had invaded the camp. Sonchis had turned base metal into gold; he could control the weather. Hadn't Ethan said something about a freak sandstorm that had struck on his way back from seeing Sir William? Sonchis had even raised the dead, turning them into his servants, and his ultimate aim was to reawaken the great serpent, Apophis, and summon him to the surface of the world. Then he would command him to destroy the armies of Akhenaten, so that he, Sonchis, could take the throne and rule all of Egypt.

As she read, Madeleine was vaguely aware of the tent flap opening and closing behind her, but she did not look up. Ethan and Alec, no doubt, eager for more information.

'You will 'ave to be patient,' she said. 'I am finding out more and more about this 'igh priest, but I need to finish all the scrolls before I can tell you any more.'

No answer, but she was aware of soft footsteps and measured breathing. Somebody was standing right behind her, looking over her shoulder, and she smelled the sharp tang of sulphur, as though somebody had struck a dozen matches all at once.

She started to turn in her seat, but in that instant a powerful hand clamped over her mouth and an arm locked around her chest in a hold that felt like a steel cable. She tried to struggle but the arm lifted her up as though she weighed no more than a rag doll. She kicked her legs, managing only to knock over her chair, and then she was being swung round towards the tent flaps.

She caught a glimpse of her reflection in the mirror that stood against one side of the tent. The man who held her looked hardly human – a bald head, dark piercing eyes and a naked chest and arms that seemed to pulse with unnatural power, his lower half wrapped in mouldering bandages. She saw him for only an instant and she would have screamed, but the hand across her mouth allowed her to emit no more than a soft grunt.

Then a mouth was beside her ear and, most terrifying of all, it spoke to her in the unmistakable Lancastrian tones of Doc Hopper.

'Don't struggle,' said the voice. 'We're going to take a little trip, you and I. There's someone I want you to meet.'

And before she could even wonder what that might mean, she was carried, kicking and struggling, through the open tent flaps and out into the night.

CHAPTER EIGHTEEN

Crash

Alec woke for the second time that night, and once again he was sure he had heard something outside. He glanced around the dark interior of the tent. Coates was still snoring like a walrus, clearly dead to the world. Alec yawned, got up and went to pull open the tent flaps. He looked groggily through the mosquito netting into the night. Across the way, he could see figures moving around the Crossleys . . . No, not moving exactly. Struggling.

He gave a grunt of surprise and pulled aside the netting. Now he could see more clearly. Madeleine was out there and she was being bundled into the car by two men who . . . Alec's jaw dropped open and he asked himself if he wasn't still asleep and dreaming. For the two creatures that held her were not men at all, but two shambling, wizened manikins wrapped in filthy bandages, their faces gaunt and hideous to behold, their eyes glittering with feral malevolence.

Another such creature was already clambering awkwardly into the passenger seat, while beside him, a fourth figure was climbing in behind the wheel; this one not as wasted as his companions, his arms and chest bare and apparently pulsing with life. As Alec watched in frozen terror, the man turned his head to look towards the tent and a triumphant smile etched itself across his cadaverous features. A shock of recognition lanced through Alec like the blade of a knife. He had seen that face before, staring up at him from the wooden sarcophagus in the tomb.

'Sonchis!' He heard himself say it, not really believing, but having to accept what his eyes were telling him. Sonchis and three of his lieutenants. They were alive. They were abducting Madeleine. Alec stumbled forward, unsure for a moment what to do. He glanced around desperately, but there was no weapon to hand and all he could do was bellow for help.

'Ethan!' he yelled. 'Everybody! Wake up, wake up!'

Then the Crossley's engine roared into life and the headlights flicked on to send two beams of light arcing though the darkness. The vehicle was moving away onto the road and Alec caught a glimpse of Madeleine's terrified face as she struggled in the grasp of the two mummies. He began to run after them, dimly aware of people stumbling out of the tents behind him, but the Crossley's tyres had hit the surface of the road with a screech and it was accelerating away up the hill.

Then, from out of the darkness ahead, two more headlights appeared as another automobile crested the rise and came rattling down the hill. Alec recognized Mohammed's old Ford, its rusting metalwork clattering in protest at the speed it was doing. Alec felt his spirits lift because he knew that there simply wasn't room for two cars to pass on that narrow road: the Crossley would surely have to stop.

Alec continued to run, not knowing what he would do if he caught up with them; and then he saw Sonchis lift an arm and make a brief gesture, and the Ford suddenly lurched sideways, as though swept aside by a giant's hand. It smashed headlong into the boulders at the side of the road. The tail end lifted and the automobile turned over and came crashing down with an ear-splitting rending of metal. The Crossley did not slow for an instant. It raced on up the hill and dropped away out of sight.

Alec ran over to the Ford and looked inside to see three people tangled together. He stooped and grabbed the nearest of them – the photographer, Charlie Connors – and began to pull her free of the wreckage. She was barely conscious and had a deep gash in her temple, but she was holding onto her precious camera as though her life depended upon it.

Now other people were coming over to help. Ethan appeared, pulling a shirt over his head, and then Coates, looking ridiculous in his striped pyjamas.

'What the hell's going on?' bellowed Ethan. 'I thought I heard the Crossley . . .'

'You did,' Alec assured him, helping him to drag Charlie to a safe distance. He was all too aware of the smell of petrol coming from around

the Ford. 'Madeleine. They took Madeleine. They
were driving away in the Crossley and
Mohammed's car came down the hill—'

'Who was driving away?' yelled Ethan.

Alec could see that Coates and Mickey were
pulling Biff Corcoran from the wreckage now,
his face a mask of blood.

'Sonchis,' he said. 'Sonchis took her.'

Ethan looked at Alec. 'Have you any idea how
crazy that sounds?' he said.

'Oh yes,' said Alec. 'Absolutely.' He ran back to
the Ford and ducked down to reach for Mohammed, who was conscious but clearly in pain.

'My Ford!' he groaned. 'My beautiful Model T!'

Alec grabbed him under his arms and tried
pulling, but Mohammed gave a shriek of pain.
'My leg . . . my leg is caught.' Alec glanced
nervously at the large puddle of fuel that was
spreading beneath the wrecked automobile. He
took a firmer grip and renewed his efforts. Ethan
dashed over to help him.

'I think the car's gonna blow,' he said quietly
and his voice was surprisingly calm. He went
down on his chest and reached in past
Mohammed, trying to manoeuvre the man's leg
out from where it was caught.

'Leave me,' gasped Mohammed. 'Leave me with my automobile. Without it I cannot make a living!'

'Aw, we'll get you a new one,' Ethan assured him. 'And this time we'll buy you something decent.'

'Who was that maniac in the Crossley?' groaned Mohammed. 'I caught a glimpse of his face but he looked . . . he didn't look . . . human . . .'

'Is that right?' Ethan glanced at Alec.

Alec looked at the spreading pool of petrol, noting with a sense of dread that it was beginning to smoke.

'Ethan . . .' he said.

The American followed his gaze and nodded. He gripped Mohammed around the waist and braced himself for one monumental effort. 'All right, Mohammed,' he said. 'I'm going to count to three—'

'Forget the count!' yelled Alec. 'Do it now!'

Ethan pulled with all his might and Mohammed bellowed in pain, but suddenly the foot came free and they were able to pull him out onto the road.

'Did the foot come off?' gasped Mohammed,

too afraid to look himself. Alec looked for him and saw that it was bloody and possibly broken at the ankle, but still attached to his leg.

'It's all right,' he said, and he and Ethan began to pull him across the road. 'I think you're going to be—'

And then there was a flash and a great blast of heat and Alec was thrown backwards as the Ford exploded in an orange burst of flame. He crashed into Coates, who flung his arms protectively around him as he fell. A great wave of hot air soared over them and then there were just the huge flames blossoming beneath the night sky, and Alec heard Mohammed bellowing that his Ford, his wonderful Ford, was gone for ever and a curse on those who had caused it to crash. Then he heard Ethan telling him to shut up and he knew that the three of them had survived. He lay there for a moment, catching his breath, until Ethan's face came into view. He was looking down at Alec with an expression of disbelief on his face, and said, 'Alec, just run it by me again, will ya? Who did you say took the Crossley?'

Seated at the wheel of the speeding car, Sonchis had time to marvel at the ingenuity of the people who had created this amazing horseless chariot, while the part of him that was still Doc Hopper went through the routine of actually driving the thing. He glanced over his shoulder and saw the woman's pale face between the shrivelled, decomposed bodies of her two captors, and for a moment he almost felt sorry for her. When he spoke, he chose to use the gentle, cultured tones of Tom Hinton, thinking that this would be the most appropriate voice for her to deal with.

'I'm sorry we had to be so rough with you back there. It was necessary to get away as quickly as possible.'

She continued to stare at him as though she was in shock – which, he reflected, she almost certainly was.

'Who are you?' she asked at last.

He paused for a moment, and when he spoke again, his voice was deeper, strangely accented. 'Oh, come, I think you know who I am. Weren't you just reading about me?'

She shook her head. 'I was reading about a man who died three thousand years ago!' she protested.

'Ah no, that's where you are mistaken. I was

imprisoned three thousand years ago . . . but I did not die. That is to say, my *ka* did not die. I had long before that time conquered the concept of death. I had already made myself immortal.'

'What nonsense is this?' protested Madeleine, not wanting to let herself believe the evidence of her own eyes. 'You . . . you cannot be Sonchis.'

'But I am; and I am more than that. I am in fact the sum total of four spirits.' His eyelids flickered and then the voice was back to its earlier cultured tones. 'I am Tom Hinton, in whose voice I am speaking to you now.' He paused for a moment and then spoke in a broad Lancastrian accent, the voice she had heard back in the tent. 'I am the man you knew as Doc Hopper,' he said; and then, after another pause, his voice emerged as an oily Welsh burr. 'And I am one Wilfred Llewellyn, private detective of London, formerly of Carnarvon. An odd choice, but who knows, he may come in useful for something.' He laughed and his voice slipped effortlessly back into the deep tones he had used before. 'So you see, I am many things, but one thing I most definitely am is *alive*!'

Madeleine glanced sideways and then looked

away with a gasp of revulsion. 'And these . . .
things?'

'My most devoted servants. Fine men once, all
of them . . . but don't expect a meaningful conversation from them. I gave them just enough life
to aid me in my next task. I did not want to drain
my own reserves. Ah, now, if memory serves me
correctly . . .'

He slewed the car sideways off the road onto
a rough dirt track that angled away across the
desert. The Crossley started juddering and buck-
eting across the uneven surface, shaking the
occupants of the car.

'Where are you taking me?' protested
Madeleine.

'My dear *mademoiselle*, have you not guessed?
We are going to the Gates of Apophis to awaken
the great serpent!'

Madeleine laughed. 'Then you are clearly as
mad as you ever were,' she said. 'Even if there
were a great serpent, do you really think 'e would
still be alive after three thousand years?'

Sonchis laughed again, a cold, heartless
sound. 'Apophis is a *god*!' he said. 'Gods do not
die because of the passing of a few millennia.
Of course he is alive! He sleeps beneath the

sand, waiting to be called back to the world. We go to do exactly that. And, of course, on such occasions it is customary to offer a suitable sacrifice.'

Madeleine stared at him for a few moments and then her eyes widened as she understood his meaning. She began to struggle with renewed ferocity. 'Stop this automobile!' she bellowed. 'Let me out at once!'

'I don't think so,' he said.

'I am warning you, if you do not stop now, you will be sorry!'

Sonchis gestured to the bandaged thing that sat to her right. 'She's beginning to be tiresome,' he said.

The creature nodded. It released her for an instant, lifted its arm and punched her hard across the face, the impact causing bits of withered flesh and dried bone to fall from its hand. But it did the job. Madeleine slumped forward, unconscious, and Sonchis was able to concentrate on driving, applying all Doc Hopper's undoubted skills as a motorist in an attempt to get the automobile to its destination without shaking it to pieces.

* * *

Ethan stared at Alec for a long time before he spoke. Then he said, 'Kid, that sounds absolutely nuts!'

'I know exactly how it sounds,' Alec assured him. 'I'm only telling you what I saw. I saw Sonchis and three . . . *things*.'

'The boy speaks the truth,' Mohammed assured him. He was stretched out on the ground nearby, and a workman was trying to wrap a length of bandage around his injured leg. 'I saw the people in your automobile, Mr Wade. Only for an instant, but I saw them. They looked like things from a . . . a nightmare!'

'You're telling me that some three-thousand-year-old mummies just stole my automobile?' cried Ethan. 'For cryin' out loud, how would they even know how to *drive*?'

It was a good question; but Alec had a far more pressing matter on his mind.

'They took Madeleine!' he cried. 'We have to get after them before they get too far.'

'I don't know how you're going to do that,' said Mickey. He was standing by the other Crossley, peering dejectedly under the bonnet. 'Before they left they tore the guts out of this engine.'

'What? Well, you've got to fix it!' cried Alec. 'Now.'

'You don't understand, son. They've really torn it up.'

Ethan strode across to him. 'Give it your best shot anyway,' he told Mickey. 'It's our only chance.' Mickey nodded and started work. Ethan quickly glanced around, assessing the situation.

Mohammed's Ford was still blazing beneath the night sky. Coates was tending to the two injured journalists, while the Arab workmen ran backwards and forwards with buckets of water, trying to extinguish the blaze. Archie, meanwhile, was marching up and down shouting orders at them, as though he was back in the army. Charlie was fully awake now, sitting up and cradling her camera in her lap, but Biff Corcoran was still unconscious.

'Just what the hell is going on here?' Ethan asked aloud.

'I don't have the foggiest,' said Coates quietly, 'but I think Mr Corcoran here would benefit from some professional medical attention. Has anybody seen Dr Hopper?'

Alec thought for a moment and then remembered the sounds that had first woken him up.

'He went to the tomb,' he said.

'At this time of night?' said Ethan.

'Yes. At least, I'm pretty sure it was him. I'll . . . I'll go and find him.' He turned and ran to his tent to pull on a pair of boots. When he emerged again, he asked Mickey, 'How's it coming along?'

'Not great,' muttered Mickey.

Alec turned away helplessly and headed for the rocks.

'Please go with him, Mr Wade,' said Coates. 'Who knows what dangers might be out there? I'll hold the fort.'

Ethan looked around quickly, as if to reassure himself that there was nothing else he could do here. He nodded and strode after Alec.

'Hey, hold up there, pard!' He fell into step. 'Is it just me, or has everything gone screwy around here?'

Alec couldn't relax enough to make light of the situation. 'What are we going to do about Madeleine?' he asked anxiously.

'We'll go after her, of course, just as soon as Mickey gets that engine running.'

'What if he can't fix it?

Ethan had no answer for that.

They clambered through the opening in the

rocks and descended into the valley beyond. As they approached the tomb, they could see the glow of light emerging from the opening in the ground; but as they drew nearer, they saw Hassan's figure slumped on the sand beside it.

'How does anybody sleep through that kind of racket?' muttered Ethan.

Alec went straight down the steps to the tomb but Ethan paused to prod Hassan with the toe of his boot. There was no response.

'Hassan?' he said. He stooped, gripped the man's shoulder and turned him over. Hassan's dark eyes stared sightlessly up at the stars and Ethan noticed that his head was lying at a strange angle. He snatched in a breath and rocked back on his heels. He had known this man for years; he had considered him a friend. And now . . .

A yell of terror from down in the antechamber jerked his senses awake.

'Alec?' he yelled. '*Alec!*' He jumped back to his feet and, without a moment's hesitation, went charging down the steps.

The Crossley was suffering terribly on this rough, half-buried track, but now the cliffs were in sight and Sonchis told himself he only needed to keep it going for a few more miles.

He was thinking how sweet it would be to revenge himself on a world that had treated him so cruelly; and his only sorrow was that Akhenaten himself would not be there to witness the destruction of his empire. But the great pharaoh was so much dust now; he was lost in the great passing of time like a handful of chaff thrown on the wind. In the end he had been no more than a man.

Sonchis remembered how they had taken him captive the night before he planned to awaken Apophis – creeping up on him when he was asleep and at his most vulnerable. He remembered how they had chained him with forged copper and how they had put his servants to the sword as he stood there, helpless. And then they had burned his beautiful palace. On his knees, chained like a slave, he had watched it burn, his eyes filled with tears. Finally they had carried him in a humble ox cart through the city, still chained for all to see; and those who had feared to look him in the eye now mocked him openly as he passed by. They had thrown stones and handfuls of dung at him; they had jeered him as though he was some lowly commoner being taken to a place of execution.

Only at the end, after they had wrapped him in bandages and nailed down the wooden lid of his sarcophagus, did he find words. Emerging from his drug-induced sleep and still bound by the copper manacles, he had cursed them, the people who had done this to him and those who had commanded it; and he had sworn an oath that one day he would return to fulfil his destiny; to take his place as pharaoh of all Egypt.

Steam was now pouring from the radiator of the Crossley, but Sonchis kept the speed up, thundering along the rocky track that unwound like a ribbon between the dunes, aiming at the limestone cliffs rearing up from the sand, with the high jagged outcrop that resembled the head of a cobra. Soon he could even make out the dark opening of the cave: the Gates of Apophis.

And then the engine gave a last convulsive shudder and the car slewed to a halt. It could go no further but this was of little consequence. They were close enough now to walk the rest of the way. Sonchis got out and gestured to his minions to follow him. The last of them lifted

Madeleine's unconscious figure with one arm and flung her over his shoulder.

Sonchis looked around. The cliffs looked eerily magnificent in the first rays of the rising sun. A perfect day, he thought, to finish what he had begun three thousand years ago.

He started walking and the others followed.

CHAPTER NINETEEN
The Guardian

The first thing Alec saw when he stepped into the tomb was a carpet of shiny scarab beetles swarming around what looked like a pile of rubbish that somebody had dumped beside the empty sarcophagus; then he realized with a jolt of horror that the rubbish was actually a large pile of bones wearing Doc Hopper's clothing.

He opened his mouth to shout something; but in the same instant he became aware of something moving behind him. He turned as if caught in a nightmare and saw the figure approaching him: a gaunt, shrivelled creature shrouded in filthy brown bandages, its teeth

320

exposed in a hideous grimace, its tiny dark eyes glittering with deadly intent. Alec's recent nightmare came back to him and he realized that this was the unseen thing that had been chasing him through the darkness of his dreams.

Alec managed to scream, but the mummy's hand shot forward and grabbed him by the throat, cutting off his cry. He was lifted bodily from the ground, his legs kicking helplessly, and it felt as though a band of steel was tightening around his neck.

Then Alec saw Ethan running into the tomb. For a moment the American froze, looking in stunned disbelief at what was happening in front of him; then he flung himself forward and leaped onto the creature's back, locking his arms around its neck.

The mummy gave a grunt of baffled rage and threw Alec against the wall. The impact slammed all the air out of his lungs and he slid to the ground, gasping for breath. The creature lifted its arms, grabbed Ethan and heaved him over its head, then threw him down onto the earth floor. Ethan yelled in pain, and the mummy raised one foot to stamp on his face; but he rolled aside and scrambled to his feet, looking around helplessly for some kind of weapon. In an instant the mummy was on him again, grabbing for his throat.

He twisted round and aimed a punch at the creature's face, breaking several of its teeth and making it retreat a couple of steps; but the blow seemed to have had little real effect on it and it shambled forwards again, emitting a hideous grunt as it tried to tear at Ethan's face. He ducked under its arm and backed towards a corner of the tomb, trying to lead it away from Alec, who was now getting groggily to his feet.

'Get out of here, kid!' yelled Ethan, but Alec shook his head. He wasn't going to leave his friend. He too was looking around for a weapon and his gaze fell on an oil lamp, standing on the floor beside the main sarcophagus. He ran towards it, horribly aware that Ethan was now trapped in a corner. Snatching up the lamp, he ran over and aimed a kick at the creature's backside.

'Hey, ugly!' he bellowed.

It roared in fury and jerked round to glare at Alec before lumbering after him.

'Alec, what are you doing?' yelled Ethan.

Alec backed slowly away, waiting until the

mummy was in the middle of the room. Then he lifted the lamp above his head and flung it as hard as he could at the creature's chest. The glass smashed to pieces and the lamp reservoir fell to the mummy's feet, spilling kerosene as it went. At first Alec thought his plan had failed; but then there was a bright flash and the kerosene ignited, setting fire to the mummy's bandaged legs.

It paused for a moment, looked down in dull surprise and then emitted a shriek of terror as it began to burn. It tried flailing at itself with its skeletal arms but the flames flicked upwards, and all at once it was a walking torch, the fire licking towards its chest and head. It gave an angry roar and came stumbling towards Alec, blazing arms outstretched. He backed away, telling himself that it couldn't keep going for very much longer . . .

Ethan bent down to pick up the heavy wooden lid of one of the sarcophagi and, staggering forward with it, slammed it down on the mummy's head, driving it to its knees. In an instant, the dry wood of the lid was blazing too.

The tomb was beginning to fill with acrid black smoke. Alec ran round the kneeling figure to rejoin Ethan. The two of them stood there, looking down at the flailing, shrieking mummy. Its tinder-dry body was nearly completely consumed and Alec could see the exposed bones. As they watched, its struggles finally weakened and it slumped forward, its black skeleton mingling with the remains of Doc Hopper.

'Now do you believe me?' yelled Alec as they backed towards the exit.

Ethan nodded. He had the look of somebody who had just awoken from a deep sleep. 'And those things have taken Madeleine?' he cried.

'Yes. Ethan, I already told you. We have to go after them.'

Ethan was nodding, but he still seemed to be sleepwalking. 'Those bones on the floor . . . Doc Hopper. What happened to him?'

They hurried through the antechamber and up the steps to the fresh air.

'Sonchis happened,' said Alec. 'He's back. I don't understand how, but he's back. Come on!' He started to run towards the campsite, and after a few moments' hesitation Ethan hurried after him.

'We'll have to take something to burn them,' said Alec. 'It seems to work.'

'Burn them?'

'The other mummies. We'll take some petrol from the fuel supply.'

'Uh . . . but wait, we don't even know where they were headed.'

'Yes we do,' said Alec, pausing to look at the American. 'Isn't it obvious? They're going to the Gates of Apophis.'

He moved on and Ethan stood for a moment, staring after him. 'My God, Alec, are you saying that . . . ?'

'Yes. I think Sonchis has gone to do what he always planned to do. He's gone to awaken the great serpent.'

The dawn was breaking as Sonchis and his followers approached the cliffs. This at least had not changed: it was exactly as he remembered it, a huge limestone outcrop rising sheer from the sand dunes. Set in its very centre, at the top of a steep hill of broken shale, was the large semi-circular opening of a cave mouth. He glanced back at his companions and pointed a finger at one of them.

'You stay here and stand guard,' he said, speaking in his own tongue. 'Anybody tries to get into the cave, kill them. You two, come with me.' As they followed, the woman draped across one mummy's shoulder moaned and shifted a little. Sonchis reached out a hand to stroke her hair. 'Patience, my dear,' he said. 'You will soon be keeping your appointment with destiny.'

He turned away and began to climb the steep escarpment that led up to the mouth of the cave.

Back at the crash site, there was total confusion. Coates was tending to Biff Corcoran, who was still unconscious. Charlie had actually put down her camera and was trying to help, holding a cloth against a deep cut on the reporter's face. Mickey was still tinkering under the bonnet of the remaining Crossley and Archie was wandering about as though he didn't have the first idea what was going on. The Arab workers had almost put out the blaze and all that remained of Mohammed's Model T was a burned-out, smoking wreck.

Coates looked up hopefully as Alec and Ethan approached. 'Where's Doc Hopper?' he asked.

Ethan shook his head. 'He didn't make it,' he said.

Coates looked confused. 'What are you talking

about?' he snapped. 'This isn't a Tom Mix Western drama we're in. What do you mean, *he didn't make it*?'

'I mean he's dead. Hassan too. Killed by . . .' Ethan looked distinctly uncomfortable. 'Killed my mummies,' he said.

'Killed by—?' Coates looked up at the American. 'Have you gone quite mad?' he asked.

'I'm beginning to wonder,' he admitted.

'Ethan, there's no time for this,' Alec told him. 'We have to get after Madeleine. You go and fetch your gun, I'll find the petrol!'

'Er . . . right.' Ethan headed for his own tent.

'Guns? Petrol? Will somebody please tell me what's going on?' roared Coates. 'Alec, what are you doing over there?'

Alec had lifted the tarpaulin that covered the fuel supply. He grabbed an empty petrol can and began to fill it from the main fuel tank. 'It's for burning mummies,' he explained. 'We just set fire to one in the tomb. It went up like a bomb!'

'You . . . set fire to a priceless relic?' roared Coates. 'Why would you do a thing like that?'

'Because it was alive. Well, not exactly *alive* . . . but coming after us anyway. And some of the other mummies have kidnapped Madeleine and taken her in Ethan's Crossley, so we need to go after them.'

'You may as well forget that,' said Mickey, stepping away from the Crossley and wiping his oily hands on a rag. 'I can't fix it, Alec, they've done too much damage.'

Ethan emerged from his tent, strapping on his holster. 'What are you saying?' he asked.

'I need to buy new parts. It'll take me days to get it running again.'

Ethan said something colourful under his breath. He looked at Alec. 'That's it then,' he said flatly. 'There's nothing we can do.' He pointed across the road to the still smouldering remains of Mohammed's Ford. 'That was the only other vehicle for miles and it's in no condition to go anywhere.'

'Don't remind me!' wailed Mohammed.

Alec slammed down the petrol can. 'But we *have* to go after her. They are going to sacrifice her, Ethan, I'm sure of it.'

'Alec, there's no way. They've already got a huge start on us and we can hardly walk all the way to the Gates of Apophis. We'd die of thirst before we even got anywhere near the place.'

Alec paced around for a moment, racking his

brains. *There had to be some way*, he told himself. *There just had to be!* He couldn't leave Madeleine to whatever fate Sonchis had in store for her. She was his friend − she had hugged him. Then it came to him in a flash of inspiration and he turned back to Ethan.

'The biplane!' he yelled.

'What?'

'Madeleine's plane. It's only a short distance from here. You remember − we passed it on the road.'

'A plane? Alec, I don't know . . .'

'Didn't you tell me you flew planes in the war?'

'Uh . . . yeah, but that doesn't mean I can fly *her* plane.'

'Well, why not? They're all pretty much the same, aren't they?'

'Umm . . . well . . . I guess so . . .'

'Come on then!' Alec snatched up the petrol and turned to leave.

'Hold on!' roared Coates. 'If you think for one moment, Master Alec, that I'm going to let you go up in an aeroplane with . . . *that man*' − he pointed an incriminating finger at Ethan − 'you are very much mistaken.'

'It's not up to you,' said Alec defiantly. 'Madeleine's in trouble and we have to help her. Besides, I'm only taking Ethan to the plane . . . I didn't say I was going to go up in it, did I?'

Coates frowned. 'And who will accompany you back?' he asked. 'There are dangerous animals out there – hyenas and Lord knows what else.'

'Mickey can come with us,' said Alec. 'You'll come, won't you, Mickey?

Mickey nodded, looking baffled.

'That's settled then. Now let's go, we're wasting time!' Alec picked up the petrol can and started along the road. Ethan and Mickey exchanged looks and then hurried after him. Coates stared dismally at their retreating figures, wondering what Alec's father would say if he knew about this latest turn of events. Then somebody tapped him on the shoulder.

'Did they say somebody has been kidnapped by mummies?' whispered Charlie, her face very pale in the dawn light.

Coates looked at her. 'I do believe they did,' he said.

Charlie looked down at Biff and shook her head. 'Would you believe it?' she said. 'He finally gets the story he's been dreaming of and he ain't even conscious!'

Sonchis stepped into the cave. The first light of dawn was beginning to illuminate the interior. He stopped for a moment to stare up at the high vaulted roof, where hundreds of large, leathery bats clustered like strange fruit. He knew that they had travelled far to be here and that they were now starving to death, denied the food that they needed to survive, but it mattered little. They had come to do his bidding and would obey him until they had drawn their last breath.

He walked across to the place where the stone floor ended in a sheer drop. He looked over the edge, straining his eyes to peer down into the void, but it was dark as the blackest night down there, and who knew how deep?

He remembered the first time he had come here as a child – how he had stood at the edge of the chasm and gazed down into the darkness: he'd known, even then, that Apophis slept down there in the bowels of the earth, and that one day he, Sonchis, would be the one to call him back to the surface. He had been anticipating this moment ever since. Now there were a few necessary rituals to perform and everything could begin. The first step was the initial sacrifice. He turned to the mummy carrying Madeleine.

'Set the woman down,' he said. The creature obeyed him and Madeleine groaned and rolled onto her side. Her eyes opened and she looked up at Sonchis. It took her a few moments to realize where she was.

'Why have you bought me here?' she whispered, and he saw fear in her pretty blue eyes.

'You are going to help me achieve my ambition,' he said. 'Here is the lair of Apophis. Now, there are rituals to observe, spells to cast and finally a sacrifice to be made.' He saw her expression turn to one of terror and he waved a hand at her. 'Oh, don't worry, it's not your turn yet. No, first we offer our initial sacrifice.'

He beckoned to the nearest of his disciples. The creature shambled forward and stood looking calmly at its master.

Sonchis smiled. 'This man was once my friend,' he said. 'We spent many long hours talking together, advising each other. But of course, now, wasted and wizened as he is, I cannot even tell which particular friend he might be. I suspect that he is a man called Selim,

THE EYE OF THE SERPENT

once my closest and most trusted ally . . . but of course, I cannot be certain. It is of no consequence.' He reached out a hand and placed it on the mummy's shoulder. 'Goodbye, my loyal servant,' he said. And with one swift movement, he threw him over the edge of the crevasse.

Madeleine gasped in horror as the flailing bandaged figure fell silently down into darkness. She waited for the sound of a thud but it did not come for a very long time; when it finally did, it was barely audible.

Sonchis turned away from the edge with a smile of satisfaction.

'Now,' he said. 'Let us prepare.'

CHAPTER TWENTY

Flying Blind

By the time they reached the biplane, they were sweating and gasping for breath after a frantic half-mile dash along the road. Wasting no more time, Ethan clambered up into the pilot's seat and Alec, still lugging the petrol can, climbed into the passenger cockpit in front of him. He stowed the canister by his feet and put on the goggles and leather helmet he found hanging on a hook beside him.

'Alec, what the hell do you think you're doing?' snapped Ethan. 'You promised Coates you wouldn't go up with me.'

Alec glanced back over his shoulder. 'I'm not

letting you go on your own,' he said. 'You'll need all the help you can get.'

Ethan looked down at Mickey. 'Maybe you should come instead?' he suggested.

Mickey's face turned pale and he shook his head. 'I'm sorry, Mr Wade, I'm terrified of heights. I wouldn't go up in one of those things for a hundred pounds.'

Ethan scowled. 'Great,' he said. 'I don't know about this, Alec. This plane is totally new to me. Supposing something happens to you?'

'Never mind about that. We've got to think about Madeleine. If Sonchis is planning to summon Apophis, I feel sure that part of that ceremony will be a human sacrifice.'

Ethan stared at him. 'You really think so?' he said.

Alec held his gaze.

Ethan considered for a moment, then nodded. 'Then I guess we have no choice,' he said. 'OK, belt yourself in.' He put on his own goggles and helmet and started fiddling with the unfamiliar controls. 'It's all in French,' he complained. 'I think this is the magneto' – he threw a switch – 'and this looks like it should be the fuel pump . . .' He turned a tap on briefly and then switched it off again. Then he looked down at Mickey. 'Now, we need to prime the engine,' he shouted. 'Grab the propeller and turn it once.'

Mickey ran round to the front of the plane and did as he was asked. 'Now what?' he asked.

Ethan flicked another switch. 'Contact!' he said. 'OK, Mickey, I want you to grab that propeller and spin it as hard as you can, anticlockwise. And make sure you jump out of the way of it.'

Mickey nodded. He reached up, grabbed the propeller and gave it a try. It turned a couple of times, spluttered, threw out a puff of smoke, then stopped.

'I need to re-prime it,' shouted Ethan. He flicked more switches, opened the fuel valve again, then shouted, 'Contact!' Mickey tried a second time. This time the propeller actually spun a few times before coming to a halt and spilling out a bigger cloud of smoke.

Mickey looked up at Ethan and spread his hands in a gesture of helplessness. 'It's not working, Mr Wade!'

'No, trust me, we're getting there,' yelled Ethan. Again, the maddening fiddling with the controls, then: 'Try it again, Mickey – hard as you can!'

Mickey took hold of the propeller and spun it with all his strength. The engine nearly caught but died again after a few seconds.

Ethan said something very colourful and slammed his fist against the plane's dashboard. 'OK, *this* time!' he bellowed. He set the controls and yelled, 'Contact!' Mickey spun the propeller: it belched out a big cloud of black smoke and then started spinning in earnest. Ethan opened the fuel pump and revved the engine to a thunderous roar. He lifted a thumb to Mickey.

'Chocks away!' he yelled.

Mickey looked up at him, not understanding.

'The chocks!' yelled Ethan. 'The wooden blocks in front of the wheels!'

Mickey scrambled to pull them aside and the plane immediately began to move towards the road.

Ethan leaned out of the cockpit. 'We're heading for the Gates of Apophis,' he yelled. 'The cave system due west of here. You know where that is?'

Mickey nodded.

'Get help to us. As soon as you can – I don't

care how you do it, but send help. We may need it.'

Mickey gave Ethan the thumbs-up, then lifted a hand to wave.

'What do we do for a runway?' shouted Alec over the roar of the plane's rotary engine.

'We're already on it,' Ethan bellowed back at him. He aimed the snout of the biplane at the horizon, opened the throttle and they accelerated along the bumpy dirt road, while he struggled to master the unfamiliar controls. In moments, the plane was moving at an alarming speed but showed no sign of leaving the ground.

'We're not going up!' yelled Alec.

'Yeah, I'm working on it!' Ethan was hunched down, trying to work out how to deploy the flaps.

Then Alec saw something on the road ahead of them. At first it was just a series of shimmering images in the rising heat of morning, but as the plane drew nearer, the shapes became more distinct and Alec saw to his horror that an Arab drover was leading a small herd of camels along the road towards them.

'Ethan!' he cried. 'Ethan, ahead of us!'

But Ethan was intent on the controls, trying to work out how to lift the Caudron from the ground.

Alec could only sit and stare at the potential disaster awaiting them. They were closing on the camels at incredible speed.

'ETHAN!' he screamed, and this time the American looked up. He said something, but whatever it was, it was lost in the rush of wind around them. Alec could now clearly see the look of terror on the drover's face as he saw what was approaching him along the road.

'Get out of the way!' roared Alec, gesturing frantically, but the man just stood there, frozen to the spot, his eyes huge in his sunburned face, his mouth hanging open. Behind him, the camels seemed to be mimicking his expression.

Ethan slammed down the wing flaps and the plane finally began to rise from the ground, but the camels were looming up fast. Alec wanted to close his eyes but he could only stare, his heart pounding in his chest, as the plane rose gradually higher . . . higher . . .

At the last moment the drover ducked and the wheels narrowly missed the heads of a couple of his prized camels; and as the plane skimmed over them, Alec was aware of the terrified creatures veering off the road in all directions and stampeding into the desert.

Looking back over his shoulder, he saw that the drover had turned and was waving his fist at the departing plane.

'What an idiot!' shouted Ethan. 'Who brings a herd of camels down a main highway?'

Alec shook his head. He considered saying, *That chap down there*, but decided against it. For one thing it was difficult to talk with the wind pounding into his face, snatching his breath away; and for another, he was all too aware that Ethan needed to concentrate on what he was doing. How, for instance, were they going to change direction? No sooner had this occurred to him than the plane banked suddenly and, making a wide sweep to the left, headed out across the desert.

Alec looked down and was shocked to see how high they were already: the great dunes below them looked like the surface of a child's sandpit beneath the rapidly lightening sky. He felt a strange mingling of emotions within him. A sense of exhilaration, because he had never flown before and had always wanted to; apprehension, because he liked Madeleine immensely and was aware that she was in great danger; and, most of all, the feeling that he was asleep and all this was some fantastic dream, prompted by the things that had happened to him over the past few days.

And then another thought occurred to him. The Gates of Apophis were out in the middle of the desert. Putting the biplane down on the bumpy surface of a road would be hard enough, but the cliffs where the cave was located would be surrounded by sand dunes. *How were they ever going to land?*

Sonchis was kneeling at the edge of the great chasm. He had just begun speaking the words of reawakening when he felt something stirring down in the bowels of the earth; something huge and incredibly powerful. But another sensation had interrupted his thought processes: something was coming.

He stood up and walked back to the cave entrance, staring out across the desert at the early morning skies. Yes, something was wrong. He concentrated, closed his eyes and saw a strange, bird-like machine speeding towards him, closing the distance much faster than the automobile had done. The parts of him that were the spirits of the recently departed gave him the machine's name – an aeroplane. It wouldn't take long to reach him.

He opened his eyes, turned away and gazed up at the cavernous roof, where hundreds of his minions roosted. He knew it was against their instincts to leave the cave by daylight but he concentrated his powers and willed them to obey him.

The creatures began to stir and flap their leathery wings. A couple of them released their grip on the craggy rock and fluttered towards the cave entrance, intent on obeying the high priest's commands. Then more of them followed, and more and more, until there was a great stirring mass of them, speeding out into the pale sunlight and arcing upwards into the sky, seeking out the thing that Sonchis wanted them to destroy.

He turned to watch them go, saw them receding into the distance like a twisting, swirling sand devil stirred by the wind; and then in the distance he heard an unfamiliar sound: the snarl of the plane's engine as it sped to its destruction.

He allowed himself the ghost of a smile. Then he turned back to the chasm and resumed his kneeling position. He became aware of somebody staring at him and saw that the woman was now fully awake. She was lying on her side, her hands securely tied behind her back.

'You . . . you made those bats leave 'ere,' she said. 'You must also 'ave sent them to attack us that time.'

Sonchis bowed his head slightly. 'From child-hood I have been able to make certain creatures do my bidding,' he said. 'So as soon as I emerged from my burial place in the body of another man, I called to them to help me. My scarabs came instantly. The hyenas took longer because they had to travel so far. And the bats have always lived here in the lair of Apophis. Sending them against you was good practice for me . . . a way of seeing if I could still command the creatures of the earth and air to do my bidding. But now, if you'll excuse me . . . there is one more creature I must summon from his sleep.'

Madeleine laughed. 'You cannot believe that this is going to work,' she told him. 'A giant snake? It is preposterous.'

He looked at her for a moment. 'And if some-body had told you only a few days ago that a man who had lain entombed for three thousand years would get up and walk – would you have thought that preposterous also?'

She gazed at him, the expression on her face telling him that she had no ready answer for him.

'The great serpent *will* rise,' he assured her. 'And I shall be lord of all Egypt. You can depend on that.'

They were getting close now. On the far horizon, Alec could see the limestone cliffs rising from the sand, tiny at first, but rapidly growing in size as they approached. He looked back over his shoulder and pointed at them. Ethan nodded: he had seen them too.

'How are we going to land?' yelled Alec. He was not altogether encouraged by the reply he got − a shrug of the American's shoulders and a worried expression.

In their rush to leave, there had been no time to ponder questions like that. Now they were almost at their destination and they would have to put down as best they could. A crash landing. The only alternative was to turn round and head back without Madeleine and that, Alec knew, was unthinkable.

Then he noticed something in the air ahead of them; what he at first took to be a trail of brown smoke. Only this smoke appeared to be speeding towards the plane in a long, shifting column, and as it drew nearer, he could see that it was made up of dark, flapping shapes. He opened his mouth to shout to Ethan, but as he did so, one of the shapes hurtled into the plane's propeller and exploded in a burst of crimson. Alec felt drops of warm liquid spatter his face, misting his goggles.

The plane lurched under the impact and then more shapes were zooming towards them, skimming just above their heads, bouncing off the fuselage. Alec threw up an arm just in time to ward off a savage set of jaws and the bat went tumbling away. He twisted round to see Ethan crouched down in his cockpit, trying his best to shake a couple of the creatures off his shoulders. Ahead, it was as though the biplane was plunging into a forest of flapping wings and snapping teeth. A series of heavy impacts rocked Alec in his seat as more of the creatures blundered into the propeller, their blood coating his goggles. He tore them off, flung them aside and then heard the plane's engine give a faltering, coughing squeal as it began to clog with furry bodies. The plane lurched abruptly sideways and then flipped over on to its back. Alec yelled in terror as he felt his own weight tugging on his lap strap. The petrol can seemed to float up past him and he grabbed hold of it and hugged it to his chest, knowing that if he lost that, he would have no means of defeating Sonchis.

Leathery shapes glanced off his head and thudded into his shoulders and then, quite unexpectedly, the plane emerged from darkness into clear air. Ethan struggled to right it, but the engine was making a hideous screeching din and Alec was horribly aware of the ground whizzing past just a short distance above his head. They had to right themselves. If they didn't turn back over in time . . .

He glanced back and saw Ethan struggling to make the turn, his blood-spattered face set in an expression of grim determination; and then Alec whipped round again as something exploded right in front of him. Fire and smoke began to belch out of the engine – he could feel the heat of it blasting back into his face. Ethan was still trying to bring the plane back up, but it didn't seem to be responding to the controls . . .

It had swung back to perhaps a forty-five-degree angle when the starboard wing ploughed into sand. Alec felt an abrupt impact that seemed to thud into every part of his body. A flurry of sand flew into his eyes, the lap strap snapped open and he was thrown forward; then his head struck something hard, lights seemed to flash in front of his eyes and he was falling into darkness.

CHAPTER TWENTY-ONE
The Gates of Apophis

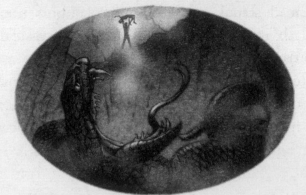

A lec opened his eyes. He was lying on the sand and his head felt like it was splitting open. He lifted the fingers of one hand to assure himself that this was not the case and found nothing more alarming than a large bump. He lifted his face from the sand and looked around warily.

To his surprise, he saw that the cliffs they had been heading for were now only a few hundred yards away. He turned his head and saw something more worrying. Sticking up out the ground were the remains of what had once been a biplane, now little more than a jumble of broken wood and flapping canvas. Flames were licking up from the shattered engine casing and trailing back along the fuselage towards the place where Alec had been sitting. He experienced a brief feeling of relief that he was no longer in harm's way, but this turned to horror as he registered the fact that Ethan was still sitting in the cockpit. There was a splash of blood across one shoulder of his khaki shirt and he appeared to be unconscious.

'Ethan!' Without a moment's hesitation, Alec was up and running towards the biplane. He clambered up the fuselage to look down into the cockpit, grabbed Ethan by the shoulders and began to shake him violently. Nothing happened. He tore off the American's helmet and goggles and slapped his face hard.

Ethan's eyes opened. He sat there for a moment, groggy, looking at Alec. 'Why are you hitting me?' he asked.

'You've got to get out!' yelled Alec.

'Out?' Ethan looked puzzled. 'Out of where?'

'The fuel tank could blow at any moment!' Alec grabbed Ethan under his arms and started trying to pull him free.

Now Ethan looked around and it dawned on

him exactly where he was. The grogginess went out of him in an instant. 'Holy mother of God!' he said.

Alec was horribly aware that the cockpit in front of them was already consumed by fire. He could feel the heat on his face.

Ethan began to try and lever himself out of his seat, but didn't seem to be getting anywhere.

'The lap strap!' said Alec. 'Hurry!'

Ethan reached down and unclipped it. Then he was able to scramble up, and he and Alec fell over the side of the fuselage onto the sand.

'Come on,' said Ethan, starting to crawl away on his hands and knees. 'We daren't stay here any—'

He broke off as he found his way blocked by a pair of withered, skeletal legs and he looked up in surprise to find one of the mummies looking down at him, an angry scowl on its hideous face. Ethan reached instinctively for the pistol at his waist but the mummy launched a savage kick at his chest, sending him reeling back towards the wreckage. Alec jumped to his feet and ran at the creature, knowing that he had no weapon of any kind and all too aware that the flames were now consuming the cockpit where Ethan had just been sitting. How the plane had not yet exploded was a mystery.

Operating on instinct, Alec dived between the creature's legs, rolled forward and came back to his feet. The mummy spun awkwardly around, reaching out its arms to grab for him; as it did so, Alec dived head first at its chest, delivering a powerful head butt. It reeled away with a baffled grunt and Ethan rolled against its legs, tipping it backwards with a bellow of rage.

Ethan looked at Alec. 'Run for the cave!' he yelled, getting to his feet.

Alec needed no second bidding. As he ran, he glanced back over his shoulder and saw the mummy getting clumsily to its feet. It was now standing only a few yards from the wreckage of the plane; then it began to stagger after them—

Alec felt the explosion an instant before he saw it – a burst of hot air that swatted him forward like a giant's hand. Then there was a flash and a great orange ball of flame engulfed the spot where the mummy had been standing. Alec hit the sand and Ethan landed beside him.

There was a moment of utter silence and then things began to rain down around them: bits of burning canvas, shards of splintered wood and, most alarmingly, several pieces of smouldering mummy. The creature's head tumbled past them and came to a halt, one cheek against the sand. As Alec stared at it in mute horror, the mummy's lips curled into a snarl and it uttered a last feeble grunt of rage.

Alec grimaced in revulsion. He turned and saw that Ethan was now sitting up and pulling aside his shirt to look at the wound in his shoulder.

'How is it?' asked Alec.

'Just a gash,' said Ethan. 'I guess I'll live. Come on.' He got to his feet and started towards the cave entrance.

'Wait!' said Alec. He had just spotted something lying in the sand a short distance away from the wreckage. He gave the mummy's snarling head a wide berth and ran over to pick up the petrol can. He was glad to see that the lid was still firmly on, and now he noticed something that he had missed when he had filled the can in the darkness. It was made of copper. It had been a total accident but now it seemed significant. He remembered the lining of the sarcophagus and the manacles that had bound Sonchis's wrists. Both had been made of copper.

'We might need this,' he said as he and Ethan ran towards the Gates of Apophis.

'I'm not sure it's a good idea trying to rescue Madeleine,' muttered Ethan.

Alec stared at him. 'What do you mean?' he cried.

'She'll probably kill us when she sees what we've done to her plane!'

In different circumstances, it would have been funny; but the open cave mouth lay ahead and neither of them felt like laughing. They didn't know what they might find there.

They came to the steep pile of scree below the cave mouth and began to climb.

Madeleine watched Sonchis in mute disbelief. He was on his knees and his lips were moving as he chanted the words under his breath – words she could not quite hear; and she told herself that she must be imagining things because she thought she could feel the ground beneath her shuddering, as though deep beneath the earth something immense was moving, shifting, coiling . . .

Meanwhile she was using the sharp jagged rock just behind her to saw through the ropes that secured her wrists. She kept glancing at the mummy that stood guard over her, but she could not be sure how much intelligence lay behind those gaunt, wasted features. The creature was watching her as it had been instructed to, but did not seem to be taking much notice of what she was actually *doing*.

She returned her attention to Sonchis, noticing – not for the first time – the two objects that hung round his neck on a leather thong. One was a small statue of Apophis; the other was like a Wadjet eye, a popular ancient Egyptian talisman, only the pupil of this eye was long and snakelike; and she remembered what she had read in the papyrus: the eye of the serpent was the charm that other high priests had created to keep Sonchis's spirit prisoner. But now, it seemed, he was using it as some kind of amulet, perhaps deriving some of his power from it.

Another shudder rippled through the stone beneath her, too strong to be her imagination –

and Sonchis broke off from the ritual for a moment to stare at her in triumphant delight. She noticed how he lifted a hand to stroke the amulets as he spoke, his eyes blazing with triumph.

'Did you feel that?' he cried. 'The great serpent stirs! *Now* try to tell me that I am deluding myself!'

Madeleine gazed steadily back at him, but when she spoke, her voice lacked conviction, even to her own ears. 'That was nothing more than . . . an earth tremor . . . they 'appen 'ere every day!'

Sonchis laughed; a most unpleasant sound. 'Apophis is rising!' he said. 'He is emerging from his lair of dreams to take his place as the lord of our world.' He smiled at Madeleine. 'He will be hungry after such a long sleep,' he said. 'You will provide him with sustenance.' Then he turned back and continued his chanting. He was speaking in his own language, his voice louder, menacing, and she could understand only a few words and phrases.

'Awake, great serpent!' she heard him say. 'The power of Sonchis commands you! The power of Sonchis compels you!'

And then, from the depths of the abyss, she

heard a sound that seemed to freeze the blood in her veins. It was a deep, resonant hiss that seemed to fill the cave. The earth shook again and she knew that there really was something down there; something massive and powerful and deadly. It was awake now and moving towards the surface . . .

Terrified, Madeleine continued to saw frantically at the ropes that bound her.

Near the top of the pile of scree, Alec and Ethan paused and looked at each other.

'Did you hear that?' whispered Alec.

Ethan nodded but said nothing and continued to climb. They reached the top of the incline and were able to peer over the threshold into the gloom of the cave. They could see the weird, half-naked figure of Sonchis on his knees, and beside him, two figures: the tall cadaverous shape of a mummy standing a short distance from the high priest and there, stretched out on the ground, Madeleine. She was moving, apparently trying to free herself.

Ethan crept into the cave and Alec followed close behind. As they moved forward, the mummy sensed their presence. It turned and began to shamble towards them, arms outstretched. Ethan drew his pistol and shot the creature in the chest, blowing a sizeable hole through it. It faltered for only an instant. Ethan fired twice more but it kept on coming.

Sonchis had turned his head and directed a mirthless smile at Ethan. 'You're too late!' he cried.

He got to his feet and moved towards Madeleine, grabbing her by the throat and lifting her to her feet. Then he returned to the chasm and pushed her to the very edge.

The mummy closed on Ethan and wrapped him in its hideous embrace, its arms clamping around his ribs and crushing the air from his lungs. He fell back against the wall and Alec ran to try and help him. He lifted the heavy copper petrol can by its handle and swung it with all his strength at the mummy's head. There was a dull thud and the head came clean off and went bouncing along the ground. The mummy, blind now, reeled away from Ethan and stumbled towards Alec. He sidestepped and the creature continued towards the mouth of the cave. It reached the edge, plunged over and went tumbling down the shale incline out of sight.

Alec and Ethan turned back and cautiously began to approach Sonchis, both of them horribly aware that one push from him would send Madeleine to her doom. But he seemed to be waiting for something. The ground was shaking constantly now and the cave filled with that eerie hissing. Alec was aware of something moving in the abyss beyond; something immense that was rising rapidly to the surface.

Ethan lifted the pistol and aimed it at Sonchis. 'Let her go,' he said.

Sonchis laughed. 'You think your puny weapon can defeat me?' he cried.

'Sure, why not?' said Ethan, trying to be cool.

'You made a valiant effort,' said Sonchis. 'But you are too late. Apophis comes!'

'Use the gun!' screamed Alec.

'I can't!' said Ethan. 'I might hit Madeleine.'

'You've got to try!'

But in that instant Madeleine's arms came round from behind her back and the fingers of one hand clawed at Sonchis's face, the nails gouging the flesh around his eyes, while with the other hand she grabbed something that was hanging around his neck on a leather thong and pulled hard. The thong snapped and he released her. She fell to the ground and rolled quickly away.

Sonchis looked down at his chest in dull surprise, realizing that the source of his power was gone. He extended a hand towards Madeleine, his face contorted in rage.

'Give them to me!' he roared; and his voice seemed to fill the cave.

Alec knew he had one chance and he took it. He ran forward, hefting the heavy copper petrol can like a shot put; and summoning all his strength, he launched it straight at the high priest's chest. It struck him hard, driving the breath out of him, and his hands closed instinctively around the can as he stumbled backwards towards the edge of the chasm.

Alec registered the look of shock on his face as he realized he was clutching a piece of copper to his chest – the substance that had held him bound for so many thousands of years.

'Now, Ethan!' yelled Alec. 'One shot!'

Ethan had only a split second in which to fire. He lifted the pistol and took quick aim at the petrol can as Sonchis teetered on the brink. Alec heard the crack of the gunshot an instant before the priest disappeared over the edge of the crevasse.

For a moment there was just silence and Alec told himself that the shot must have missed; but then he felt the impact of an explosion and saw a great flash of light as the petrol ignited. The blast slammed him and Ethan to the ground and a huge gout of oily flame blossomed up over the lip of the abyss.

Whatever had been rising to the surface fell back into the void with a mighty crash, and the ground began to shudder as though in the grip of a mighty earthquake. The movement caused rocks high in the roof to dislodge and rain down. Alec scrambled to his feet and ran to help Madeleine up. She opened her hand to reveal the two objects lying in her palm. She seemed to hesitate for a moment, as though considering taking them with her; but then she turned and flung the amulets into the chasm.

She and Alec started to run for the cave mouth and Ethan joined them. The ground bucked and shuddered as something below the surface thrashed and crashed around the stone labyrinth. As they ran, Alec was aware of the roof above them, sagging, buckling, ready to fall and crush them to a pulp. They emerged from the cave and threw themselves down the incline, tumbling head over heels, not even feeling the impact when their knees and elbows connected with hard scree.

Behind them, the cave roof came down with a thunderous roar and thick clouds of dust enveloped them, but they went on falling. When they finally hit the sand at the bottom of the slope, they leaped up and ran as huge boulders came crashing down behind them.

Glancing fearfully over his shoulder, Alec caught a glimpse of the headless mummy stumbling blindly back uphill before being struck by a boulder the size of an automobile. He didn't stop to see any more.

They kept on running until they were clear of the last rolling boulders and were able to stop and catch their breath and look back at the devastation behind them.

The Gates of Apophis were gone. As the dust began to settle, all they could see was a great pile of stones where the hillside used to be. A thick red cloud hung in the air above it.

Nobody said anything. They stood there, letting their breathing settle to something like a normal rate, and then glanced at each other, grinning. They kept looking back at the heap of stones, asking themselves what had really happened back in the gloom of the cave.

'It *was* real, wasn't it?' gasped Alec after a while. 'We all heard it.'

'We *heard* something,' said Ethan. 'But we didn't *see* anything.'

'Something was coming up through that crevasse,' persisted Alec. 'Something big and powerful. The ground was shaking!'

Ethan frowned. 'Good job you insisted on bringing that gasoline,' he said. 'Whatever was in there must be buried under a hundred tons of rock.' He laughed incredulously. 'Maddie, do you realize that if Alec hadn't—' He broke off.

Madeleine was standing a short distance away, studying the smouldering remains of her plane. 'My beautiful Caudron,' she said. 'Destroyed.'

Ethan winced, then nodded. He and Alec went to stand with her.

'I'm sorry,' muttered Ethan. 'But there was just no other way to get to you.'

She forced a smile. 'Under the circumstances, I suppose I'll have to forgive you,' she said.

She turned to look at them. 'Thank you,' she said. 'Both of you. For saving my life.'

Alec smiled. 'Our pleasure,' he said. 'It was a fluke really. The can was made of copper. I didn't even notice when I was filling it.' He looked at the other two and then pointed back towards the place where the Gates of Apophis had been. 'But I don't suppose we'll tell anyone . . . what really happened in there?'

Madeleine laughed. 'Not if we want anybody to believe us,' she said.

'We'll do what we've been doing all along,' said Ethan. 'We'll keep a lid on it, and if anybody asks us awkward questions, we'll just look like we don't know anything.' He jerked a thumb at the devastation behind them. 'We'll put that down to an earth tremor,' he added.

Alec looked around slowly. They were in the middle of the desert and the heat was intensifying. There was no habitation anywhere near them and they had no water.

'I'm not sure how we get out of this one,' said Ethan.

'It can't end like this,' said Alec. 'Not after everything that's happened.' He remembered something. 'Wait! You . . . you told Mickey where we were going, didn't you?'

'Well, yeah, I guess if we wait around long enough, he—'

'What's that?' yelled Madeleine, pointing.

Something had appeared on the far horizon: a shimmering mirage against the white sand dunes, tiny at first but rapidly growing in size; and as they watched impatiently, the mirage took on shape and substance. At last they were able to see that it was a group of camels. As the creatures approached, they could see Mickey perched awkwardly on one of them and, riding beside him, an Arab whom Ethan soon identified as the drover they had nearly killed with the plane. They were leading three more camels behind them.

Ethan chuckled. 'How about that for service?' he cried.

They sat down on the sand and waited more patiently now. After what seemed like an age, Mickey was grinning down at them.

'You all right?' he asked them.

'We are now,' said Alec; and he noted with joy that both Mickey and the drover were carrying water canteens over their shoulders.

'Sorry it took a bit of time,' said Mickey. 'We had to catch the camels and then I had to explain to Malik here that I needed his help.' He looked around, first at the remains of the biplane and then the great heap of rock and dust where the Gates of Apophis used to be.

'What the hell happened here?' he asked.

'It's a long story,' said Alec. 'We'll tell you all about it on the way home.'

EPILOGUE
One Week Later

The steamship *Sudan* was still waiting when they got to the port but it was obvious from the bustle on the quayside that it would soon be leaving. Mohammed brought the Crossley to a halt and sat there proudly for a moment, taking in the admiring glances of his friends and neighbours. Then he got out and limped around to the back to unstrap the luggage.

Alec helped his uncle out of the automobile. He was still frail and subdued, and needed the help of a walking stick, but he had improved considerably since Alec had last seen him; and the doctors had decided that he was now strong enough to make the trip back to Cairo to continue his convalescence. Perhaps in time he would be up to making the long journey back to England. Madeleine got out too and linked her arm with Uncle Will's.

'Let me 'elp you aboard,' she said.

'Thank you, my dear,' said Sir William.

There was a grinding noise behind them and Alec turned to see that Mickey was coaxing what was left of the other Crossley to a halt. Mickey had found it abandoned on the sands when he rode by on his camel and had somehow managed to get it towed back to base. He had patched it back together, but after being gunned headlong across that desert road it would never be the same again. Steam boiled from the radiator, but Ethan, sitting beside Mickey, didn't seem to care. He left Mickey and Coates with the rest of the luggage and hurried over to say his goodbyes. Alec watched as he shook hands with Uncle Will.

'It's great to see you looking so much better, sir,' he said. 'Now, listen, before you go . . . are you absolutely sure you don't want to keep *any* of the antiquities for your own collection?'

Sir William shook his head. 'I've already told

the people at the museum – they can have every last bit of it,' he said. 'I'm finished with archaeology. Now I just want to sit quietly at home and rest. And we stick to the story, Ethan. We found an antechamber and an *empty* tomb. Nothing more. Right, Alec?'

Alec nodded. 'I don't think anybody would believe us if we told them the truth,' he said. 'I'm still not sure what Ethan is supposed to say to the authorities, though. All those people gone without a trace – Tom, Doc Hopper, Llewellyn – and all of them linked to the dig. How will he ever explain all that?'

Sir William sighed. 'He'll just keep insisting that he doesn't know anything,' he suggested.

Ethan nodded. 'Maybe that ain't so far from the truth,' he said. 'Oh, don't worry about me, pard. They ain't gonna pin anything on me!'

Now he turned to smile at Madeleine, and Alec could see the look of regret in his eyes.

'I'm real sorry you have to travel home the slow way,' he said.

'I'm not,' she assured him. 'I so very nearly wasn't travelling 'ome at all. It was a good plane, but there will be others.'

'It's a shame your first assignment was

something you won't even be able to talk about,' Ethan observed.

She shrugged. 'But it is something I will never forget,' she told him. 'It was an incredible adventure and nobody can take that away from me.'

'You'll write to me – let me know how you are?'

'Of course.' She leaned forward and kissed him lightly on the cheek. 'Goodbye, Ethan Wade,' she said. 'You are a good man. I 'ope you will come to Paris one day so I can show you the sights.'

Ethan grinned. 'You can bet on it,' he told her.

Now Madeleine turned to Alec and smiled at him. 'The same goes for you, Alec Devlin. And I want you to write to me just as soon as you can.'

'I will,' he promised.

She reached out and hugged him tightly for a moment. 'I'm going to miss you,' she told him; and a slight catch in her voice betrayed the fact that she was close to tears. She turned away quickly, took Sir William's arm and led him towards the *Sudan*. Alec and Ethan watched her fondly.

'Why don't you ask her to stay?' asked Alec under his breath.

Ethan snorted. 'What makes you think I

haven't?' he muttered. 'But she has her own life in Paris — stuff she needs to do. And neither of us is ready to settle down. Maybe I'll meet up with her another time.'

'Hey, Wade!' They turned their heads and saw Charlie Connors pushing Biff Corcoran towards them in a wheelchair. Biff had one leg encased in plaster and he still bore the marks of an injury on his forehead.

'You going on the *Sudan* too?' cried Ethan.

'Yeah. Can't wait to get out of this hole. The *Post* has got a nice quiet story lined up for me in New England. Suits me fine.' Biff took the stub of a cigarette from his mouth and, leaning forward, lowered his voice. 'Come on, Wade, off the record. What really happened out there in the desert?'

Ethan shrugged his shoulders. 'Your guess is as good as mine, Biff.' He looked at Alec. 'You know anything, kid?'

Alec shook his head. 'Not a thing,' he said.

'You figure?' Biff clearly wasn't convinced. 'We got at least three missing people, a car crash, a photograph of a guy that looks like his face is made of bugs.' He jerked a thumb over his shoulder. 'And I got Scary Mary here telling me that she saw a bunch of mummies driving off in your automobile. You telling me you don't know anything about it?'

Ethan kept his expression blank. 'No comment,' he said.

'Aw, forget it!' said Biff, waving a hand in dismissal. 'You know what? I ain't even interested no more. I wouldn't please ya to ask any more questions. I just wanna go home.' He looked up at Charlie. 'Let's get aboard this tub before it leaves without us.'

Charlie glanced at Ethan as she went by. She looked harassed. 'Remember me?' she said. 'I used to be a top photographer. These days I'm Biff's nurse.'

'Yeah? Well, look after him anyway,' said Ethan, and he and Alec watched as she pushed the reporter up the gangway.

Now Coates bustled forward, all businesslike. He shook Ethan's hand but not with any real warmth. 'Mr Wade,' he said, 'I'd like to say it's been a pleasure, but really it's been more of an education. I *won't* speak to Alec's father about some of the exploits you got up to. I wouldn't want to unnerve him.'

'I'm glad to hear it,' said Ethan. 'You know,

we're going to miss you up at the dig. We'll be back to Archie's cooking for the next few weeks while we get the last of the antiquities packaged up.'

'I've left him full instructions,' said Coates proudly. 'I think you'll be pleasantly surprised by his culinary skills.' He turned his head. 'Come along, Master Alec,' he said. 'The boat will be departing at any minute.'

'*Please* don't call me that,' pleaded Alec. 'And could I have a few moments to say goodbye?'

Coates rolled his eyes but obligingly left him to it.

Alec turned to look solemnly at Ethan. 'Well, I suppose this is it,' he said.

Ethan nodded. 'It's gonna seem kind of quiet without you, Alec.'

Alec laughed and glanced over at Mohammed, who was chatting to Mickey and proudly polishing the bonnet of his new automobile. He lifted a hand to wave. 'I can't believe you gave him your best Crossley.'

Ethan shrugged. 'I won't be needing it,' he said. 'The old one will see me out for the last few weeks. And how else was I gonna swear Mohammed to silence? Don't forget, he knows quite a bit about what happened.'

Alec chuckled. 'What are your plans once you've finished here?'

'Well, I'm getting out of Egypt, that's for sure.'

'Where will you go?'

'Haven't decided yet. What about yourself?'

'Father mentioned Mexico in his last letter,' admitted Alec.

'Yeah? I know Mexico like the back of my hand. Say, if your pop needs any help, remember me to him. Tell him to get in touch with me. You can always get a message to me at the Winter Palace – I'll be around for a while.'

'I'll do that,' said Alec. 'I'll talk to him just as soon as I get back.'

'Good.' Ethan glanced up at Coates, who was staring frostily at him from the deck of the *Sudan*. 'Might be a good idea not to mention it while ol' Coates is in hearing range. For some reason I still don't think he approves of me.'

They laughed together and Alec reflected that he was going to miss that.

There was a great honking blast as the steamer sounded its whistle, and somebody shouted the 'All aboard!' for the last time.

Alec glanced back to the gangway. The crew

were getting ready to remove it. 'I have to go,' he said. 'Take care of yourself, Ethan.'

'Always.'

They shook hands one more time and then Alec hurried aboard. He joined the others at the rail and the *Sudan* edged slowly away from the quayside and headed out into mid stream. Ethan stood looking out across the water, an easy grin on his face.

'Well, that's the last we'll see of Mr Wade,' said Coates, with some satisfaction.

'I wouldn't bet on it,' said Alec, smiling; and he lifted a hand to wave.

Follow the further adventures of Alec Devlin in Empire of the Skull.